ANYA KELNER

Hunt

Rise of the Red Claws (Book 2)

Copyright © 2024 by Anya Kelner

All rights reserved. No part of this publication may be reproduced, stored or transmitted in any form or by any means, electronic, mechanical, photocopying, recording, scanning, or otherwise without written permission from the publisher. It is illegal to copy this book, post it to a website, or distribute it by any other means without permission.

This novel is entirely a work of fiction. The names, characters and incidents portrayed in it are the work of the author's imagination. Any resemblance to actual persons, living or dead, events or localities is entirely coincidental.

First edition

*This book was professionally typeset on Reedsy.
Find out more at reedsy.com*

Contents

Rise of the Red Claws series	v
Prophesy	1
Prologue	2
Chapter 1	5
Chapter 2	19
Chapter 3	34
Chapter 4	41
Chapter 5	47
Chapter 6	51
Chapter 7	65
Chapter 8	70
Chapter 9	78
Chapter 10	84
Chapter 11	93
Chapter 12	107
Chapter 13	120
Chapter 14	128
Chapter 15	144
Chapter 16	146
Chapter 17	153
Chapter 18	163
Chapter 19	167
Chapter 20	172
Chapter 21	176

Chapter 22	182
Chapter 23	199
Chapter 24	203
Chapter 25	220
Chapter 26	223
Chapter 27	232
Chapter 28	242
Chapter 29	250
Chapter 30	256
Chapter 31	262
Epilogue	270
The story continues	277

Rise of the Red Claws series

Part 1: Awake
Part 2: Hunt
Part 3: Legacy

Note for readers: Rise of the Red Claws is a three-part vampire romance and suspense story with no cheating. Book two ends with an unresolved plot element, which is completely resolved in book three. All three books have been released.

Prophesy

Creatures of the night will come together to fight as one. Unlikely allegiances will be forged. They will be tested. They will be sacrificed. They will be broken. Creation teeters on a perilous balance between light and dark.

Salvation lies in one soul. A death-walker turned young. One of tainted blood. He will endure a betrayal, a loss and an awakening. He will love, as no other of his kin has before. He will abandon those he serves. He will develop abilities unknown while reverting to the origin. These abilities can corrupt and besiege, for they stem from the transmutation of loss, the most powerful emotion. He must drain the one he loves, filling his essence and ending theirs. This act alone brings forth the genesis.

Extract from a prophecy found in the ancient vampiric text *Cimmerian Prognostications*, contained in the book *Adumbrate Invictus* (date and author unknown).

Prologue

Hands clutched at her throat. They clawed at her face. Fingernails like knives ripped at her skin. Her entire body felt raw. On fire. It had been this way since she left the safety of Vhik'h-Tal-Eskemon in the Blue Ridge Mountains. Constant, unyielding torture. Even when she was left alone, on those rare occasions she wasn't being mutilated or maimed, her body screamed in pain. The aftermath of the sheer brutality she faced.

The same hands that wounded her now dragged her across the floor. Fingers intertwined in her straggly hair, pulling her across the uneven concrete. She was hauled across the space like a ragdoll, lacking the energy to fight back. There was no point screaming or yelling. It didn't get her anywhere. It usually made matters worse. An extra set of teeth clamping down on her body, another slice along her abdomen. More ridicule. More taunts.

Nell wasn't sure how long she'd been held captive in the dank basement. The days and nights blended seamlessly into one when you were underground. When she was alone, her time was spent flailing in and out of dreamless sleep that left her feeling even more exhausted. Periodically, the main vampire who fed on her would look down through the open hatch in the ceiling and sneer at her broken, crumpled form. She remembered his name. Zachariah.

This wasn't who she was. She was a fighter. But each time she tried to resist, her captors would subject her to the most horrific pain. So eventually she stopped fighting back. Visions of Christopher, the one she loved, would occasionally provide a little respite. She'd done this to keep him safe. To protect him from harm.

Her jailers continued to grab at her. But this time it was different. The hands that usually tore her skin to shreds now pulled her upwards, through the open hatch as if she weighed nothing at all. They didn't bother to protect her from the bangs and scrapes as she hit the sides of the trapdoor. Nell couldn't help but cry out as her hip bone smashed into the wooden frame. Finally, she was pulled fully out and deposited onto the rough wooden planks. Her eyes burned in the light, after having been in darkness for so long. She had to squeeze her eyelids tight shut.

It was colder up here. The air smelled of rain. It reminded her of holidays she used to take with her mother and father when she was little. She could see herself laughing as the waters of Niagara Falls sprayed into her face, making it burn with an icy cold. She loved those holidays. Her mind was drifting off again. To a happier time. It was using its innate protection mechanism to blot out the horrors of her present situation. Her brain wanted to take her far away from this Godforsaken place.

She was dragged through a door and out into the open. The ground was covered in snow. She could feel the powdery cold as her feet dragged along the ground. The hands holding her up suddenly let go. She collapsed onto the ground in a heap.

Her hands instinctively clutched at her head. She felt bare patches where clumps of hair had been ripped from her scalp.

"Red Claws!" a voice shouted. "Behold, the secret to our salvation. This human..." Nell felt a kick to her ribs, the freezing snow heightening the intensity of the pain. "... will help us take our place in the new order."

Nell was hoisted off the ground and raised high in the air. She had no strength left and so hung limp like a marionette with broken strings while raucous chanting erupted around her.

"Ridicarea ghearelor roșii...Ridicarea ghearelor roșii... Ridicarea ghearelor roșii..." was shouted over and over again.

Nell tentatively opened her eyes. They still burned in reaction to the light and tears streamed down her face, but she could make out hazy shapes. A sea of Red Claws. Cheering at her suffering and humiliation.

Why haven't they killed me yet? Nell thought, not for the first time, as a set of teeth clamped on to her neck. This was surely the end. If this was death, then at least Christopher didn't have to suffer the anguish of killing her as instructed in the prophecy. She would at least spare him that.

With that final thought, Nell's world went black.

Chapter 1

It had been more than two weeks since Nell had simply left through the front door. Since she'd been tricked and stolen from Christopher. His blood still boiled when he thought of her willingly walking into the clutches of the Red Claws. The reason why she'd gone was clear, but it didn't make him feel any better. Heat rose in his face, yet his color remained the same. Corpse white.

Christopher slammed his fist into the bedroom wall, making a dent in the stone. It was one among many. He waited for the anger to subside. It wouldn't make the situation any better. He knew that. He needed to be as calm and rational as possible.

If he'd only kept his feelings inside in the first place, Nell would be safe at home with her Aunt Laura, not kidnapped by a band of evil blood-sucking bastards. Her aunt, meanwhile, would have been spared a cruel death and the indignity of being hastily buried by the roadside.

The Red Claws had played to Nell's weakness. The fact that she would always put others before herself. But she had promised Christopher in her letter that she would stay alive. That she would be ready when the opposing army was strong enough. Christopher knew in his heart that she was still alive. She had to be.

Devan had left the vampire headquarters to track the Red Claws and try to find help. He rang from payphones as often as he could but, in this day and age, they were few and far between. There wasn't much point taking a cell phone if you were tracking a brood of vampires in wolf form through the undergrowth. Nowhere to charge your battery. No Wi-Fi, no pockets. Christopher had to survive on the intermittent phone calls. Each time he waited with bated breath for Devan to say that he could still smell her trail. That she was still alive. Those phone calls were all that kept Christopher going. He took a long moment to regain his composure and headed downstairs to the cavernous basement library.

There was a buzz of activity in the air. Amara was seated at her large oak desk with books spilling around her in what Christopher could only assume was organized chaos. Only one of the Council of Elders remained at the headquarters — Loris Valkari, the most recently recruited member. Kavisha Devi, the High Chancellor, was also still at the imposing gothic building. The other Elders — Dragos Vacarescu, the Speaker, along with Gustav Nielsen, Loshua Dascălu, Zulima Vargas and Shing-Lei Zan — were sent on a recruitment drive across the country. They were trying to find supernatural allies to join the fight against the Red Claws. So far, it appeared that they'd had little success as no one had arrived at headquarters.

Thankfully, Amara had been experiencing better luck in her search for recruits. The Vampire Hunters had sent an email explaining they would be arriving in the next few days. It had taken lengthy persuading on Amara's part, but luckily the Hunters had heard of the infamous Red Claws and wanted them eradicated. It never failed to amaze the Council just how clued-up the Hunters were on vampire affairs. Their

CHAPTER 1

skills extended far beyond the arena of combat to intelligence gathering and reconnaissance.

Scanning the room, Christopher's eyes fell on Kavisha and Loris, who were engrossed in an animated but hushed conversation. The High Chancellor was, as always, sitting in her motorized wheelchair. She was dressed in a green and gold sari and had a thin gold chain hanging between her ear and nose. Loris knelt beside her, dressed in dark pants and a formal jacket. Their voices would be barely audible to human ears. Both the speed and low volume of the discussion would make their words incomprehensible. But Christopher was no human. He picked up every word.

Kavisha had managed to pull some strings with 'old friends' she'd met on her earlier travels. They would be arriving at Vhik'h-Tal-Eskemon today. Unfortunately, they weren't particularly fond of some of the other creatures of the night. Kavisha and Loris were furiously planning how to keep tempers even before the battle commenced.

The battle in which I'm supposed to kill Nell.

Christopher's mind continued to betray him. Every thought, every rumination, brought him back to Nell. To the fact that she'd been thrown into the middle of a series of catastrophic events, all beyond her choosing.

"But what about the Hunters?" said Loris. "What happens when they discover there are a lot more preternatural beings in the world than just vampires? Are we turning our allies into targets?"

His question was met with silence. Nobody knew what would happen when you placed Vampire Hunters, vampires and other supernatural creatures in the same room. It seemed like the opening to a bad joke. *So, a vampire, Hunter and a fairy walk into a bar...*

But the question was a serious one. For the first time in known history vampires, Hunters and various creatures Christopher hadn't even known were real were coming together. It could have a ripple effect upon the entire supernatural world. Something else Christopher hadn't known very much about. He'd heard of werewolves — or 'werwulfs' as Devan insisted they were actually called — but didn't know of fae, lamia, witches, abarimon, elves, nymphs and about a dozen other groups that Kavisha, Loris and Amara (whose nose had been permanently stuck within the pages of various books since Nell and Devan left) had reeled off. It left Christopher's head spinning. He'd yet to meet any of these races and he was anticipating it with quiet trepidation. Christopher could sense that both Loris and Kavisha were nervous about the new arrivals, and this had rubbed off on him.

He sank into one of the plush chairs in the corner of the vast library, putting his feet up on the matching footrest.

"So," he broke the eerie hush. "Seeing as we can't predict what will happen when our guests arrive, there's little point dwelling on it."

Loris gave him a cagey look.

"Is there any further update from Devan?" continued Christopher. "Or Dragos, Gustav, Loshua or Zulima for that matter?" He tried to hide the edge in his voice.

"No," Loris replied, looking slightly downcast. "But we have heard from the remaining Magisters."

Christopher felt fury at the word 'Magisters'. It was thanks to one of them, a puffed-up and scornful ancient called Fabian Bamford, that Nell had been taken from him. Bamford had

CHAPTER 1

defected to the Red Claws and tricked Nell into leaving the safe confines of the headquarters. Poor, fragile, human Nell. If the damn Magisters had only managed to control their own kind, things would be much different now.

"They're coming to see us," explained Loris. "Apparently they are profusely sorry for the 'ex-Magister's' actions. Yes, they actually called him an 'ex' Magister. Bamford has been kicked out of the club." Loris snorted a little. No one else found it funny. "They want to apologize in person for his actions," continued Loris, more levelly. "I quote, '*They do not reflect the opinions of the group as a whole*'. Now that they know we are preparing for war, they want to support our cause."

"They have quite the nerve," said Kavisha. Anger hardened her usually soft features.

"Allies must be found," said Loris, turning to her. "We need all the help we can get. In the best interests of Nell and that of our kind, I suggest that we might appease them."

"You're really allowing them to come here?" exclaimed Christopher, leaning forward in his chair. "What if it's a set-up? One of them went rogue. What's stopping the others? How do we know it's safe?" Sometimes he was sure that the Council of Elders didn't actually think before it acted. "How is this good news?" he added.

"It's good news because we have a lot to learn from them, Christopher," replied Loris, looking mildly exasperated. "They were tracking the Red Claws long before Devan set off on his one-wolf quest. Their knowledge can help us. Now that we're on the same team, as it appears, we can use them. They are very old and very powerful vampires, Christopher. I don't have to tell you that."

Loris looked at Kavisha again.

"But we too are old. We will be prepared," he added.

The High Chancellor gave a resolute nod in return.

Since Nell's vanishing act, Loris had been tiptoeing around Christopher, giving the young vampire his space to mourn. If anything, it made Christopher feel even worse about the situation. Not only was the love of his life in the clutches of the enemy, but those around him seemed to be side-lining him. *They don't trust me,* he mused, bitterly.

"I trust you." Loris spoke softly so that only Christopher could hear.

Christopher looked at him quizzically.

"You were thinking out loud," Loris added, with a wry smile.

Christopher just shook his head in response. He didn't think it was entirely true that he was trusted.

"Erm, guys..." said Amara, without removing her face from the pages of the large book she was studying intently. "I've found something."

All eyes turned to her.

"Go on, Amara," Kavisha encouraged.

The librarian's research skills were proving invaluable in the search for an effective battle strategy. Her opinion was considered one of the most valuable in the room. Far above Christopher's, he would wager.

"I've been looking into the history of the Red Claws," she said, peeling her eyes briefly away from the imposing book. "We know that their leader is named Zachariah." She glanced at Kavisha.

"Yes, that's correct," confirmed the High Chancellor.

"Well, I'm not sure exactly what this means for us, but I'm certain it's relevant," said Amara, the enthusiasm in her voice now unmistakable. "I've been reading the census ledger entries for territories all over North America, cross-checking spates of unexplained deaths with the population records of the time. This one is from the year 1910."

Amara held up the hefty book. It was a hardback with hundreds of pages and looked like it weighed a fair few kilos. On the open page was a picture of a creased and yellowing sheet of paper with neat cursive handwriting covering the entire surface.

"I must have scanned tens of thousands of names over the past week, but I've finally got a hit."

Amara brought the hefty tome over to Kavisha. "What do you notice?"

Kavisha's finger traced the many columns of names filling the page. It wasn't long before her mouth dropped open.

"Zachariah Redclaw. Age 44. Son of Lucianu." She read slowly as her finger traced the ornate writing.

The room fell completely silent at Kavisha's words. Amara had been clutching at straws trying to find leads in the old census records, without knowing exactly what she was hoping to find. She just had an academic hunch and followed her nose. But the resourceful librarian-turned-detective had made a breakthrough.

"He was too proud to even alter his name," said Kavisha.

"Why would he?" replied Loris. "What was there for him to fear?"

Kavisha passed the bulky book to Loris for further inspection.

"Wait," Loris said, after studying the text. His finger had stopped lower down the page. "He had a brother, older than him…and a sister, too. Damien Redclaw, age 62. Mary Redclaw, age 41. No entries for the parents in the document."

"Well done, Amara," said the High Chancellor. "This could be very useful."

Amara smiled, a little self-consciously. She wasn't comfortable with the spotlight.

"If we can learn more about Zachariah, then maybe we can discern something about his strategy," mused Loris. "It could help us to figure out where they plan to go."

"Where is the census from?" asked Kavisha.

Loris quickly shifted his gaze to the top of the page.

"Whittier, Alaska," he read.

The room fell silent for a long moment as the occupants digested the new information.

"Makes sense," said Amara, contemplating. "Harsh terrain. An isolated populace. If people went missing fewer questions would be raised compared to a larger urban center. Easier pickings."

"Devan needs to know this information," said Loris.

"I'll tell him when he phones next," Christopher said.

Devan should be checking in soon, Christopher thought, but it depended upon when he stumbled across another payphone or if he could borrow someone's cell for an emergency call. Being a young guy with a swarthy complexion, many people were reluctant to hand over their cherished device. He was calling every two or three days. The waiting bored a hole into Christopher's stomach. It felt like acid was leaking over his organs sometimes when the anticipation got so great.

Christopher's brooding was interrupted by Sanford, the impassive human butler. He cleared his throat and then introduced the group of people behind him. Actually, mused Christopher, "people" was probably an insult to the colorful array of visitors who had just arrived through the library door.

CHAPTER 1

From his conversations with Kavisha and her vivid explanations of what to expect, Christopher could see that the tall woman standing at the front of the throng, with her head held high and bosom squared, was fae. She had bright blonde hair, sparkly blue eyes and was wearing a tight scarlet dress. Her fluid movements made her appear as if she was dancing. That was part of her 'special appeal' which made men so susceptible to her charms.

"Miss Odette," Sanford managed to choke out as he surreptitiously looked her up and down.

Was the usually unflappable butler actually blushing? Christopher was sure Miss Odette wiggled her hips just a tad more forcefully as she walked away from him towards Kavisha.

"My dear, dear old friend. Still a bloodsucker, I see." Miss Odette smiled in a way that was almost sincere.

Her words were met by an equally trite response from Kavisha.

"My dearest Odette. Still luring innocent men to their deaths?"

"Oh, you know me, Kavi. A girl's got to get by." The sickly-sweet smile returned to her face. "How long has it been, darling?"

"Not long enough," said Loris under his breath. Christopher's hyper-sensitive hearing registered the quip.

"You look as…exotic…as ever, still *sitting* pretty, I see," said Miss Odette, glancing askew at the electric wheelchair, before bending down and kissing Kavisha on both cheeks.

The fae looked around the room before spotting Christopher. She sauntered over and settled on the chair next to him. Christopher immediately rose to his feet and went to stand on the other side of the room beside Loris. He was not one to judge a book by its cover, but Miss Odette gave him a bad vibe.

"Charming," mused Miss Odette. "Seems decorum is dead around here."

"Master August," announced the butler. Sanford spoke more harshly this time as a very young boy walked up and took the freshly vacated seat beside Miss Odette.

"An imp," Loris whispered

This was not a species Christopher had discussed with Kavisha, but something about the boy was just plain wrong. August's face was contorted into a childishly sinister rictus smile. He wore white trousers with a white shirt that was buttoned all the way to the top and had slicked down black hair that was severely parted to the side. He looked like a prefect in a school for creepy misfits, thought Christopher, who was a little shocked that these two individuals wanted to help defeat the Red Claws. What motive could a boy have for joining the battle?

"What's with the child?" asked Christopher, almost silently, still looking straight ahead. He knew Loris would hear.

"He's not a child," replied Loris, equally quietly but rather sternly. "He only appears that way. Remember that, Christopher."

A small shiver ran its way down Christopher's spine.

Christopher took in the rest of the arrivals as Sanford announced them. He noticed another fae, a male this time. He had that same ethereal aura and fluidity of movement. There were two female spell-casters, who looked like friendly bohemian seniors. They were unmistakably twins. Their names were Sanya and Yansa. Both wore flowing floral dresses and their arms were adorned with dozens upon dozens of bracelets, each one colorful and unique.

Christopher smiled and nodded at each of the new arrivals, avoiding all further eye contact with Miss Odette and her little imp. It felt more reassuring to pretend that they weren't there.

After the introductions, Christopher decided to take his leave. Loris and Kavisha were more than capable of handling the welcomes. No doubt Kavisha would ask Sanford to show the guests to their rooms after. Christopher wanted to enjoy the quiet of the grand building while he still could. Before it was transformed into a bizarre menagerie of supernatural residents.

He walked somberly to his room, taking the long way around the headquarters to clear his mind.

"Christopher?" Amara approached as he began to close the door to his room.

"Oh, yeh...hi," Christopher answered, chastising himself for being so inarticulate. He was a vampire for God's sake, the unearthly evolution of man. He should be able to string a simple sentence together. But Nell had broken him when she left. She'd taken half of his heart with her, and apparently much of his brain.

"Can I talk to you?" She sounded concerned. Her grave tone made Christopher agree, even though all he wanted to do was sulk in his room. He gestured for her to follow him in.

Amara perched herself on the bed and Christopher plonked himself down heavily on a cushioned chair. They sat facing each other.

"I wanted to see if you were okay, I mean really okay?" Amara said. She looked into Christopher's eyes just as he pulled them away from her, not wanting her to see the tears welling inside the pink rims.

"Yeah, I'm fine." He nodded and smiled at the wall, but he was fooling no one.

"You need to talk," Amara urged, not unkindly, her voice low. "These emotions that you're experiencing. You're not used to them. They must be overwhelming."

Christopher swallowed and looked back at her.

"I'll manage," he said, simply.

He stared down at his hands. He'd not had anybody to talk to since Nell left him. It was only two weeks ago, but it felt like an eternity. But how could he talk about something that hurt him so much? He didn't think he'd be able to get the words out coherently.

"It's okay. I miss her like crazy, too," assured Amara. "Nell is like family. But we *are* going to find her." Her tone was defiant, leaving no room for doubt.

It heartened Christopher to know she was as determined to fight as he was. In his downward spiral he'd forgotten that not only was he mourning his love, Amara was missing her friend, too. This wasn't just about him. There was also Devan, also. He was out in the wild right now putting himself on the line. If he didn't come back, if the Red Claws got to him first, that would be devastating. Christopher had come to actually like the wolfman and there was no question of Devan's dedication to Nell.

"I'm sorry. I just can't do this," said Christopher as he continued looking at his hands.

"How do you mean, Christopher? What can't you do?"

"All of this, Amara. All of it." He met her eyes again, not caring about the tears dripping down his face now. "This whole thing is so fucked up. On the one hand I'm scared that she won't ever come back. But I'm also petrified that we *will* find her. What will I do if... when we get her back, Amara? Kill her? Fulfill the fucking prophesy so we can wipe out the Red Claws. What's the point in that?" His eyes pleaded with the librarian.

"We don't know for sure that you'll have to do that yet," said Amara. "Yes, the Council and Magisters seem pretty certain that's how it has to go down. I know that. But I've been doing my own research. I'm trying to find a way out. I promise you. There's wisdom in those books."

Spoken like a true librarian. Christopher couldn't help but give a half smile.

"Thank you for trying, Amara."

Christopher leaned forward and grasped her hands. He squeezed gently. He knew that she was trying her hardest, but he also knew that the likelihood of finding a way out was slim.

"Don't keep this bottled up, Christopher," she counseled. "We have to be there for each other. It's what Nell would have wanted. We're the only ones here who love her. The rest of the vampires can't love, you know that. They're helping because it saves their own skins and prevents their food source from being eliminated. I'm not saying that they have no noble intentions, but we want to save Nell because we love her. We know Devan feels that way, too."

Christopher was a little stung by that last comment, but he couldn't deny the truth of it. He scanned Amara's face and saw the fierce resolve etched on her features. Who knew librarians were made of such stern stuff?

"Thank you again, Amara. You are a blessing." He squeezed her hands a little tighter.

"Don't get twisted into knots about the prophecy," said

Amara. "Put that on the back burner for now. First things first. Let's get our girl back."

Chapter 2

"We should camp here for the night. The foliage is thick and will provide good cover," the wolf next to Devan said.

Lupita's coat was rust colored, compared to Devan's deep brown. She was the largest of the werwulfs Devan had recruited in the wild. Both were currently in their full wolf form. To the human eye they would look like two unnaturally large feral wolves.

He'd come across Lupita and her pack just outside of Fort Wayne. At this point, Devan had only managed to persuade five other werwulfs to join his search for Nell and ultimately the war against the Red Claws. The wolves he'd recruited were all for killing vampires, that was a given. But they were more reluctant to get thrown headfirst into a supernatural war. That part definitely took some convincing.

Devan was feeling the pressure of trying to find recruits as well as track Nell's scent across the country. So when he met Lupita he was thrilled to have somebody else he could trust to take the lead. She had quickly become his beta in the pack, tracking the scents of other colonies while Devan kept his nose to the ground for Nell's trail.

Werwulfs in the wild were traditionally peaceful and un-problematic creatures, preferring to live amongst their own in full wolf form, far removed from human gazes. Out of Lupita's pack, only her younger brother, Lupo, and her father, Lupertico, had joined Devan's ranks, bringing their total number to nine. He knew he'd need as many reinforcements as possible when they finally caught up with the Red Claws. Now with nine, he was feeling quietly optimistic about his chances of at the very least taking Nell back, and hopefully turning a few Red Claws to ash in the process.

Devan had remained mostly in full wolf form since leaving the vampire headquarters, as it was by far the swiftest way to travel. When they passed a populated area, he would transform into human form, steal clothes and try to call back to Vhik'h-Tal-Eskemon with an update. The whole exercise took precious time away from the hunt, but Devan knew that headquarters needed to keep track of his whereabouts. He also knew that Christopher longed to hear that Nell's trail was still warm. That there was hope.

Werwulf packs had long family trees, with most of the members related. Devan had been adopted by a human mother so his family hadn't been able to prepare him for what was coming as he grew from infant to boy to man. It was a frightening yet exhilarating journey as his true nature slowly unfolded through the years. Not being a part of an established pack, he had been surprised when he stumbled across werwulf colonies in the wild on his hunt for Nell. They welcomed him with open arms and open minds. Literally. They could talk amongst themselves by mental projection. The words were as clear as if they'd been spoken aloud. He could hear the thoughts even in his human form. Wild.

"I think we should keep going a little longer," Devan projected out to the pack.

CHAPTER 2

The answer was always the same at this point of the day as the last rays of light dissipated from the late evening sky. A collective groan sounded among his brethren. They were tired. He couldn't push them too hard. They needed to rest.

"Fine," Devan acquiesced, slowing down his pace and moving towards more dense tree cover. He finally came to a stop and sat on his haunches.

Lupita came to sit next to him, as she did each night.

"I'm not sure we're getting any closer." Her thought projected only to Devan.

That neat trick had been a surprise, too. Within a pack, you could isolate one individual when communicating so only they heard your thoughts. There had been other revelations as well. Such as the ability to project images, both actual things he was seeing and also pictures he could vividly conjure up. If Devan ever got lost, which was highly unlikely, he'd be able to show his pack his surroundings, making it easier for them to find him.

"We have to try harder. Run faster, for longer tomorrow," Devan answered as he curled himself into his usual fetal sleeping position.

"You love her, don't you?" Lupita's voice, even in his mind, faltered a little. "This isn't just about the big battle and that prophecy. That's why you're driving yourself, and us, so hard."

This was new. Until now they'd only talked strategy. But his hastily-assembled pack were taking a leap of faith and placing their trust in him. He owed them something. Plus, he was curious to learn more about Lupita, too. He hadn't had much interaction with his own kind previously and now, living as the alpha in a pack, he had a lot to learn.

"Yes, I think so," he said.

"I thought as much," Lupita said quietly, before she closed her eyes and began to slow her breathing.

"Devan?" She said after a few minutes of silence. "If you truly loved her, you wouldn't have to think. You'd know."

Devan didn't respond. He let the sentence float around the edge of his consciousness. He loved Nell. Of course he did. He wouldn't have followed her halfway across the country if he didn't.

***

The next morning the wolves were awake bright and early. As the big orange sun rose over the dense trees the wolf who had taken the final night watch, a russet-colored youngster by the name of Flint, stretched his body, pointing his nose to the sky and smelling the damp, heavy air. Devan followed suit, reveling in the sensation of extending his sleek limbs after his slumber.

"Food?" Devan heard in his mind.

Flint was always hungry. As a teenager and the youngest of their makeshift pack, he was growing faster than Devan thought was possible. His stomach was a bottomless pit. Devan saw an image of a rabbit as clear as day inside his own head. Flint preferred smaller furries to larger predators.

Now fully awake, the small pack bounded off soundlessly to find fuel for the day. It was something Devan needed to get used to, eating in wolf form all the time. The first bite of the sinewy rabbit was tough and slightly acidic in his mouth, but his primal instinct soon took over and he made short work of the tough flesh. He had a preference for elk, but in the wild you took what the land provided.

CHAPTER 2

It didn't take the pack long to satiate their hunger and they quickly moved back to the job at hand: tracking Nell and the Red Claws. For Devan, recruiting for the army was a secondary task at the moment, but every set of paws counted. The nine wolves were currently in North Dakota after running for three solid days, only stopping to feed, double-check the scent trail and allow Devan to make his call. Every so often one of the wolves would branch away from the pack after sensing another group of werwulfs in the vicinity. The peace overtures had to be made and the local colony needed to be reassured that Devan's pack would be passing through as opposed to making a claim on the territory.

They had been making good progress, but the Red Claws had a big lead. Luckily, the vampires had been so eager to flee quickly that they hadn't masked Nell's scent. This was a saving grace for Devan. Life would have been a hell of a lot harder if the Red Claws had taken steps to hide Nell's distinctive odor. As the days went on, Nell's scent became stronger and stronger, which indicated the pack was closing the gap. But it also meant the Red Claws were not allowing Nell to bathe or take care of herself.

Nell had walked into the hands of the Red Claws freely. One part of Devan had been hoping that would mean the vampires would be allowing her the courtesy of traveling in comfort. But who was he kidding? The fact that she seemingly hadn't been able to clean herself for a couple of weeks meant that she was likely being held captive with force. If only the wolves could catch up, they'd be able to assess what was happening to her. But that was a double-edged sword. If Devan stumbled on the Red Claw Family and discovered that Nell was being mistreated, he knew he wouldn't be able to hold himself back.

He'd likely get himself killed which, no doubt, would make the situation worse.

The pack picked up speed through the dense foliage. Trees and shrubs whipped past Devan's muzzle, barely leaving a mark as he cascaded through the pine forest. The rich smell of the trees wafted through Devan's nose but did nothing to hide the traces of Nell. He had locked on to that particular scent as if his life depended on it. Devan momentarily looked up. Dark storm cloud hung overhead. It wouldn't be long until the Heavens opened.

The vampires had been taking some precautions. They'd kept to back roads and forest trails out of the sight of prying human eyes. A merry band of blood suckers with a female captive would likely draw a lot of unwanted attention. Despite the fact that werwulfs were quick and could cover a lot of ground in a day, the vampires had the advantage. They could run unnaturally fast and didn't need much rest. But what the werwulfs lacked in speed, they made up for in strength, which would help them further down the line. Hopefully.

"We're averaging over one hundred miles a day, but we're still no closer to her," Lupita shouted into Devan's mind as she flew through the forest alongside him.

"Yeah, it seems like they might even be stretching their lead, though I hate to admit it," Devan responded, his lips never moving. He didn't once take his eyes off the ground before him.

He and Lupita ran at the front of the pack. The rest stayed close behind. With such a small pack it was pretty easy to track your packmates in your peripheral vision. The nine werwulfs hadn't known each other for more than two weeks, but they had found a working rhythm together.

CHAPTER 2

"They have to stop at some point and we'll find them when they do," Lupita projected.

She had a strange way of knowing when Devan's thoughts had run away from him and he was thinking the worst. He'd been spiraling a lot in the quiet hours and it was happening more and more lately. When his mind grew dark, Lupita was there with a placating word or two.

That evening, after traversing another hundred or so miles through rain, mud and sludge, Lupita made the call that they would have to stop. Devan begrudgingly agreed. The rest of the pack were looking dirty, ragged and were in need of well-earned rest. They'd crossed the boundary into Canada and had settled at a spot in the Boundary Dam Reservoir to spend the night. The sun was setting low over the water, turning the entire surface into a glowing red plateau. It was actually beautiful, but Devan's agitated state of mind didn't allow him to appreciate the splendor of their surroundings. The rest of the pack had gone hunting, leaving Devan alone with his thoughts. He padded through the forest around the circumference of the reservoir before finding a small, golden-red pool of water about the size of a small backyard swimming pool.

Dipping his muzzle into the pool, Devan drank for a long while. The water was refreshing, cooling his dry mouth and tongue. He then tiptoed into the water until his body was almost fully submerged. After a few minutes of peace, his thoughts were interrupted.

"It's beautiful here, isn't it?"

Lupita's voice was clear inside his mind. It concerned him a little that he didn't know she was there before she spoke. His roiling thoughts were distracting him from observing his surroundings. He needed to be on high alert or else they were all in danger. He mentally kicked himself.

"What are you doing here? Aren't you going hunting?" he projected.

Devan wasn't ready to leave the cool water just yet. It was just starting to work its soothing magic.

"They can manage without me. I came to find you. You left in a rush. It worried me."

"And why would that worry you?" Devan asked, his tone too harsh. He immediately felt lousy.

"Because you're our alpha, Devan," she replied, matching his stern tone. "I left my pack, my friends, to come on this mission with you. I'm trusting you. I'm here to save your girlfriend and then save the fucking world, okay? So I think I have a right to be worried if I think you're losing it."

Lupita turned to leave.

Devan felt worse than ever. He was letting his emotions cloud his judgment. He liked to think he was pretty level-headed, but Lupita seemed to push his buttons sometimes.

"She's *not* my girlfriend and I'm *not* losing it," he replied.

Devan took a breath, realizing his tone was still overly harsh.

Lupita paused.

"I know I said I loved her," he continued. "And I do, just not in *that* way. She's not mine."

Lupita remained still for a moment, then slowly walked away.

"I'm sorry. Don't go," Devan pleaded, hoping it would be enough to earn her forgiveness.

He needed her. She was critical to this mission for one thing.

Lupita tensed her haunches. Then she slowly turned back around, eyeing Devan.

CHAPTER 2

"You're pretty new at this, aren't you?" Lupita's huge hazel eyes bored into his.

"New to chasing vampires across the country? Yup, you bet I am."

Devan tried to keep his voice light. But, of course, Lupita saw through him.

"You know that's not what I meant."

Her tone was gentle. Her eyes softened. She dipped her head slightly.

"Yeah, I'm pretty new," he conceded.

"How new?"

Lupita was relentless, Devan thought.

"Four years."

"Woah." Lupita's surprised voice was loud in Devan's head. "That's, like, really new. I thought you were older. You seem older. Erm, you're just a kid!"

"Kid? I'm twenty-four, in human years."

Devan was a little weirded out that Lupita thought he was so young.

Lupita considered for a moment.

"You can't be twenty-four, that doesn't make any sense," she replied. "If you first made the change four years ago you'd only be about sixteen or seventeen now, maybe eighteen tops, if you were a late bloomer."

Lupita's confusion projected clearly into Devan's mind. She seemed hurt at the prospect of him lying to her.

"I didn't lie," he insisted. "I'm twenty-four! I changed for the first time just after my twentieth birthday. Something happened and I snapped. I couldn't control it. I remember it clearly. It scared the living daylights out of me."

Devan could feel his temper rising again. He fought to keep

a lid on it

"Seriously?" asked Lupita, unconvinced. "The change always happens at puberty, that's just the way it is." She paused for a moment. "Maybe your pack is different. When did the others change?"

Lupita's words were hitting Devan like stones. Each new utterance was a reminder that he didn't really know what he was doing and was way out of his depth here. He remained silent to gather his thoughts.

"You were alone," she said, more to herself, when there was no reply forthcoming.

The silence stretched out.

"Devan." Lupita's voice softened again. "I think that explains a lot about you. I can't imagine not being brought up in a pack. We are social animals. It must have been a lonely, bewildering experience, not having any guidance."

"What about you?" asked Devan, keen to take the focus off himself. "How was it?"

Lupita pawed at a twig on the ground, slowly rolling it back and forth.

"I was twelve," she said. "The time when girls, well some girls, start going through some quite bewildering physical changes anyway. Add being a werwulf to the mix and you have an explosive recipe. I didn't handle it well, at all. I put dad through hell, in fact. But he was always there for me. Always patient and understanding. He wanted us, me and Lupo, to have the skills necessary to navigate the human world. Reading, writing, driving etc. So even if we ultimately chose to live in our primal form, we could still get by in both realms. I can't even imagine what I would have done without dad's guidance."

CHAPTER 2

A long silence stretched out, filled only by the gentle sloshing of the reservoir and birds chirping nearby.

"I always knew I was different growing up," said Devan, finding his voice at last. "The heightened senses, being faster and stronger than the other kids. The restlessness when the moon was full. I could tell that it wasn't exactly normal. But the change threw me for a loop when it finally happened. But at least it explained why I was the way I was."

Lupita seemed deep in contemplation, head bowed.

"I think I know why you've been feeling so shitty," she said, finally. "Have you ever stayed in wolf form for this long before?"

Devan shook his muzzle.

"I think the experience is doing strange things to you," she said. "Messing with your brain chemistry or something. Being in a primal, feral state continually when you're not used to it must be taking a toll. You need to change back to your human form, Devan, for a while at least. It might reset your system or something."

She turned around, ready to pad away. "I'll leave you to it."

"Stay."

The word escaped from Devan's mind before he could control it. But the truth was he didn't want to be alone. Lupita was right. He was losing it. He was letting his fear and anger get the better of him. He needed to pull himself together, for everybody's sake. The alpha had to take care of the pack. That was the way it was. He knew that much.

Lupita tilted her head to consider his request then padded slowly into the pool. Before Devan realized what was happening, Lupita's body was contorting. Her limbs grew in length. Her thick russet fur receded into her skin. Her animal features softened and morphed into a human nose, mouth and eyes. She quickly ducked down to preserve her modesty, only keeping her head above the dark water.

Devan's sharp wolf eyes widened as he took her in. Light brown skin with a smattering of freckles on her cheeks, clear hazel eyes, a sharp nose and long straight black hair. She had an oval face with full lips and a high forehead. She was beautiful in a natural, earthy way.

Devan drew in breath then ducked completely beneath the water. A few moments later his human head popped above the ripples. His dark hair was matted to his forehead. He ran a hand through it to push it back.

Lupita took a moment to assess him. A smile slowly crept across her cheeks. Water clung to her long lashes and she blinked it away.

"So, this is you," she said. Her voice was deeper than Devan had expected, yet still soft. He was a little disorientated listening to words coming out of her mouth after communicating by thought for so long.

"I know," she said, registering his confused look. "This is odd for me, as well. I don't really spend much time like this."

"You're not how I expected," Devan said, without really thinking. He was suddenly very aware of his own body.

"Oh!" Lupita responded, taken aback. "I hope that's not crushing disappointment I can detect." She looked a little crestfallen.

"No, no," Devan reassured, quickly. "Far from it."

Her smile returned.

"Well, you're not totally offensive to the senses, either," she said, playfully. "For a human, anyway."

"Um, thanks," were the only words he could muster.

CHAPTER 2

They stood in silence for what felt like an eternity. Their eyes locked, both grinning. A full moon hung low in the sky. Devan moved forward. She did the same. He leaned his head towards her, gently tilting it so that their lips would meet. Neither closed their eyes as Devan gently kissed her, placing a hand softly behind her head and curling it into the wet hair that clung to the nape of her neck.

Devan's world seemed to shift as their lips caressed. Eyes closed now, their lips found a rhythm. He could sense a primal hunger emanating from Lupita. She was ferocious with her kisses, forcing his mouth open with her own. Their bodies moved against each other as though pulled by a magnetic force. He felt her breasts against his chest. With his free hand, he discovered the curves of her body.

Lupita's hands enveloped Devan's neck. She jumped up and her legs wrapped around his waist. A primal hunger now overcame Devan under the large glowing moon. He deepened his kisses, biting at Lupita's neck. She moaned as Devan pulled away, looking at her for confirmation before he went further.

"Please." Her voice was ragged, her cheeks flushed.

Without removing her legs from around his waist, Devan lowered her hips and gently guided himself inside her. Her gasp was loud in his ear. Soft moans left her mouth with each rhythmic push of Devan's hips. The water rippled around them, reflecting the moonlight in the small waves. He moved slowly at first, following the rhythm she was setting with her own hips. He moved his lips back to Lupita's mouth and she met him eagerly. Her mouth opened against his. He quickened his movements as their tongues danced together. Lupita squeezed her legs tight around his waist and threw her head back, releasing the energy building inside her into the universe. Devan stiffened then buried his head into the nape of her neck, holding on to her for dear life.

Lupita kept herself wrapped around Devan as he pulled his head away from her. His eyes searched her face. She smiled, delicately kissing his lips one final time before placing her feet back onto the floor of the pool. They both took a moment to catch their breath.

"That was…" Devan's voice was gruff. He cleared his throat as Lupita finished the sentence for him.

"Unexpected?" She smiled again.

She was beautiful. The word actually didn't seem to do her justice. Lupita was something else entirely. Patient, kind, trusting, open, empathetic and free as nature itself. Wise as well, as clearly she was right about being in wolf form for too long driving Devan a little stir crazy.

They moved to the edge of the water, sitting in the shallows.

"Devan," Lupita took his hands in hers.

"Yes," he replied, a warm feeling coming over him as Lupita said his name.

"I'm really sorry that you had to go through life alone."

Devan was relaxed, in what felt like the first time for an eternity. Even though it had been terrifying at times growing up as a werwulf alone, right now, in this moment, he was thankful for it. That experience had brought him to Lupita.

Devan answered by squeezing her hands tightly.

They sat for a while, watching as the moon rose higher in the night sky.

"I think it's time to go back, don't you?" Lupita broke the silence. "The others might be wondering."

They changed back into their wolf forms and trotted back to the pack. If the rest of the wolves noticed or sensed anything, they were too diplomatic to mention it.

"Our little secret?" Lupita asked him, her words sensual in his mind, as she settled close to him for the night. She projected an image of Devan waist deep in the water as seen through her eyes.

"Our little secret," Devan confirmed.

Just as sleep was about to claim him, Devan thought about Nell. They *would* find her. They would save her and then they would figure out the rest.

Chapter 3

The Magisters arrived at Vhik'h-Tal-Eskemon exactly when they said they would, down to the precise minute. They followed Sanford into the cavernous library, where the majority of residents were settled, each focusing on their own particular task. Some more than others.

Miss Odette and her pet imp August, who insisted on being called 'Master August', lounged on a plush couch looking thoroughly bored. Master August would growl under his breath whenever Christopher walked past and Miss Odette would pat the imp on his head each time, like a good little boy. It was infuriating. However, Christopher kept reminding himself that they were there to help, no matter how self-centered or indifferent they appeared.

The spell-caster twins, Sanya and Yansa, were huddled around a stack of books researching various spells and incantations that could disorientate, incapacitate, hurt or even kill vampires. Poor Kavisha had taken a break from being their test subject for the tamer spells. She had the scars to prove it.

It took every ounce of self-control for Christopher to remain calm when the Magisters arrived. If that old fool Bamford hadn't defected to the Red Claws, Nell would probably be safe in the headquarters right now. It seemed like ruminating was all Christopher was doing lately... *If this hadn't happened then...* Over and over again. Christopher analyzed how every choice made led to a chain of consequences. If he'd not met Nell. If she hadn't discovered his secret. If the prophecy didn't exist. And so on and so on. There were too many 'ifs' to count.

"Good evening." The female Magister named Jiangshina spoke in her sing-song voice.

"Good evening, Magister," said Kavisha, kindly. "Please make yourselves comfortable."

"Thank you for your hospitality. However, that will not be necessary. We prefer to stand."

"As you wish," Kavisha assented, staring up at the four robed figures from her wheelchair.

"First of all, we wish to apologize for...what transpired," began Jiangshina, looking genuinely pained. "Fabian's betrayal is unforgivable. He misled us all. As you so perceptibly recognized at the time, High Chancellor, he wanted Christopher to drain Nell before the army of the night was assembled. This was out of sequence with the prophecy and would have rendered it ineffective, thus giving the advantage to the Red Claws."

The library was completely quiet.

"Fabian has sided with darkness and deviated from the values that, as Magisters, we have held sacred for centuries," continued Jiangshina. "For this, we are deeply sorry."

She looked around the library.

"I see that you are readying yourselves for war," Jiangshina added. "We wish to join you in your fight. We must ensure that the prophecy is fulfilled, for the sake of all that is."

The Magister gave a pointed look at Christopher before continuing.

"The only way to do that is to bring back the girl and allow this young man to do what needs to be done. But at the right time, when we are at strength."

Christopher balled his hands into fists, but was determined not to make a scene. If the Magisters wanted to help get Nell back, then that was fine. But as soon as Christopher had her in his arms, the rest was undecided. He still held out some hope that they would find a way out of this. That the Red Claws could be wiped out without having to sacrifice Nell.

Christopher caught Loris's eye. The older vampire smiled proudly, seemingly impressed with Christopher's feat of self-control.

"Thank you for your offer of help," said Kavisha. "Your wisdom and insight are always much appreciated." The high Chancellor spread her arms. "As you can see, the first of our recruits have arrived. We are anticipating many more. As a first measure, we need to strengthen the perimeter of this building from psychic attack, so there's no repeat of Bamford's infiltration. Your assistance in this matter would be invaluable. If you would follow me."

Kavisha gestured to the door then pushed the joystick on her wheelchair forward so she trundled slowly towards it. The four Magisters followed her.

On a whim, Christopher reached out with his fingers, lightly grazing the female Magister's hand as she moved past him. Jiangshina gave him a curious glance before continuing on her way.

It worked. There was a flash in Christopher's mind as he recalled events from Jiangshina's perspective. The surprise

CHAPTER 3

and bitter disappointment on realizing Bamford's treachery. The shock turning to anger and then to a firm resolve to atone for his actions. The pain of having to tell the other Magisters what had transpired. Christopher breathed a sigh of relief. He didn't trust the Magisters, but at least Jiangshina was telling the truth. She was not complicit.

He wished that he had more opportunity to practice his little skill. Seeing somebody's life experience when you placed your hands upon them was filled with possibilities. But the skill worked on some and not on others. The memories shown were sometimes a little random, too.

Loris walked over and placed a hand on Christopher's shoulder, squeezing gently. Nothing sparked in Christopher's mind. It seemed the older vampire was immune. Either that or Christopher's gift was irritatingly sketchy.

Mind-reading aside, Christopher was really starting to appreciate Loris, seeing him as a kind of father figure. He had also warmed greatly to Kavisha, who seemed tireless and didn't allow her disability hold her back. For two vampires who would never know true love they sure were warm-hearted, Christopher mused. He sometimes thought about why vampires couldn't fall in love. Was it a defense mechanism in case the object of their desires wasn't also immortal? Was it something to do with casting off a human weakness? And what made Christopher different? Was it purely because he was the subject of some prophecy? Was it something about Nell? These questions were too big for him.

"You miss her badly, don't you?" Loris asked. His words stung but the tone was kind.

"More than anything," Christopher admitted.

Every moment of every day he missed Nell. But it wasn't

only that. He was terrified that something would happen to her and he wouldn't even know it. That was his worst fear. That he was already in a world where Nell no longer existed. It was agonizing to think about.

"We're doing everything we can to get her back, you know that right?" assured Loris. "She's just as important to us."

His words were meant to be comforting, but Christopher found them anything but.

"Important to you so that I can kill her myself," Christopher spat. "So she can die the 'correct' death."

"Whatever needs to happen, will happen," said Loris, somberly. "I know Amara is working tirelessly to try and find another way." He turned to look at the librarian. "That one is not to be underestimated, for a human."

Loris turned back to face Christopher, sympathy in his eyes. It was still strange to Christopher that the vampire before him, who was God-only-knows how old, was unable to love, yet was so understanding.

"We both know how unlikely a get-out clause is," Christopher said, sullenly.

He knew he was behaving like a petulant child. He was also well aware that he had an audience, namely Miss Odette and creepy Master August, but he didn't even care at this point.

Loris grabbed Christopher by the shoulders so quickly that it took him by surprise. Even with Christopher's heightened vampiric senses, Loris's hands moved faster than the eye could register.

"I want you to listen to me carefully," said Loris, his grip firm. "Yes, this entire situation is a diabolical mess. It is probably the worst thing imaginable for you. It's cruel that you are the only one of us who gets to love somebody, and that fate would decree that you have to be the one to end her life. Frankly, it's sick. Nobody is questioning that. But you have to be strong." Loris loosened his grip a little. "By all means hold out hope that something might change," he continued. "But if not, you have to be the one to…make things right." Loris took a step closer. "At least you get to feel love, Christopher. Even if it's part of a cruel God's even crueler joke. Do you know how long it has been since any of us have felt love? I can't even remember what it feels like. So please, in the name of the Omni-Father, pull yourself together. Do you think you can do that?"

Christopher blinked. He'd never stopped to consider that other vampires might be jealous that he could feel love, even in these most grotesque of circumstances.

"Yes," Christopher answered. "I can try."

He knew his response wasn't sufficient but it was all he could give at that moment. To see Loris so animated, fragile even, was bizarre. Christopher reached up and patted one of Loris's hands that was placed on his shoulder. He was trying to see if he could catch a glimpse inside his mind. Nope, nothing.

His concentration was swiftly broken when Miss Odette piped up from her position sprawled on the couch.

"Now boys. You could at least kiss. Provide us with some entertainment." The words slithered from her mouth like venom. Master August widened his sinister grin.

Loris stiffened.

"Thank you for the suggestion, but you'll have to find your entertainment elsewhere," he replied, without a hint of animosity. "You know, if you're bored, you could perhaps help out one of the others."

"Of course, I *could* help out," replied Miss Odette. "But the fact that I'm even here should be enough. Surely you're not going to force your happy helpers to *work* for their keep, are you?"

"Perish the thought," said Loris, "What was I even thinking?"

Loris winked at Christopher, who couldn't help but smirk.

Chapter 4

The next morning more guests arrived. The Vampire Hunters.

They reached Vhik'h-Tal-Eskemon just as the sun began peeking up over the horizon. Christopher, who only entered his sleep-state in fits and starts since Nell left, came down to the first floor and leaned over the banister to take in the scene in the grand hallway.

Ten humans, six men and four women wearing tight-fitting black fatigues, were grouped near the door. Christopher noticed they were all well-muscled and looked like they could handle themselves in combat. Each wore some kind of high-tech earpiece as well as a thick leather utility belt, upon which was arranged an array of weapons. Christopher saw guns, knives as well as objects whose function he couldn't fathom. They looked poised for battle. Christopher had to admit that he felt a little anxious at the sight.

Even more disturbing was the fact that lined up in front of them were the four Magisters. The vampires were barring the humans from moving any further into the building. Christopher was sure that he heard the Magisters hissing, which brought a wry smile to his lips. For all their high-mindedness and grandiose ways, it seemed that the ancient vampires had reverted to type when confronted with a threat.

The atmosphere was tense. For once, Christopher didn't entirely rate the vampires' chances in a standoff with humans.

Just then a flustered Amara came bounding down the stairs, wearing a yellow robe over her flannel pajamas, matched with pink fluffy slippers. She glanced at Christopher, who raised an eyebrow, before bolting down the remaining stairs in a huff. Christopher looked on.

The gaggle of Vampire Hunters stood very still. Statuesque. While they had a pretty easy time killing vampires when they were ensconced in their sleep state, or picking them off one by one, the four Magisters before them would give them pause. The situation was finely balanced. One wrong move could tip the scales in the direction of chaos.

Amara pushed her way through the Magisters, mumbling pardons until she was situated between the opposing sides.

"Excuse me, Magisters. Please allow me to welcome our *guests*," Amara said, emphasizing the last word.

The Magisters didn't move.

"I do apologize," Amara said to the Hunters, smiling. "Our esteemed friends seem to have forgotten their manners temporarily."

"They're no friends of ours," said one of the Vampire Hunters. He looked about thirty and had long black hair tied into a ponytail and a sharp roman nose. His skin was so pale that he could have been mistaken for a vampire himself, Christopher thought.

"I can see why you would feel that way, but we're all on the same side here," said Amara, unconvincingly and clearly out of her depth. "Just allow me a minute. Loris! Kavisha!" she screamed into the depths of the building, as if she were calling for her mom and dad after answering the door to a grown-up.

CHAPTER 4

Christopher recalled the words of the prophecy — *'Unlikely allegiances will be forged. They will be tested. They will be sacrificed. They will be broken'.* The scene before him was both slightly comical and somehow ominous. These were truly the strangest of times.

After a few moments the High Chancellor and the Elder arrived. Christopher noticed the cool veneer of a few of the Hunters cracking slightly when they took in the docile-looking Indian lady rolling towards them in a motorized wheelchair. This was a morning of surprises all round. Christopher also noticed Amara keenly eyeing the black-clad females of the group. They looked fierce in their fatigues and combat gear. He wondered if the studious librarian ever wished that she was more than just a mild-mannered keeper of knowledge.

Amara stepped forward.

"Would you kindly ask the Magisters to step back and allow our guests to enter?"

Amara was addressing Kavisha and Loris, but didn't turn her head as she spoke. Instead, her eyes remained fixed on the Magister Jiangshina.

"Magisters," said Kavisha, in a placating tone. "This might be…"

"You decided to bring our enemies here?" Jiangshina interrupted. The edge to her voice was as sharp as a knife. This was very unlike her.

"It was a detail I was saving for a more opportune time to discuss with you," said Kavisha, resigned. "I didn't anticipate our guests would be arriving so early today." She looked up at the black-clad group, appraising each member.

"The enemies of your enemies can sometimes be your

friends," said Amara, not taking her eyes off Jiangshina. "The Hunters have agreed a truce for the greater good, namely eliminating the Red Claws before they wreak havoc on the world."

Loris stepped forward.

"Desperate times have called for desperate action, Magister. As you can see," he said.

Jiangshina snapped her head around to look at him.

"What gives you the right to side with those who have so tirelessly worked towards our destruction?" she hissed.

"We have the right to do what is best for all of us, vampires and humans," Loris replied. "I'm sure you cannot argue that, right now, this comes down to exterminating the Red Claws."

Jiangshina was silent, seemingly caught off-guard for a moment.

"It seems we've intruded on a domestic squabble," said the long-haired Hunter. "Aren't you 'evolved beings' meant to be above all that?" His comments raised a few sniggers from his colleagues. "We'd be happy to leave if we're not welcome. All bets off. Let the hostilities resume."

Amara shot him a glance of reproach. His comments and tone weren't helping.

"That is not necessary," said Kavisha. "There's simply a misunderstanding."

"We will not side with the *nocturnae hostium*," said Jiangshina, looking down at Kavisha with barely disguised disgust. The Magister straightened her shoulders, as if squaring up for a fight.

"Esteemed Magister, while I value your opinion, it is not required at this moment," said Kavisha, her tone level despite the strong words. "Those who you see in front of you are both very knowledgeable and very capable. We require their assistance to win this battle, for all our sakes. If you cannot be civil, I will have to ask you to leave."

"You would have *us* leave so that you can welcome these... *monsters?*"

"That's rich," said the Vampire Hunter.

"Yes," was all Kavisha had to say, looking directly at Jiang-shina.

"You'll regret this. Siding with this murderous scum." The Magister turned on her heel and walked out of the front door, followed by her three companions.

There was a long silence in the hallway as everyone regained their bearings.

"Now we have that out of the way, perhaps we can start again," said Loris. He smiled and turned to the Vampire Hunters. "Welcome to Vhik'h-Tal-Eskemon. I hope your journey was relatively painless."

"Yes, thank you." One of the older Vampire Hunters responded. His hair was salt and pepper gray but he was built like a brick outhouse. He looked like he pumped some serious iron.

Loris made the introductions before handing over to Amara.

"Thank you all for coming," said the librarian. "I've chatted with you over email but it's a pleasure to meet you all in person." She stepped forward and shook each hand, listening as they reeled off their names. Christopher noted that the sarcastic one with the ponytail was called Haiden while the older brute was called Ezra.

Amara led the Hunters to their make-shift lodgings at the far end of the headquarters on the ground floor. Kavisha had wanted them stationed as far away as possible from the supernaturals, for everyone's safety. And, suspected Christopher, like him she didn't entirely trust Miss Odette and her little pet.

Chapter 5

After a mentally draining afternoon filling the Hunters in on the Red Claws, other creatures of the night and the search for Nell, Amara returned to the library for some late-night research. She wasn't used to doing so much talking and found it wearing being around other people for so long. She was an introvert by nature and needed quiet time to recharge her spiritual batteries. Herbal tea and books had always been the perfect combination to rejuvenate her soul.

The sun had disappeared over the horizon. It was her favorite time of day. Dusk. She should have been in seventh heaven surrounded by so many amazing books in this magnificent library with a steaming cup of cardamom and chamomile tea in her hand, but her thoughts betrayed her. She tried so hard to be positive throughout the day when she was surrounded by others. But at night it was a different story. The weight of the situation bore down on her. Unrelenting. She had been thrust into circumstances that her logical mind said shouldn't exist. But here she was. The fate of all existence seemingly at stake.

She sat down at her large oak desk and gently put her cup down. The books she had been studying previously were still laid out on the desk, opened to the familiar pages. She ran a hand through her long black hair, pushing it away from her face and smoothing it at the nape of her neck. She sighed, then picked up the tea, inhaling the spicy scent as she cradled the warm mug in both hands.

This was where Amara felt grounded. Not necessarily in an immense vampire lair, but in the company of paper and words. The words had filled her mind over the past two weeks as she learnt all she could about the Red Claws, various supernatural creatures and possible battle strategies. The old, archaic texts were difficult to digest, but perseverance paid off. She had made some interesting and useful discoveries, but she still had so much to learn and so little time in which to learn it.

As well as planning how they could win the war, Amara spent a great deal of time reading about prophecies, specifically how to break them and what the consequences of breaking them might be. Oftentimes, the consequences were bloody and unpredictable. But she wouldn't let this stop her. There had to be a way to save Nell from being sacrificed as well as defeating the Red Claws. She wouldn't give up, no matter how futile her search seemed at times.

She took a small sip of tea then jumped in her seat when she heard footsteps. The warm liquid sloshed in the cup then spilled over the rim, wetting her fingers. She hurriedly put the cup down and licked her fingers, before looking up.

"Oh, sorry. I thought you'd be in bed like everyone else."

It was Haiden, the Vampire Hunter with the ponytail and sarcastic streak. His hair was now free. It framed his angular face and fell smoothly around his neck.

His voice was a lot softer than she remembered. But perhaps it was because he was in a library and opting to display the correct etiquette. If so, he had at least one redeeming quality.

CHAPTER 5

"Oh…um…hello," said the librarian, not really knowing what to say and feeling a bit annoyed if truth be told.

This was the only time Amara usually got to be alone. She craved her quiet time. The headquarters could be pretty loud, especially with the new additions. She looked forward to the late evenings when she could finally be herself.

The Vampire Hunter must have seen it in her face.

"I can go."

Haiden's words were halfway between a question and a statement.

When there was no reply, he turned to leave.

"No, it's okay. I'm afraid I'm not very good company, that's all," said Amara, suddenly accosted by a pang of guilt. This wasn't how you treated guests. Especially those that were here to help you.

"That's not a problem. I'll just grab a book and sit way over there."

Haiden pointed to a seat on the other side of the library.

He walked over to the small fiction section off to the side of the library. Amara watched him from the corner of her eye. He picked up a battered paperback from a pile of books on a table. Amara could tell from its distinctive cover that it was *Time Immemorial* by Thomas Proust, one of her favorites. Haiden quietly walked to the seat and began reading. He flicked through the pages soundlessly, allowing Amara to get on with her work.

The problem was that she couldn't. Her concentration was broken. Her eyes roamed from the pages before her up to the ivory contours of Haiden's face. His hair fell in a curtain near his eyes, which was good, as he wouldn't be able to tell she was staring. But suddenly he lifted his head and looked her way, catching her off guard. Amara was grateful for the abundance of melanin in her dark skin. Had she been paler, her face would have been a dangerous shade of red right now.

"It's rude to stare."

Haiden's eyes flashed with humor as he said the words.

"I…I wasn't staring," said Amara, defensively. "I was looking at the book."

She hoped that this was sufficient explanation to preserve her dignity.

"Of course," said Haiden. "Of course."

Haiden winked at her. He actually winked. Who did that in this day and age? This wasn't a classic black and white movie from the fifties. Feeling both embarrassment and irritation, Amara focused back on the pages before her. She really did need to get on with her research. She mentally slapped her wrist for allowing herself to be distracted. Lives were at stake.

Amara managed to study for another hour before she decided to finally call it a night. Haiden was still reading quietly in his seat. She'd have to find somewhere more private to study if he planned to make this a regular occurrence.

"Goodnight," Amara said a little harshly as she passed him on her way out.

She was well aware that she was being unfair to her silent guest, but her feelings didn't seem to want to remain bottled inside, for once.

"Goodnight Amara," he replied, calmly, looking up.

She noticed his eyes following her as she walked away. A teeny weeny, minuscule part of her had to admit that it felt… well nice. But a Vampire Hunter? Just forget it.

Chapter 6

"Do you smell that?" Devan shouted into the minds of his pack. Blood. It wasn't any animal he had encountered before. No. This was human. He was certain. His stomach lurched as Lupita confirmed what he dreaded.

"Human."

Lupita's voice was edged with disquiet. Her mind projected a picture of an injured girl lying on the cold forest floor. The girl in Lupita's mind was breathing heavily and clutching her side, pain etched on her face. As quickly as the grim portrait flashed in Devan's mind, it dissolved and then vanished. Lupita didn't acknowledge her indiscretion. It had clearly been a mistake. Her imagination getting the better of her.

Devan raised his sensitive nose and inhaled deeply. His heart began to thunder in his chest.

"It's Nell's blood," he confirmed.

Devan raced off, forgetting to pace himself with the pack. The ground was sludgy after recent snow, but it didn't slow him down. If Nell was dead, it would be his fault for not getting to her quickly enough. They'd had too many breaks. Too much sleep. They hadn't run fast enough. If they could have just pushed a little harder, maybe they could have made it in time.

"Hey," Lupita called, only to Devan.

When he didn't answer she tried again, louder.

"Hey! Devan. Calm down. Can't you smell that it isn't enough? There's not enough blood for her to be dead. Slow down, will you. Try to let the others keep up. You need them. This isn't how you lead a pack. Devan…DEVAN!"

Devan slowed down at Lupita's words. But only slightly. She was right, of course. The panic of smelling Nell's blood had stopped him from acting rationally. She was also right that it didn't smell like there was a lot of blood. But then another thought occurred to him and the heat quickly rose in his face.

"There wouldn't be much blood if the fuckers drank it," he projected. "Come on."

Devan flung himself through the forest, almost doubling his speed. It wasn't something he could maintain for long. But the blood smelled close. He wouldn't need to.

After a few minutes he came to a clearing. About the size of a large backyard. A ramshackle wooden hut stood in the middle of it, leaning precariously as though drunk. The high sun was melting the last remnants of snow on the ground.

Lupita arrived just behind him, panting for breath. The rest of the pack wasn't far behind. She padded forward and took in the scene.

"Devan," Lupita's urgent voice reverberated in his mind. "Look."

Thick blood, almost black in color, covered a grassy verge. Devan took a deep breath. This wasn't human. The scent was very faint, but it smelled off. Wrong. But he could still smell Nell's blood in the air. Stronger now. He didn't know what to make of this other blood.

CHAPTER 6

The rest of the pack exited the trees and converged on the clearing.

"Nell. Find her," Devan commanded the wolves. "She's what matters."

The wolves stalked forward slowly, smelling the air as they approached the hut. They held Nell's blood scent in the back of their throats, tasting it as they moved forwards. The smell became thicker and thicker on their tongues and in their nostrils as they proceeded.

It was Lupita who nosed the door open. The brittle wood began splintering, some falling to the ground. It was completely rotten.

Devan followed behind. He knew he should be leading from the front, but he was terrified that he'd stumble upon Nell's body, as broken as the building housing it.

"Devan. Come here." Lupita's voice was sharp.

Devan stepped tentatively through the door into the decaying wooden shack. The wolves were circled around an open trapdoor in the floor. A single beam of sunlight coming from the broken roof lit a patch of rough concrete in the room below.

"The smell's coming from down there." It was Flint, the youngster, who projected his voice now. "I can go down. I'm the lightest." He sounded so brave.

Devan felt a pang of guilt that the teenager was involved in this battle. He was still so young.

The pack were on edge as they peered into the void. Hackles were raised. The wolves were ready for a fight if necessary. If there were vampires present they would shift into werwulf form, where they would be at their strongest and fiercest.

Devan looked at Flint again before finally acting like a pack leader.

"No, stay back, Flint. I'll go," he said with authority.

Devan shifted into human form.

"Cover me," he instructed. "Watch your backs to make sure we're not ambushed from outside."

He sat next to the trap door and placed his legs through the gap, no more aware of his nakedness than the rest of the pack. They had a job to do. Being a werwulf meant that you got used to seeing naked bodies.

He eased himself down into the void while grabbing the wood on either side of the trapdoor, so he was dangling above the concrete floor below. Luckily the wood was holding and he hadn't come crashing down. He held his breath and then let go, landing with a thud on the cold concrete. He shifted back to wolf form as he needed his senses sharp. The smell of blood immediately assaulted his nostrils.

Don't let her be dead, please.

He was frozen for a moment, mesmerized by the dust particles dancing in the ray of light coming from above. One part of him didn't want to move. It wanted to remain oblivious to the truth. He felt like he was at a crossroads.

"What do you see?" projected Lupita.

Devan snapped out of his dark thoughts and began tentatively padding around the dank enclosed space. Wolves could see pretty clearly in the dark thanks to their sharp eyesight.

Blood. Lots of traces of blood. But no Nell. The blood stained the floor in patches. Some were still a deep red, while others had turned a thick maroon. He felt relieved and terrified at the same time at what it meant.

He heard a series of thuds behind him as others landed on the concrete floor. Like Devan, they quickly shifted back to wolf form, using their animal senses to scope out the small space.

"She's not here." Lupita exhaled, the relief palpable.

Her father was bent over a patch of dark blood, his muzzle close to the ground.

"Some of this is two weeks old," said Lupertico. "This bit here and more over there." He lifted his muzzle and pointed at another dark patch close by. He padded over to another area where the stains on the concrete were brighter in color. "This part is the newest," he said, carefully scanning the pattern of blood against the dark gray concrete. The old wolf paused for a long moment before speaking again. "I know this is difficult to hear, son." He looked at Devan. "But it looks like spillage from a vampire feeding. When a vampire pulls his head back up, you tend to see this pattern. The way the droplets fall in this way. I've seen it before."

"So they *were* feeding on her?" Devan's voice trembled through the pack's minds.

Tension filled the air. Despite him never mentioning his feelings for Nell, Devan knew the pack had guessed there was more to the story than supernatural warfare and prophecies.

"I'd say definitely," projected Lupertico, scanning the ground. "And it looks like multiple feedings."

"Very tactful, Dad." Lupita nudged her father with a shoulder.

"The boy needs to know the truth, Lupita," he countered.

"Thank you, sir," Devan spluttered, his eyes gazing apprehensively around the rest of the uneven floor. "Some of it is pretty recent, then?" He was clutching to whatever hopeful signs he could.

"Yes, son," replied Lupertico. "Some of it is just a day or two old, at the most. They didn't leave here long ago."

"Which means we can still catch them," said Devan, with renewed vigor in his voice.

The pack all chorused their affirmation. The mood was suddenly energized. Devan was confident they would be catching up with the Red Claws soon. But that was as far as the plan went. Finding the Red Claws. After that, everything was left open.

Devan quickly shifted back to human form and stood directly under the trap door.

"Arm up," he shouted above him.

After a few moments two human hands reached down. Devan grabbed them and was hoisted up out of the basement. After a few more minutes they were all back up and in wolf form once again, ready to resume the hunt.

Flint was exploring the back of the rotten shack, pawing at the wooden slats. He suddenly lifted his head.

"Wait, do you smell that?" Flint projected.

His nose was up-turned. Before anybody could stop him, Flint ran out of the hut, excitedly. Such was the recklessness of youth. The rest of the pack took off after him.

Flint sprinted around to the back of the hut before abruptly stopping in his tracks.

"Woah! Erm, guys," he projected as the rest of the pack caught up with him. "Look..."

Flint gestured with his nose at the body lying crumpled on the ground.

Lupita approached cautiously, sniffing at the body from a distance.

"A vampire." She spoke with apprehension, eyes wide, then instinctively backed away a few steps and bumped into her brother Lupo.

"A Red Claw," Devan spat. "Or what's left of him, at least."

He remembered the black-looking blood at the front of the hut. There was a lot more around the motionless vampire, with that same 'off' smell. The creature's body lay battered and broken. Its clothes were torn to shreds and deep gouges riddled its body. The horrific wounds looked like they had robbed the vampire of most of its blood, which meant death would be coming. But a stake through the neck wouldn't go amiss just to make sure, thought Devan. To him, the only good Red Claw was one floating away in a cloud of ash.

Devan transformed back to human form to inspect the vampire. It would be easier to manipulate the body with hands and fingers, and there was nothing to fear now. He felt eyes upon his back as he approached the body and lent over it. He could sense that the pack were wary.

The body was lying face down in the cold grass and dirt. Blood matted its hair. Devan took a deep breath, braced himself and then rolled the crumpled form onto its back.

His heart jumped, then a long exhalation escaped his lips. The vampire's eyes were open, staring vacantly up at the sky. He had deep green irises that Devan for some reason hadn't expected on a vampire, but his deathly pallor confirmed that a vampire was exactly what he was. The skin looked shredded and raw, as if it had been stripped.

"Son, I think you need to back up there." Lupertico spoke slowly and clearly inside Devan's head. "Right now," he added, more urgently.

"What? Why?" Devan began to ask.

Then he saw it for himself.

Movement.

A twitch of the vampire's finger was all it took for Devan to flick the switch. He erupted into his werwulf form, ready to attack. He didn't mean to growl, but did so nevertheless. Devan's muscular lycan body towered over the limp vampire. He immediately felt much safer and his emotions quickly turned from surprise to anger. This vampire was part of the Family that had taken Nell and tortured her, drunk her blood. And now the bastard wasn't even dead. That didn't sit right with Devan.

The vampire's eyes blinked.

Devan froze in place.

"Zachariah...please," the vampire mumbled, barely audible. "D...d...don't do it. D...don't..."

The words were broken. Filled with fear. Fear so intense that Devan thought for a moment that he couldn't possibly be a vampire. He sounded so pathetic, so broken, so...emotional.

The vampire lifted his head a little way off the ground. It seemed he was slowly regaining strength, using his healing factor, or hadn't been as badly injured as Devan first thought. The Red Claw looked tentatively around him then dropped his head back onto the ground with a thud. A grimace came to his lips.

"Filthy werwulfs," he whispered. "I knew you *dogs* wouldn't be far behind."

Flint lurched forward and growled in the vampire's face, seemingly stung by the insult.

"Get back. Now!" Devan ordered.

Flint backed away, head held low. Devan could see a lot of himself in the impetuous young wolf.

Slowly and with great effort, the vampire pushed himself backwards. He was gaining strength, slowly recovering, that much was obvious now. In time, his wounds would heal, Devan realized. Even so, one vampire was no match for nine werwulfs.

The vampire leaned against the hut and then pushed himself up into an awkward sitting position. He clutched at a deep gash in his side, pain etched on his face.

Flint growled loudly again.

"You know I can't understand you dogs," the vampire spat at the youngster. "Do you hear me, mongrel? *Vampire speak human.*"

He scanned his surroundings once more, taking in each of the wolves with disgust before looking up at Devan in his towering werwulf form. His eyes widened with recognition.

"You," he said, before coughing and spitting black blood onto the ground. "Foul beast. It's thanks to you that I'm here. You abomination."

The harsh, mocking words were dampened by the fact that he winced and clutched his side more tightly, coughing up more of the black blood.

Devan looked closer at the vampire, for the first time noticing the strands of red hair matted with blood. His mind flashed back to the ambush on the road out of Angel Falls.

"You're the bastard who killed Nell's aunt," Devan said in his deep, lycan voice.

He stepped forward, sharp claws raised high. His pack formed a protective semi-circle around him. Each one of them had their lips drawn back from their teeth, deep growls emanating from their chests.

The vampire held up a hand, as if that was going to stop the pack from ripping his head clean off his shoulders.

"That's rich," said the vampire, talking quickly, realizing his life was hanging in the balance. "What about Ramone and Corbyn? I seem to remember things not ending so well for my brethren."

"After you attacked us!" replied Devan, who moved in for the kill. He drew his arm higher, ready to slash down and decapitate the vampire.

"Think, son," projected Lupertico. "If you end him, you end any chance of knowing what he knows. Consider the war, son. Not just your personal battle."

Devan kept his arm in the air. The vampire looked away with his eyes shut, braced for the death blow. It never came. Devan slowly lowered his arm and stepped back.

After a few moments the vampire slowly opened his eyes and then turned his head to face the pack again. Confusion was etched on his face.

"You don't get to check out that easily," said Devan in his gravelly voice. "Not yet, anyway."

The vampire straightened his body and tried to stand. He placed his hands on the muddy ground, palms down, and heaved himself into a crouching position. He stayed there for a moment, looking pained, before trying to stand. His legs buckled and he crashed back down to the ground. Resigned, he sat back down against the rotted boards of the shack.

"Stay down," ordered Devan, pointing at the ground. "I didn't say you could move. From now on you do exactly as I say."

The vampire looked humiliated, but didn't argue.

"What's your name, blood-sucker?" Devan asked. "And think carefully before you decide to lie. I have a hotline to the Council of Elders and one particularly fastidious librarian there. If you're telling porkies I'll find out, and then it's ashtray

CHAPTER 6

time for you. Trust me, nothing would give me more pleasure."

The vampire had given a look of disgust when he heard the words 'Council of Elders', but decided to keep his hostility in check. Wise move, Devan thought.

"Klaus…Klaus Red Claw," the vampire almost whispered, still worn out from his attempt to stand.

"Where's Nell?" Devan decided to forgo any small talk. Time was of the essence. "What have they done to her?"

"The girl is still alive," said Klaus. "Unfortunately."

Devan growled, then relaxed a little. Nell was alive. That was the main thing right now. He needed to keep his emotions in check.

"Where are they taking her?"

"Why should I tell you anything?" countered Klaus. "You want to steal her from us. That's not happening. We need her."

"So you know about the prophecy?" asked Devan, his tone level.

His tactic was to try to ascertain what rank Klaus had been within the Red Claws. If he had been in the lower tiers then he likely didn't have a lot of information that would be helpful. But if he was in the inner sanctum of the Family then he'd be extremely useful.

"As I said before, why should I say anything, especially to a bunch of savage hounds?" Klaus's tone was defiant. The fact Devan had stopped himself from delivering the death blow seemed to have emboldened the vampire.

That was when Lupita swiftly approached the Red Claw and slapped him around the face with her huge paw.

"I think she's asking you to be more courteous," Devan chided, proud of his side-kick. "Trust me, if you're no use to us then we *will* kill you."

The words sounded foreign on Devan's tongue. Never had he threatened to kill another soul. But he did mean it. He would kill to save Nell.

"I can't wait for the day when my Family tears you dogs limb from limb," said Klaus, coolly.

Before Devan could reply, Lupita launched herself at the vampire. She bit into his shoulder with such ferocity that black blood spurted into the air when she finally released her grip. Lupita spat in disgust. Clearly the blood tasted rancid.

"Control your *bitch!*" Klaus screamed at Devan. The vampire winced in pain.

"Tried that once," said Devan, casually. "Didn't get me very far. Free spirit, that one. Now, tell me what you know about the prophecy."

Klaus was silent for a long moment. He seemed to be torn.

"What's the point?" he said, finally, looking down and sounding uncharacteristically subdued. "You'll still kill me. And if you don't, there's no point in me living anyway. My Family won't take me back." Klaus rubbed his shoulder and let out a cry of pain. The shoulder didn't seem to be healing like the rest of his wounds.

"Werwulf saliva," Lupita said inside Devan's head. "It slows down the healing and, as an added bonus, burns like hell."

Devan smiled, which looked rather jarring on a werwulf.

"We don't have to kill you," said Devan. "As you can see, and no doubt feel, we can make you suffer…a lot. Your destiny is in your own hands, blood-sucker. As for the Red Claws, we can see how much you mean to them. Nothing says family like being hacked to shreds and left for dead in the wilderness."

Devan could see he had hit a raw nerve. The torment in Klaus's eyes was palpable. The vampire looked down again,

CHAPTER 6

not wanting to expose his vulnerability to the pack.

"Zachariah," said Klaus, to himself more than anyone else. "I failed him…sometimes his temper…he…"

"Help us to help you, Klaus," said Devan, almost sounding sympathetic. "If you join the right side, if you renounce the Red Claws, then you won't share in their fate. Were you always this…callous? Even as a human? Even as a child? Is there no decency in you, Klaus?"

Devan knew he was clutching at straws in trying to appeal to his better nature, but he didn't have any better ideas.

"My Family," Klaus said, dejectedly. "My Family…my Family…" He kept saying the words, as if turning them over in his head to see what they meant anymore.

Devan realized that he'd guessed correctly earlier. Klaus had been attacked by the Red Claws as a punishment. He also knew that the vampire had never considered life outside of the Family. Why would he? Devan just hoped that Klaus's self-preservation instinct was greater than any misplaced loyalty.

The vampire looked up again.

"If I tell you what I know you won't kill me?" he asked, not convinced.

"We won't kill you," Devan said, levelly. "I give you my word on that, for what it's worth to you."

Klaus remained silent. He looked more conflicted than ever.

"Alaska," he said finally, squeezing his eyes shut, as if speaking the word hurt him. "They're taking her to Alaska." He grimaced. Betraying his Family seemed to inflict as much pain as his physical wounds.

"What's in Alaska?" Devan tried to recall what he knew about the state. All he could come up with was people with too much money skiing.

"Zachariah's family home," said Klaus, his tongue loosening. "It's the one place he feels safe. It's isolated and built like a fortress."

"What does he plan to do with Nell?" asked Devan.

"I honestly don't know," said the vampire. "I wanted him to kill her straight away, so the prophecy couldn't play out, but Zachariah had a reason to keep her alive."

That last word 'alive' reverberated in Devan's mind.

Nell could still be saved.

Chapter 7

Christopher heard a sound from the depths of his sleep state. It was fuzzy and muffled. After a few moments he recognized what was making the noise. He quickly forced himself out of the restorative trance and flung himself out of bed. He dived over to the nightstand where his phone was charging. He grabbed the device and jabbed the green icon.

"Devan…" Christopher shouted into the mouthpiece, before the person on the other end of the line had a chance to speak.

"Thinking of me, I see," Devan laughed. "That's cute. Anyway, we have a development."

"Oh God, is any…"

"Woah, woah…calm yourself, dude," reassured Devan. "It's nothing bad. In fact, I would say it's a positive, on balance, as long as we can manage the sit…"

"Devan, please just get to the point!" Christopher shouted.

As much as he'd grown to like the werwulf, despite their obvious differences and the fact they were both smitten with the same girl, God, could he wind Christopher up.

Amara came running into the room. She must have heard Christopher's shrieks. He put the call on speaker.

"Well, we have a new friend," explained Devan. "He's part of your unholy fang-gang, but of the Red Claw persuasion. He'd been abandoned by his Family with some pretty spectacular injuries. We found him left for dead." Devan's tone turned more serious. "Christopher, he's the one who killed Aunt Laura, the red-haired vampire who ambushed us at Angel Falls. I know you vowed to end him, but he's been co-operative. I think we can use him. But that's for the Council to decide. It's way above my pay grade. He says their leader, Zachariah, has a place in Alaska and that's where they're taking Nell."

Christopher was stunned into silence. It was a lot to process. His mind flashed back to fighting the flame-haired vampire, of pushing him away from Aunt Nell's crumpled body on the road and then being flooded with his memories. Klaus Redclaw, he recalled. That was his name. Christopher didn't know what to do with this new information, but one thing stood out above all else.

"So she's still alive?" Christopher exhaled into the phone. Even though he didn't need to breathe, for some reason when he was stressed he found himself holding air.

"Yes, Christopher," said Devan, flatly. "Don't you think that if she was dead I would have opened with that?"

"But why?" asked Christopher, giving voice to the question he was afraid to confront. "What's their plan? Surely it would have made more sense to…you know…so that the prophecy can't play out. Why are they keeping her? Did you ask?"

"No, I didn't think to ask that." Christopher could almost feel Devan roll his eyes through the phone. "Klaus didn't know the answer," continued Devan, more levelly. "In fact, he agreed that it would have been in their best interests to…deal with…Nell. I think that's probably part of what led to his abandonment, but he won't come clean on that one."

"Hi Devan, it's me," Amara interjected. "I've been listening in."

"Hey word-nerd, good to hear from you," he replied, brightly.

"Ditto furball of fury," said Amara. "What's your plan of action?"

"Well, that's what I want to talk to you guys about," Devan explained. "I think the best way forward is to send Klaus back to you. There's no point in him tagging along with us. We don't have the resources to guard or interrogate him. We can't use him as a political prisoner or hostage, as the Red Claws couldn't care less about him. Amara, you might be able to extract something useful from him."

Amara considered.

"We have to see how Kavisha and Loris feel about it," she said. "But you might be right. Learning from books is one thing, but hearing from a live witness to events is quite another."

"How will you get him to us?" asked Christopher.

"With escorts," replied Devan. "It's the only way, even though it means ending up with a smaller hunt team. I'll send two from my pack. The vampire is pretty beat up and isn't much of a danger right now. Lupita, my right-hand woman, will bring him along with Flint, the youngster who found him."

"How long will it take to get here?" asked Christopher. "And, more to the point, how?"

"Well, I've done a bit of pre-planning on that score," said Devan. "I've located a chop-shop that can make some fake plates for the right incentive. I just need to liberate a vehicle from one of the good citizens of Canada. Lupita can drive it down after we also liberate some clothes and cash."

"You're all about liberty," mused Amara, dryly. "How noble."

"Hey, desperate times," countered Devan. "I'm not happy

about stealing, but we're trying to save your species, right? Your folks can at least pony up some wheels, threads and moolah. Think of it as a down payment on continuing to exist. Sounds like a fair deal to me."

"Me too," concurred Christopher. "Do what you need to do, Devan."

"When should we expect them?" Amara asked, not wanting to dwell on the more illicit side of the plan.

"Three days," said Devan. "A little sooner if they push it. They'll mostly be driving by night on the highways and taking the backroads during the day. I hope you have a secure room for the blood-sucker. He's pretty docile now, but who knows what he'll be like when he's fully healed."

Amara and Christopher exchanged apprehensive glances. Assuming the Council agreed, they would have a Red Claw in their midst very shortly.

***

Over the next couple of days, while Christopher waited for the Red Claw to arrive after the Council gave its approval, new creatures of the night arrived. More gothic looking black-clad Vampire Hunters joined the rest of their crew. There were also a handful of fae and even more of the creepy imps. Christopher decided that they were his least favorite out of all of the guests he'd met. The tiny demonic children made his skin crawl. He'd secretly named them 'Little Damiens'.

A few more witches also joined the ranks. Christopher learnt the hard way that male witches were called warlocks. God forbid you called them male witches. Christopher walked around with a magical 'Kick Me' sign plastered to his back for an evening afterwards. He couldn't get it to budge. But it made Amara laugh and that was worth something, considering the pressure she was placing on herself.

Christopher decided to keep himself to himself while waiting for the wolves and their captive to arrive. He could sense there was a buzz of anticipation around the headquarters. He retreated to his room to catch up on his rest. He wanted to be at full strength for what was to come. For the first time in a long while he almost felt positive. They'd managed to find a lead, as they said in those cop shows. Two leads, actually. They had a Red Claw seemingly willing to talk, and the final destination for Nell. Things were finally looking up.

Chapter 8

Amara decided to do the opposite of Christopher. While he concentrated on getting rest, she threw herself into her books and online investigations with renewed vigor. She was researching all she could about Alaska, unexplained deaths in the state throughout history and local folklore. She was in her usual spot, perched at the large oak desk, a steaming cup of jitter juice within reach. She slammed the book she had been reading on the desk, then quickly apologized to it profusely in her head.

Great example you're setting as a librarian, dufus.

"Double damn," she whispered, pushing her hands through her hair.

This was the third book in a row that had seemed promising but had provided nothing.

"Easy there. What did that book ever do to you?"

She looked across the library.

Haiden. Who else?

It was becoming a habit for him to visit the library in the evenings. He'd waltz into the room like he owned the place, pick out a book and then settle into the same chair in the far corner, not usually breathing a word as he did so. Okay, so technically he wasn't doing anything wrong. It wasn't as if

CHAPTER 8

Amara owned the library or had been given exclusive use of it. Also, Haiden was usually quiet as a mouse. But couldn't he tell that his presence was a distraction for her? She found that she would always strain to see what book he was reading. Invariably a classic. He seemed to be going through one book a night. Tonight he had selected a copy of *The Broken Children* by T.L. Lowery. Another of Amara's favorites. Damn him and his good taste (and good looks).

Instead of stewing any further in her ire, Amara busied herself with the next tome in her large pile. It was entitled *Kushtaka and Keelut: Urban Legends of Alaska*. It dated back to 1903 so would likely be a slow burner.

For a good while Amara managed to keep her attention firmly on the book as she learnt about shape-shifting Kushtakas, black hairless dogs called Keeluts, as well as Qalupaliks, Ircenrraats and the supposed UFO base at Mount Hayes. She scanned the rest of the book but nothing stood out to her as useful. She put it back on the pile with a sigh before placing her hands over her face. She closed her eyes and rubbed her fingers up and down her temples. Amara felt like she was on a treadmill, working away furiously but getting nowhere.

"Amara," his voice was low, laced with gentle concern. A feeling stirred inside her that she'd not experienced for the longest time.

Amara splayed her fingers and took a peep out between the gaps. Haiden was standing in front of the desk. She raised her eyebrows to wordlessly question the interruption. She seemed to have forgotten her manners with people as well as books this evening.

"Seriously, do you ever take a break?" said Haiden, not unkindly, his eyes fixed on hers.

She was suddenly very aware of sensations in her body. A flush seemed to travel from the soles of her feet to the top of her head. She felt warm under his gaze. Nothing good was going to come from this, she reminded herself.

"I take breaks," she said curtly, picking up her coffee and taking a sip.

Amara scolded herself for letting him affect her in this way. She had no time for this. Just because he was handsome, knew his library etiquette, had great taste in classic literature and was clearly empathetic, it didn't mean anything. Not a jot.

She took a deep breath, steadying her emotions before continuing.

"Do you ever think maybe you take too many breaks?" she said.

Haiden chuckled.

"Ah, so there we have it, at last," he said. "You really don't like me trespassing into *your* domain."

"It's not that at all," Amara fired back, defensively.

"Could have fooled me," he replied. "Your demeanor when I'm in here is as warm as the subject matter of those books you have there."

He pointed to the volumes on Alaska sitting on the desk.

Amara took a deep breath. She knew she should be the bigger person and let the comments simply wash over her. But knowing and doing were two very different things.

"I have work to do here while you…you just pleasure read like you were sitting beside the pool on vacation," she began. "Do you not realize why you're here? What's at stake? It's all of our lives. Nell's life. How on earth can you be so relaxed at a time like this? Shouldn't you be doing something useful? Drills or weapons training…something?"

CHAPTER 8

Amara found that she'd stood in the process of her monologue. She gripped the edges of the desk, trying to keep her anger from completely boiling over.

Haiden looked at her for a long moment. His cool expression never wavered.

"Did you ever stop to think that I might actually be good at what I do? That I don't need to train perpetually," he said, his voice remaining soft. "Being a Vampire Hunter is in my blood. The skills are innate, you could say." He held up the novel. "Also, had you ever considered that what I might need was to quieten the mind. That this was perhaps my way to prepare for battle…where I'll be putting my life on the line, as opposed to sitting behind a desk."

Amara was wrong-footed. It wasn't the response she was expecting. She sat back down, feeling suddenly very tired. This was more than just physical exhaustion from burning the candle at both ends. She was tired of it all. The battle. The supernaturals. Her life up until now. Being a librarian. The crazy events of the past month or so had thrown her very existence into sharp relief. She felt so unsure of herself. Of her place in the world.

"That's great for you, Haiden," she replied, wearily. "Some of us here aren't lucky enough to have 'innate skills' or Vampire Hunter genes. We're not naturals like you. We have to work at it. Every day."

"Lucky? You think I'm lucky?" Haiden's stoic veneer finally cracked.

"Yes, I do," replied the librarian. "You can go out there and fight, knowing that you're competent. You're so sure of yourself." She stretched her arms over the books on her desk. "All I have is this, what I can fill my brain with."

"The last thing I am is lucky," said Haiden. "And the last thing you are is only what you can cram into your head. You don't even know." He sighed then held up a hand in a placating gesture. "Look, I'm sorry I annoyed you. I can tell that my presence is not wanted." He seemed to hesitate, before deciding to continue. "Believe it or not, I come here in the evenings to read so you don't feel like you're totally alone. I could just as easily take the books back to my room."

Amara's eyes widened, her palms moistened. This conversation was not at all what she had expected.

"But point taken," continued Haiden. "Loud and clear. I was trying to do something…nice, but it backfired. Whatever. I'll get out of your hair. For good."

Even though he was over six-foot tall and chiseled with muscle, at that precise moment Haiden looked like a broken bird to Amara. Vulnerable. He began walking away.

"Hey," called Amara, plucking up the courage she didn't know she possessed. "If you were coming to the library on my behalf, you should have said. You could have at least made yourself useful as…let's see…my official cup-bearer for a start." She picked up her mug of tepid coffee, tasted it then frowned. "In fact, you can start your trial period right now. If you show promise then I might even permit you to have a cup."

Haiden's expression slowly softened, then a small smile came to his full lips.

"I am only here to serve the greater good, as you have so emphatically reminded me," he said, before bending low in a theatrical bow.

Ten minutes later they were seated opposite each other at a small circular reading table, both clutching a mug of hot coffee. Amara took an exploratory sip.

"Not bad," she said. "I think we've discovered another 'innate skill' of yours."

"Thank you, ma'am," said Haiden. "Maybe I can percolate a few Red Claws into ash."

Amara grinned before looking at the Hunter for a long moment. Then she recalled something.

"Earlier, you said the last thing you were was lucky to be a Vampire Hunter," she said. "What did you mean by that?"

Haiden took a big gulp of coffee before putting the cup down.

"Let's just say it's not all it cracked up to be," he replied.

"How so? You guys parade around like you're the best thing since sliced bread."

Amara once again felt a twinge of envy as she pictured the female Vampire Hunters. They looked so confident, capable and, well, sexy. There was no other word for it. It all looked damn cool from where she was sitting with her old cardigan, dusty books and ancient laptop.

"It's hard to explain," said Haiden.

"Try me," said Amara. She nearly reached out to touch his hand, but pulled it back at the last moment. "You know I'm a seeker of knowledge."

"Well, for starters, it's not something you choose," explained Haiden. "You just get thrown into it. As soon as you become a man, you're told: 'Right son, off you trot to exterminate the undead, no more school for you'. I was dragged away from my friends to travel the world with my dad and kill blood-suckers. All for the greater good. Don't get me wrong, I've seen first-hand how unchecked vampire covens can slowly lay waste to communities. I knew I was helping to save innocent lives, but to lose my own life as I knew it, my friends, my future, in the process. It's a big ask."

Amara nodded. That was all it took to encourage Haiden to continue. She was sure that these thoughts had been brewing inside him for a long time, just waiting for an outlet. She wondered if that was part of the reason he kept coming to the library.

"I had plans, you know. I wanted to be a writer," he went on. "I wanted to have a family one day. But I don't even have a home. I spend my life in hotel rooms or off-grid properties in the Hunter network. What kind of life is that? All the rest of them love this shit. They live for this. Me? Not so much. But it's all I know."

"And now you find yourself living in the very den of the enemy," said Amara. "That must be a mind-fuck."

"I'm not even sure what the word 'enemy' means anymore," he said. "We were convinced your emails were an ambush ploy by the vamps. That's why only a few of us showed up to start with. I'm still having trouble believing any of this is real." He looked around the cavernous library. "That's why I come back to the books, the classics. It's like finding peace in the familiar as the world goes bat-shit crazy. The stories and characters are like a sanctuary, taking me back to comfortable places I've explored many times before, if that makes any sense."

"I know exactly what you're saying," said Amara. "It's like catching up with old friends."

Haiden nodded.

"Can't you do both?" she asked. "Have a family and also be a Vampire Hunter?"

"It's possible," he conceded. "But what kind of life is that for a kid? To be on the move all the time and then one day to be told what you were, and that's all you were destined to be.

I've lived through that, Amara, and I can't do that to another innocent kid." His eyes looked glassy.

Amara decided to throw caution to the wind. She reached out and cradled his hand.

"I'm sorry, Haiden," she said. "I'm sorry life hasn't worked out the way you wanted. It's not fair. If it's any consolation, I know what it's like to feel you're not living the life you should. Me being here, away from my library, my apartment, my books, my quiet life. I ask myself, is that it? Is that all life was meant to be? Doing the same thing day in and day out until one day you look back in fifty years and ask, where did my life go? Was this really all I was capable of? Did I settle for a safe, mediocre existence instead of taking a risk? And now it's too late."

Amara let out a long exhale. This topic was too heavy for this time of night. Haiden squeezed her hand.

"Well, your life, however dull, has brought you to this moment right now," he said. "For that, the universe has my thanks."

Feeling her cheeks burn, Amara glanced down. She looked at her small, smooth hand in his. Her fingers were marked with ink. His were marked with scars. She turned his hand over and began to trace the raised lines that covered the surface. With the smooth pad of her fingertip, she explored the ridges and recesses across his palm. When she looked up, she saw Haiden's eyes were closed, a serene stillness on his face. A memory? If so, of whom? A mother? A lover? It didn't really matter. Amara was happy just to savor this moment amid the chaos.

Chapter 9

The scent of wolves filled the headquarters. Even though they were in human form, vampiric senses could detect the unmistakable earthy, primal aroma. Christopher was too polite to call the odor offensive, but it took some getting used to.

Devan said they were called Lupita and Flint. The young woman had olive skin, sharp features and long black hair. She wore jeans and a baseball top that were way too big for her. They enveloped her slim frame and looked like they belonged to a hefty man who liked his pizza and beer on game night. Flint was shorter and much younger, with blonde hair and bright blue eyes. He was wearing board shorts and a white t-shirt, making him look even younger. Christopher could see why Devan wanted him out of harm's way for a while.

They were accompanied by their prisoner. Though, if Devan was right, 'defector' might be a more accurate term. Klaus Redclaw. Christopher steeled himself, determined not to let his anger get the better of him. This was the vampire who had killed Aunt Laura — but he could also be the key to Nell's salvation.

Christopher stood at his familiar spot on the first floor overlooking the banister, closely watching the proceedings

CHAPTER 9

below him. If he was down there he might not be able to hold back his temper. Right on cue, Amara came bounding down the stairs. This time suitably dressed in black pants and a dark red cardigan rather than the yellow robe and pink slippers she was sporting when the Hunters had arrived at the crack of dawn.

Christopher felt unnerved. He picked at his fingernails, something he hadn't done since his human years. He was on high alert. Amara was clearly competent, but she couldn't defend herself to, well, save her life. The werwulfs could take Klaus down but it would take precious seconds for them to transform. Christopher was poised. If he needed to swoop down and end the Red Claw, as he had vowed to do after their previous encounter, he wouldn't hesitate. Truth be told, one part of him was savoring the opportunity.

"Good morning, welcome. You must be Flint and Lupita," said Amara, brightly. "And you must be Klaus," she added, more soberly.

"Amara?" said Lupita, her face lighting up with a warm smile.

Christopher had never really given much thought to female werwulfs. A rather self-centered thought crossed his mind… maybe Devan could find a werwulf partner instead of fawning over Nell. That would be just dandy all round, he concluded.

"Yup, that's me," said the librarian.

"Lovely to meet you," said Lupita, holding out a hand. "Devan speaks very highly of you."

"Thanks," replied Amara, shaking the offered hand.

"Oh, so you're the word-nerd!" said the teenager.

"Flint!" reprimanded Lupita. "We're not in the wild now! Try to show some civility." She turned to Amara. "Sorry, he's young and mostly doesn't think before he acts."

Amara chuckled. "That's quite alright. I've been called much worse. Lovely to meet you too, Flint, and thank you both for joining the team, so to speak." She turned her attention to the sullen red-haired vampire standing between them. "And thank you also, Klaus. I know this can't be easy for you."

He said nothing, just looked on dispiritedly.

"Follow me this way," said Amara. "We have a room for the two of you before you head back. And Klaus, I want to be upfront with you. We've decided to put you in one of our lockable rooms for the time being, until we can speak to you further."

"You're throwing me in a jail cell after I agreed to help you?" The Red Claw had found his voice, and it was laced with anger and resentment.

Christopher tensed.

"Given the circumstances, we think it makes sense, for now," said Amara, levelly. "We have to take precautions. Surely that's not such an outrageous proposition."

"An outrage is exactly what it is," said Klaus, indignant.

"This building has actual jail cells in the basement," replied Amara. "Trust me, a room with a lock on the door is far more desirable than being there. Though, if needs be…"

Klaus huffed before following Amara. Lupita and Flint remained at the rear, in case the Red Claw had any ideas. They moved along the hallway and began climbing the grand stairs. Christopher stepped back and blended into the shadows as they passed the first floor.

The lockable rooms were on the top floor. It was where Christopher had been sent when it was thought he might be a threat to Nell. Now that she was gone and the rogue

CHAPTER 9

Magister had fled, he was allowed his old room back on the floor below. He guessed that's where the werwulfs would be assigned accommodation also.

Christopher followed at a discreet distance as Klaus was shown to his room. The Red Claw didn't even bother to complain as the door was shut on him. He was seemingly resigned to his situation. Amara turned the large key in the lock. No keypads here. The old gothic building came with original period features. That's how a real estate agent would try to sell it, at least.

Amara, Lupita and Flint exchanged more words before the werwulfs were shown to their room on Christopher's floor. Amara wished them a restful stay and then left, no doubt heading back to her sanctuary in the basement library.

After waiting a few minutes, Christopher went to the door. He didn't want to waste the opportunity for a proper update from the field while the two of them were here. The phone conversations with Devan were few and far between and, more often than not, very short. He was also intrigued to meet other werwulfs. Were they all as impetuous and foolhardy as Devan?

Christopher knocked lightly. He could hear two voices inside. They went quiet and after a few moments the door opened. He was not prepared for the woman who stood in front of him. Even though Christopher had seen her from a distance, at close range it was quite a revelation. She was beautiful. No, beautiful felt like an understatement. With huge brown doe eyes and long, flowing inky hair that fell down to her waist, she looked like a modern-day Aztec princess.

After regaining his composure, Christopher introduced himself and was welcomed inside by Lupita, who introduced him to Flint.

"Hi," the young, skinny teenager said from the other side of the room. "So, you're the loser whose ass Devan kicked."

"Flint!" scolded Lupita. "Don't you ever learn?"

"That's okay," said Christopher, with surprisingly good humor. "However, recollections of events do vary."

"Flint here was raised mostly in the wild," Lupita said, by way of apology. "There's not much call for tact or discretion in a pack. Wolves say it as they see it."

"Good," said Christopher, more animated now. "That's exactly what I need. I want you to tell me everything that's been happening out there." Christopher knew that he was coming off a bit too intense. But he was desperate for details.

"OK, sure…" Lupita said, sympathetically. She beckoned Christopher to join her on one of the two beds.

Without pause, she launched into the story of how she'd met Devan. How he'd found her pack and had pleaded for support, outlining what was at stake. She shared how her brother and father had come along, too. There were a total of fourteen wolves now, after new recruits had joined the day before thanks to her brother Lupo catching the scent of their pack. Devan had managed to convince them that the war was worth fighting for, that if they did nothing then sooner or later it was coming for them anyway.

Lupita's eyes shone when she talked of her kin. She was close to her family, that much was clear to Christopher. What about her mother, though? Lupita made no mention of her. Christopher thought it might be rude to ask.

There was one thing that he hadn't expected. Her eyes would shine in the same way when she spoke of Devan. There was more to that dynamic than Lupita or Devan were willing to divulge. Christopher was sure of it, and also glad of it, for selfish reasons if nothing else.

Christopher left the room about an hour later. He felt better for knowing that Devan was pushing himself and the pack. Whatever the historic bad blood between them, Christopher knew that Devan was relentless in his pursuit of Nell. That much was abundantly clear from the conversation he'd just had. He held out renewed hope of once again holding her in his arms. Of course, then he'd probably still have to kill her at some point. Maybe. He offered a silent prayer to a God he wasn't convinced existed that there was another way. There had to be.

Chapter 10

Amara, Kavisha and Loris had just finished their second round of 'chatting' with the Red Claw in his room.

The librarian found that she'd developed a pretty confused understanding of good and evil. Klaus was evil. He was a Red Claw and the two were synonymous, or so she'd thought. It had been drummed into Amara's worldview that all Red Claws were fundamentally malevolent, until she sat down opposite Klaus.

He was broken. He was perhaps the saddest creature Amara had ever come across. Klaus seemed genuinely bewildered that his Family had abandoned him, injuring him so badly in the process that he was still healing. Despite herself, Amara felt sorry for Klaus. 'A pathetic brainwashed boy'. That was how Loris had referred to him after their first session.

No sinister interrogation techniques or threats were required to get to the truth. Both Kavisha and Loris, using their otherworldly senses Amara was not privy to, were certain that Klaus was divulging everything he knew after experiencing the brutality of his own Family. Yet the bonds were still there. Every so often he'd slip up and call Zachariah 'brother'. Or still refer to 'my Family', or 'we' rather than 'them'. Amara wondered what kind of war was being waged in his

CHAPTER 10

head between his old life and a now uncertain future. The guilt Klaus was feeling for betraying his Family was palpable, despite the fact that they had left him for dead.

Kavisha and Loris had decided that short sessions, fairly often, would be the best way to extract information from Klaus. They didn't want to exhaust him or put too much mental strain on him. A certain level of finesse was called for. At the end of the current session, as Amara and Kavisha turned to leave, Loris asked if he could have a few more minutes with Klaus alone. While it was an unusual request, Kavisha trusted Loris, who had shown himself to be a wise and capable Elder. Amara and Kavisha left the pair of them in the silence of the room.

Amara accompanied Kavisha in the lift to the ground floor. When the iron doors clattered open, Kavisha raised her head. Her ears seemed to prick up like an owl catching a sound in the distance. About five seconds later, Amara heard it too. Shouting. They both made off in the direction of the cacophony. The drawing room.

They found Miss Odette and Master August in their usual repose, spread lazily across one of the plush green chaise lounges. Amara should have guessed that they'd have something to do with whatever drama was unfolding. Sometimes Amara felt like she was back in high school. Miss Odette stretched her long, slender limbs across the furniture, as though she were modeling for a high-end magazine.

Amara was surprised to see Christopher was involved in the debacle. He stood on the other side of the room, his hands balled into fists.

"Don't you dare say anything about her," he shouted.

Christopher's teeth were clenched. His jaw squared.

Miss Odette laughed, throwing her head back in an over-the-top gesture that was obviously designed to annoy Christopher even more. Boy was it working.

"My child, I merely stated the facts," she said in her musical voice. "It's hardly my fault if you can't accept them, is it?"

The childish grin on her face was enough to send Amara marching into the middle of the room. She hoped her body would serve as a barrier to break eye contact between the warring parties.

"What's this all about?"

Amara looked between the two of them, silently begging Christopher to back down. He was meant to be the reasonable one here.

"I only explained to young Christopher that Nell is an inconsequential human and we are not here to save her," explained Miss Odette. "Our survival depends on her being killed by somebody other than the Red Claws, that's all. But her eventual death will be a joyful event for us all." She clapped her hands together in excitement. "Human life means nothing to us," she continued. "And it's not my fault that Christopher has contracted feelings for an insignificant human rather than wisely sticking with his own kind." The words were sickly, pouring out of Miss Odette's mouth like sweet venom.

"Miss Odette," said Amara, sharply. "While we appreciate you coming here to support us, might I remind you that we will not abide intolerance towards anyone. You might be a guest, but that doesn't give you the right to spew hatred."

"Spoken like a true human," said Miss Odette, dismissively. "Weak and deluded, and so very much expendable."

That was more than Christopher could take. He crouched down ready to launch himself at Miss Odette. A hand suddenly

CHAPTER 10

grabbed at his arm.

"Dude, chill," said Haiden.

Amara hadn't seen the Vampire Hunter enter the room. He might have been there all along. He stood beside Christopher, who remained still — for the moment.

"Christopher, man, she's not worth it," added Haiden. "Just look at her. What a sad life she must lead to derive her sense of superiority from putting others down. Others who have twice the heart and ten times the guts as she has."

Amara smiled inwardly at the unlikely sight of a Vampire Hunter trying to talk a vampire off the ledge. Her feelings for Haiden suddenly swelled.

"What did you say, scum?" Miss Odette shot back at Haiden. "You're worse than the rest of them. Failed excuse for a human. Failed excuse for a superior. You don't belong anywhere, apart from in the gutter with the rest of the filth."

Amara held her breath. After her talk the other evening with Haiden about not having a place in the world, she knew Miss Odette had unknowingly touched a nerve. Amara wasn't sure how he was going to react.

"You're right," said Haiden, calmly.

That was the last response the librarian had expected.

"Vampire Hunters are by far the worst of them all," continued Haiden. "Do you know why?"

"Yes, please confess," said Miss Odette, dryly.

"It's because we tolerate abominations like you, but kill decent folk like him." Haiden tipped his head towards Christopher. "Where's the Goddamn justice in that?"

Haiden turned on his heel and pulled Christopher out of the room with him.

"Scum consorting with scum," mused the fae. "This place is

riddled…infected."

Her little imp had a crooked grin plastered over his childlike face.

Amara glanced at Kavisha, who had been observing events from the side. Kavisha nodded at the librarian in unspoken assent.

Amara turned to Miss Odette.

"Leave," she said. Cold and final.

"Excuse me?" Miss Odette looked like she'd been slapped.

"Leave," repeated Amara. "Now."

The fae's mouth hung open in shock. She was evidently under the impression that her presence here was a blessing for all. The room was silent.

"You've been asked to leave, Miss Odette," said Kavisha. "And please take Master August with you."

"You can't possibly be serious, Kavi?" Miss Odette's voice was approaching a pitch that only dogs or werwulfs would be able to hear. "You need me!"

"You have done quite enough already," said the High Chancellor. "I'll have Sanford collect your things."

Kavisha turned to leave the room, beckoning Amara to come with her.

"If I know Miss Odette, she'll be too embarrassed to stay," said Kavisha, once in the corridor. "Give her five minutes and she'll be out the front door. You'll hear the slam reverberate around the entire building."

"Good riddance," said Amara. "The sheer spite inside that woman. How looks can be deceiving."

"Thank you, Amara," said Kavisha, turning to the librarian and gripping her hand. "I'm not sure what we'd do without you. Not just now, but throughout this unexpected journey we find ourselves on. You are living proof that human lives are worth just as much as us elderly vampires, or pompous fae."

Amara squeezed Kavisha's hand. For once, she was lost for words.

***

About ten minutes later, Amara found herself at the door to Christopher's room. He was always on edge recently and Amara was worried about the impact Miss Odette's cruel tirade might have had on him. The door was slightly ajar. She knocked before pushing it open. Then she had to blink hard a few times to ensure she wasn't seeing things.

Christopher and Haiden were sitting on Christopher's bed, talking. Animatedly.

"Hey," the vampire and the Hunter responded in unison.

"Did you know that he likes *Lazarus Unchained* too?" Christopher said to Amara as she stepped into the room.

"Am I supposed to know what that is?" Amara chuckled, cautiously.

"Only the sickest metal band in the world," said Haiden.

"I take it that means good," said Amara.

"It means fucking great, the greatest," added Haiden.

The Vampire Hunter and his sworn enemy shared common ground. It seemed that nothing was impossible these days.

"I'll leave you boys to it," she said as she backed out of the room and closed the door, not wanting to interrupt their male bonding.

She walked a few steps then paused for a moment in the empty corridor to collect her thoughts. It was nice, well amazing in fact, to see Christopher and Haiden looking at peace in each other's company. But how on Earth could that friendship be viable? It felt to Amara like they were all trapped in a bizarre bubble of time where reality was warped. If the Red Claw situation could be dealt with then would everything revert back to the old ways eventually? Were violence and mistrust the natural order of the world, or had things shifted irrevocably? Her thoughts landed on Haiden, both his stern words to Miss Odette and his empathy for Christopher. Haiden was unsure of himself as a Vampire Hunter, so was the most likely of their ilk to be able to see things from a new perspective. Perhaps he was the key to a different...

"Hi."

The sound made Amara nearly jump out of her skin. She clutched her chest and took a deep breath, trying to regain her composure.

"Oops, sorry, stealth training is ingrained," said Haiden. "It kinda becomes the default setting."

His voice brushed up against her neck. She turned to find him behind her, only inches away.

"You scared the living bejesus out of me!!"

Amara hit him playfully.

"I'm sorry. But not all my fault," he offered. "I think you were lost inside that big brain of yours."

Haiden tapped his finger gently against Amara's temple. His face was so close to hers.

"Um, fair enough," Amara conceded. "I might have to give you that."

"Were you thinking of anyone special," he asked, optimistically, leaning in a little.

CHAPTER 10

"Maybe," said Amara. "Someone I can't quite figure out."

"More fun that way," replied Haiden. "Everyone loves a good mystery, don't you think?"

He leaned even closer.

"On that topic, I better get back downstairs," she said, suddenly feeling hot and bothered. "Those books won't read themselves." She tried to sound light and indifferent.

"Can't you take a break, just for a little while," he said, suggestively. "What's so urgent?"

"Klaus mentioned something called 'familial amplification,'" Amara sputtered, suddenly very self-conscious. "He said the Red Claw leader Zachariah had talked about it more than once. I'm sure I've read about it before, some kind of dynamic within a Family or something. I just need to double-check whether it has any relevance to…" She was rambling now.

"It was a rhetorical question," said Haiden. He gently took her hand.

She looked into his eyes. He was only an inch or so away from her now. She could see a longing in his eyes. She could feel that same longing inside her.

"Amara," he said, softly. Everything was contained in the way he said that one word.

"Okay," she replied, breathlessly, not so much going out on a limb as diving headfirst into a vast ocean. "I guess a little break couldn't hurt."

Amara remained perfectly still. Haiden did not. He slowly leaned forward, touching his lips to hers delicately. Amara closed her eyes, savoring the touch. Haiden continued his soft kisses, as though the librarian was made of porcelain. It was Amara who deepened the kiss, wrapping her hands around Haiden's thick neck. He reciprocated, running his hands through her loose hair.

In a whirlwind, they found themselves in Amara's room. She urgently pulled Haiden's shirt over his head. It fell at their feet. Her hands explored every inch of his granite smooth torso. Her heart was pounding so loud that she was sure Haiden could hear it. He tugged her top over her head, exhaling as he discovered the body beneath.

Haiden worked Amara's jeans from her body, laughing a little as they became stuck around her feet. He pulled off each of her yellow polka-dot socks (she cringed a little in embarrassment).

Then he began to kiss her again. Her ankle. Behind her knee. Her inner thigh. He pulled off her underwear, revealing her full body. His eyes lit up and he scanned her from head to toe. He quickly lost the last of his clothes and took her hand, leading her to the bed.

Haiden's tongue moved delicately against hers. His fingers explored her body. Amara wrapped her arms around his shoulders and pulled him in. Time seemed to stand still as Amara discovered many more of Haiden's 'innate skills'. She was lost in a frenzy of sensations as he took his time to explore every inch of her.

She hadn't known that intimacy could feel like this. It felt like the first time. Eventually she arched her back and threw her head back in a long moment of sweet release. She heard Haiden moan and then he stopped moving. She pulled him in, encircling his firm body in her arms.

Amara folded herself into Haiden. Her head pressed against his shoulder. Her hands worked their way into his long hair. Their heavy breathing slowed as they remained entwined, their hands still discovering the curves of the other's body.

Chapter 11

Christopher found himself outside Klaus's room. The key was hanging on a hook to the side of the door. He had to smirk at the old-fashioned 'jail cell' set up, where as long as the key was out of reach of the baddie, all was good. Vhik'h-Tal-Eskemon's antiquated interior worked in Christopher's favor right now, so he wasn't complaining. He grabbed the key and took a deep breath, feeling the air moving through his body but not being utilized. He expelled the exact same air out. Unfiltered and untouched.

He'd managed to stay away from Klaus since the Red Claw had arrived, letting Amara and the Council take the lead. But now, in the dark of the night with only his roiling thoughts for company, he found himself outside this door. His questions could remain bottled inside him for only so long.

The last time Christopher had placed his hands on Klaus, he'd seen the world through the other vampire's eyes. This strange sixth sense he'd discovered was unreliable and intermittent. But he had to try again. The inside knowledge Christopher could glean would be far more valuable than anything the Council could extract just by talking.

Memories flashed into his mind unbidden of Klaus killing Aunt Laura. The way the Red Claw had casually broken her then dumped her body on the ground. Christopher bit his lip. That didn't matter right now. Those thoughts served no useful purpose here. Klaus had denounced his old life. He was no longer a Red Claw…or so he claimed.

Christopher slid the key into the lock and twisted. He turned the handle and pushed open the heavy door.

"I wondered when you'd make an appearance." Klaus smirked from the single bed in the corner of the room. He sat upright and alert, almost as if he had expected Christopher.

Christopher stepped into the room and gently closed the door behind him. Though it was dark, he could see well enough thanks to his enhanced vision.

"I guess you want to finish the job," mused Klaus as he stood up. "Rip me to shreds for killing that old-timer?" His words were matter-of-fact, devoid of emotion.

Christopher took in the other vampire, who looked younger and far less menacing than he remembered from their last encounter. But perhaps it was just this peculiar setting which gave that impression.

Christopher stepped forward.

"I don't even care anymore," said Klaus, looking resigned and keeping his arms by his sides. "Do your worst."

"No," said Christopher, surprising even himself with his calmness. "I just want to know if you're telling the truth."

"The truth about wh…" Klaus began.

"Everything," Christopher interrupted, before quickly reaching out and placing a hand on Klaus's wrist.

Christopher felt disoriented, like he was about to lose his balance. Then the images rushed into his mind.

***

CHAPTER 11

Klaus looked at the crumpled human form in the concrete dungeon below. It amazed him that a human, especially one so weak, was apparently the key to their ascension. The fate of the Red Claws rested on the shoulders of *her*. It made no sense to him.

They'd carried her all the way north, stopping only to feed. They would leave one Family member behind to keep an eye on the human. That was all it took. One vampire. The rest of the Family could go off and merrily hunt together. Not all of the Red Claws were here, of course. It didn't make sense for their entire Family to transport this measly human. The rest of them were waiting at the base in Alaska, readying for a war that Zachariah said was imminent.

It was Klaus's turn (again) to watch over the woman while his brethren were off satiating their hunger. A wave of jealousy rippled through Klaus. He wanted to be out there with them on the hunt, but always seemed to grasp the short straw. He had ended up posted to guard duty more times than any of the others. At first, he was proud of the fact. He assumed it was because Zachariah thought he was the most capable, the most trustworthy. But now, just sitting here in the shabby wooden shack in the cold while the human lay immobile below, he wasn't so sure. Another thought occurred to him. He was being pushed away.

He looked down at the woman, shivering on the floor in a fetal position. Bite marks covered nearly every part of her upper body that the thin T-shirt didn't cover. But he knew there were plenty of bite marks underneath the flimsy material, too. Klaus wasn't allowed to feed on her. He wasn't allowed to touch her when they were alone. Not that he particularly wanted to. His only job was to make sure she remained captive.

But, in the name of the Omni-Father, why the hell were they keeping her alive when her death would remove the threat hanging over the Family? How was her continued existence helping the Red Claws? Zachariah didn't confide in Klaus. Ever since he had disappointed his master by not finishing the job when retrieving the book of prophecy, their relationship had deteriorated. Klaus felt like he was being punished. He felt more estranged than ever from the one person he trusted more than anybody else in the world. Zachariah was the one who gave him the gift of eternal life all those years ago. The one constant in his life. Now Klaus felt like an abandoned child.

Saliva, full of paralyzing venom, pooled in the back of Klaus's mouth as he looked down at the human's neck. He was so hungry. Maybe he should just swoop down and kill her now. Drain her completely. Take the decision out of Zachariah's hands. That would end it all. The Red Claws would be safe.

But who was he kidding? Thinking about it was as far as he dared go. Zachariah wanted her alive, which meant he knew something that Klaus didn't, and wasn't prepared to share. That realization gnawed at Klaus with more ferocity than the hunger accosting his body.

He heard a sound behind him and turned sharply. He half expected to see a Red Claw holding a thick clump of wood that was destined for the base of his skull. But it was just the wind blowing through the holes in the shack, creating an eerie whine. Klaus caught his thoughts, forcing himself to stop spiraling down. Of course his Family wasn't conspiring against him. Family didn't do that. If Zachariah was keeping secrets, he was doing it for a good reason. And he'd tell Klaus

CHAPTER 11

before anybody else. Surely.

He stood and walked over to the door, looking out into the snow-covered wilderness. There were no signs of any filthy werwulfs. As the Red Claws continued their journey north, they twisted and turned, leading the wolves on a wild goose chase. They'd never be able to catch up. Vampires were quicker. They also didn't need to sleep in the regular sense.

Stupid, slow dogs, Klaus thought to himself as he saw the first of his Family members cresting a rise up ahead after returning from the hunt. The Red Claws planned to remain in the cabin for a brief while so they could get some rest before pushing on. They found they needed very little down time recently. After sleeping for one hundred years, you could say they were well rested.

Klaus leaned his head out of the hut to get a better look at his returning brothers and sisters. The bright sunlight felt harsh against his eyes and skin, but did no damage. The misconception amongst mortals that vampires couldn't stand the sun benefited the undead greatly. Humans naturally feared the darkness but felt safe in the light. It just made for easier pickings.

Klaus stood back as the vampires trudged into the hut, bringing dirty snow underfoot. Zachariah was at the rear. He didn't even acknowledge Klaus as he came in. The Red Claw leader simply strode up to the trap door and peered down to check for himself that the woman was still there. Klaus felt humiliated. Is this how far he had fallen in Zachariah's estimation? That he couldn't be trusted to guard a feeble human woman?

"Rest now, children," said Zachariah to his brood.

The dozen Red Claws settled around the walls of the cabin.

They sat with their backs to the rotted wood, closed their eyes and slowed their thoughts, descending slowly into the restorative trance state.

"You take the first watch," ordered Zachariah, just as Klaus was beginning to get himself settled into a vacant corner of the room.

"Brother, isn't there somebody else that can do it? I haven't even fed."

Klaus knew that his words were bold, if not stupid. You didn't argue with Zachariah. But Klaus was reaching the end of his tether. He was mentally and physically drained. And why him again? Why didn't Zachariah ask one of the other Red Claws? Some of them had never kept watch even once.

"Excuse me?" Zachariah replied, his lips pressed into a fine line.

"Zachariah, please. I've done most of the watches. This isn't fair."

Klaus wasn't sure why he was arguing. It was futile and he was only making Zachariah more angry. But something inside Klaus was beginning to snap.

"You believe so?" said Zachariah. "Because I believe everybody has taken equal turns."

The words were a dare. They were blatantly not true. Zachariah himself hadn't taken a single watch. Some other brothers and sisters had done one or two, at most. Klaus had done at least ten.

"You know that's not true, Zachariah." Klaus's voice was barely audible. He looked down.

The cabin was silent. Tension filled the frigid air.

"It's true if I say it's true," Zachariah said, with finality.

Klaus never realized how much resentment could be held

in so few words. It sounded like Zachariah truly hated him. But why? Was his previous failure so grievous? Perhaps Klaus was expected to atone, to do his penance. After that, maybe he would once again be embraced into the fold. It was worth a try.

"I'm sorry master," said Klaus, dropping his head in submission.

He quietly stood and went outside to take position in front of the cabin door, surveying the snowy vista once again. After a few minutes he heard a voice coming from behind him. He went on high alert, ready to fight or raise the alarm. But he quickly realized it was just the human, crying out again in her delirium.

"Christopher," she moaned. "...Christopher..."

Klaus pondered the humans. During the Red Claws' journey up the country they had been killing and feeding on locals from the areas they passed. Though they took care to choose victims who were alone or isolated, there could be little doubt that the humans knew something extraordinary was happening. A serial killer on the loose was probably their initial conclusion. But their musings mattered nothing to the Red Claws. The Family only saw food. They only knew hunger. But wasn't it this very hubris that had sent them to sleep for a century? Klaus knew he shouldn't care but, in this moment of weakness, of feeling estranged from his Family, he mulled the existential question.

Stop it, Klaus, he scolded himself. *Remember who you are...and what you are.*

"Christop...," the woman cried out again, weaker now. "...Chrisss..."

She was crying out for a vampire, Klaus contemplated. A

vampire. The human actually cried for her natural predator to save her. And not just that. If this particular vampire did save her, then he'd just have to kill her eventually. That was the prophecy. Yet she still called out for him. Even though he was destined to deal her death, she called for him.

More sounds from behind him. Whispering this time. Klaus narrowed the focus of his hearing to hone in on the voice. Zachariah. It sounded like he was on the cell phone he had been given. The innovations of this modern world astounded Klaus. They were as incredible to him as a vampire no doubt would be to most humans. The conversation was hushed. One-sided.

"Yes, yes." Then silence for a few moments. "We're about a week away now. Two at most depending on how many detours we have to take to keep the mongrels at bay." More silence. "Of course she's still alive, we need her, don't we?" Another pause. "She's weak, but she will arrive with blood running through her veins, of that I assure you…okay… bye."

Who was he talking to? Why is he keeping her alive? Why hasn't he told me? Doesn't he trust me?

The thoughts whirled around Klaus's head. He was suddenly accosted by a wave of jealousy upon realizing that somebody else knew the grand plan while he was kept in the dark.

At that moment Zachariah emerged from the depths of the cabin.

"I take it you heard that phone call?" said Zachariah, after noticing Klaus was standing just outside the door.

Klaus simply nodded. He didn't want to make his situation any worse by lying.

"Do not breathe a word of it to any of your brothers and sisters. Do you understand, Klaus? It is very important. I am trusting you."

"Who were you speaking to?" Klaus dared to ask, feeling he had partly regained the confidence of his master.

"That is none of your business," Zachariah shot back, his tone dismissive, as if Klaus wasn't worth wasting words on.

That drove Klaus over the edge. His hunger, mental turmoil and physical weariness combined to weaken his reserve.

"Why won't you tell me, Zachariah?" Klaus pleaded. "You used to tell me everything."

Klaus's eyes bored beseechingly into his master's. His creator.

Zachariah looked offended.

"I have never told you everything," he clarified. "Only what was useful for you to know. Just because you knew more than most, that doesn't mean you are special. My burdens are mine alone to bear."

Klaus steadied himself. He wasn't prepared to back away. Not now.

"Why is she still alive?" he asked, pointing back at the trap door in the center of the dirty wooden floor.

Zachariah narrowed his eyes and contorted his mouth into a snarl.

"You are second-guessing my decisions?" he spat. "Who do you think you are?"

"I'm worried, Zachariah," said Klaus, in a softer yet more urgent tone. "I see no reason for her to still be alive. Surely the risk is too high. If you kill her now, then the prophecy can't be fulfilled. We all live."

"That is not your concern." Zachariah's words were cold and blunt.

"How can it not be my concern?" countered Klaus. "While

she's alive there's a chance the prophecy will be fulfilled. A chance we all die."

Klaus was aware that his voice was rising in volume, but he could do very little to stop it.

"Remember to whom you are talking," Zachariah warned, holding up a finger to Klaus's face.

Klaus felt the bitterness expand within him. His feelings of abandonment and resentment over the past couple of weeks were reaching boiling point. He felt frantic.

"I am talking to the person who is supposed to keep us safe," he said. "Family above all else, is it not? We're not safe while the human is alive. In the name of the Omni-Father, Zachariah, kill her and get it over with. While we still have the chance."

Klaus took a step towards Zachariah, encroaching on his space. It was a stupid decision. He knew that. But his feet moved without any pause for thought.

"You might want to back away from me, Klaus," warned Zachariah. "I am your creator but, if you test me, I will be your destroyer. Don't make me do it."

Zachariah's warning registered, but still Klaus's feet refused to move. He remained glued to the spot directly in front of Zachariah.

What the hell am I doing? Klaus thought in a brief second of clarity. *Trying to save my Family. Trying to save myself,* a more primal part of him answered. This was about self-preservation. Klaus had already overstepped the mark with Zachariah, and there would be consequences. There was no going back now.

"Kill her, Zachariah. Now. Or I will." Klaus was as shocked as Zachariah at the words that left his mouth.

Zachariah just stared at him, open-mouthed, then raised his eyebrows. The shock had seemingly turned to amusement.

CHAPTER 11

"Don't make me laugh, Klaus," said the Red Claw leader. "You're a sheep. A follower. You were nothing before and you're nothing now. Just a clumsy, blushing boy who can't carry out the simplest of instructions. Stop your pathe…"

Klaus lunged forward before his brain had a chance to catch up with his actions. He sank his teeth into Zachariah's neck then twisted his head violently, tearing away flesh. Zachariah shrieked before grabbing Klaus and throwing him to the ground. Klaus landed heavily on his back inside the shack. Zachariah grabbed at his neck and screamed in rage, waking the other Red Claws. They quickly took in what was happening and sprang into action, crouching in a circle around Klaus, blocking him off from their wounded leader.

"Make him wish he was dead," ordered Zachariah, as black blood oozed from his gaping wound, spilling over his hand. "But don't kill him," he added, with venom. "Leave him for the mongrels to finish off. That's a fitting end for the dog he is."

Klaus's 'brothers and sisters' didn't hesitate. They threw themselves on him, lips pulled back in snarls, teeth bared.

Klaus tried to curl himself into a defensive position but it was no use. Twelve vampires were on top of him. Ripping and tearing. Biting and cutting. Their faces were quickly smeared with his dark blood.

He didn't stand a chance. Klaus screamed like a broken, scared animal as pain seared every part of his body. His so-called Family was ferocious and merciless in its attack.

Blinding agony.

Burning torment.

On and on it went.

Klaus had never known pain like it.

The attackers suddenly stopped and backed away, retreating

to the four walls, as Zachariah entered the hut, still clutching at his neck. The Red Claw leader stared down at Klaus with pure contempt in his eyes. Then his voice rang loud in the enclosed space.

"Strip him back."

Klaus registered the phrase. Within those three short words lay the worst pain imaginable for a vampire. It was the ultimate form of torture. Peel the skin away and leave the body a bloody pulp. This wouldn't kill a vampire, but re-growing the skin, nerves and veins would take days. Days of sheer agony. It was probably the worst thing you could do to a vampire short of death. Many would argue that death was kinder.

The brood descended on him again.

Klaus thought he knew what pain was before, but this was worse by an order of magnitude. It was constant, unyielding torment. Klaus imagined that this was what being burned alive would feel like…and it was just the beginning. It would be days until the torment racking his body would subside in the slightest. An eternity of pain contained inside a few days.

Amidst the unbearable agony, a darkly absurd thought flashed into his mind. He would give anything to be human right now. At least then he would be dead in a brief moment from now. There would be a swift end to the pain.

Another rip of his flesh. Another tear of skin. Red-hot torment enveloping him.

Please God…Omni-Father…Universe…anything that can hear me…make this end…make this end…

…please…
PLEASE

CHAPTER 11

✶✶✶

Christopher shot his hand away from Klaus and sank to the floor. He could still feel his body burning. The stark memory seared his brain and scorched his flesh. Then suddenly the phantom pain subsided and he was left a crumpled heap on the cold stone floor of the bedroom. He slowly looked up.

Klaus looked bewildered, mouth open, brow creased.

"Well, if that's the best you've got, I badly overestimated your fighting skills," said Klaus. "I didn't even have to land a blow."

Klaus would have seen Christopher simply grab his arm and then collapse on the ground.

Christopher tried his best to compose himself and then stood on shaky feet. He faced Klaus, the vampire who had endured such suffering at the hands of his own Family. He was telling the truth. Klaus had been cast out, attacked and left for dead. Christopher gave a curt nod before turning and leaving the room.

Klaus looked even more bewildered.

Once outside, Christopher collapsed against the wall, using it to remain upright. His thoughts quickly turned to Nell. He remembered looking through borrowed eyes down on her unmoving crumpled form in the cold basement of the shack. Limp and bloodied. He vividly recalled her flesh covered with savage bite marks. The images were burned into his brain.

One part of him had hoped that she'd be treated fairly. She'd gone to them willingly and without resistance, after all. Great heaving sobs shook his body. Nell was in pain. Hurt. Tortured. Betrayed. Alone.

Grief turned to anger. Christopher wanted revenge. The

Red Claws. He was going to kill every last fucking one of them.

Chapter 12

Devan stood at the edge of the forest clearing and used his sharp wolf eyes to scan his surroundings. He could just about make out two shapes silhouetted in the distance. One larger than the other. As the seconds ticked by the shapes grew bigger and clearer in his vision. He could see the colors of the fur now and recognized the distinctive gait of their walks. He was elated and worried at the same time.

Devan had called into headquarters two days ago to tell Lupita where the pack was headed and where it would roughly be by the time she caught up. It was up to her to catch the scent on the ground and rejoin the group. She hadn't let him down. No surprise there. It was also no surprise that Flint was accompanying her. Devan had explained to the teenager on the phone that he was too young to be putting himself in danger. He was told to grab his freedom and rejoin his birth pack. But, evidently, the foolhardy werwulf had duly ignored that advice and tagged along with Lupita anyway. Devan was uneasy (but a tiny bit proud, if he was perfectly honest) with the youngster's decision.

Though he was focused on making headway in pursuing the Red Claws, Devan caught himself longing for Lupita's return over the past few days. The fact that she wasn't there felt like a part of him was missing. When he would give a command to his pack, he'd find himself waiting for a snarky response. An opposing view. A bit of sarcasm. Maybe a word of sage advice. But instead there was nothing. Simply a whole lot of 'OK, understood' from the rest of the wolves.

Lupita and Flint finally arrived. They padded back into the embrace of the pack. The other wolves nudged and caressed them with their shoulders and flanks in the primal sign for greeting and family.

"Hi, you," Devan heard Lupita say inside of his mind.

"Hey, there," he responded, knowing his response was vastly inadequate for how he was feeling, but not knowing what to say. After a moment to gather himself, he tried again.

"Thank you for taking Klaus to headquarters. I'm glad the mission was a success."

For fuck's sake, numbnuts, he scolded himself. *That was even worse.*

"You are most welcome, pack leader," she said, a little playfully. "I am glad to be of service."

"Arghhh," he shot back. "Give me a break, Lupi. I'm not good at this."

"I missed you, too, dufus," she replied before nudging up to him.

"How was it, really?" he asked, relieved that he was off the hook.

"It was fun, actually," she projected, brightly. "A bit of a change, you know. Amara was amazing, and lovely too. I won't have any more sarcastic comments about her from you. The vampires were actually super nice, which I didn't really expect. Especially Christopher. He came to chat with us for a while. He really has the feels for Nell, huh? He's so intense

CHAPTER 12

and devoted."

Oh great, now Lupita's falling for Christopher too, Devan caught himself thinking. Before he shook himself out of it.

"Yeah great, they're all great," Devan said, perhaps a little dryly. He bravely followed it up with: "I'm glad you're back. I missed you…a lot."

Devan's heart skipped a little as he said it. He didn't want things to be weird. He needed Lupita. Her absence had driven home just how much he valued her support on their mission.

"Yeah, me too." Lupita's voice was soft in his mind. "I hear running water," she added, lifting her head.

Devan had purposely picked a spot for the reunion where there was water nearby, recalling his encounter with Lupita at the reservoir. How their bodies had intertwined under the low glowing moon. He furtively hoped that the same might happen again, but wasn't counting his chickens. In his case, absence had definitely made the heart (and other parts of the anatomy) fonder. But he couldn't speak for Lupita.

As if answering his thoughts, Lupita surreptitiously broke off from the pack and padded away towards the tinkling sound of the running water. Devan followed at a discrete distance, not taking anything for granted.

Lupita came to the wide rocky stream. When she reached the water's edge, she turned back to look at Devan. Did she know he would be standing there? She tilted her head to catch the refreshing spray coming off the water. The smooth fur on her muzzle glowed slightly as the sun caught it.

God, I've missed her, Devan thought.

She turned slowly around and placed all four paws into the moving water while crouching low to stretch her back. She then moved further into the water and turned to face

Devan again. Her body suddenly began morphing in what Devan thought was the most mesmerizing way. The manner in which the animal curves transformed into the softness of a human body was almost like a dance. Devan wondered if his transformation looked as graceful. He suspected not.

Still in wolf form, Devan approached and stepped into the water, relishing the coolness as it washed over his legs. Lupita was submerged up to her waist. She reached out and stroked his back, running a soft hand across his thick fur. Her touch felt so intimate to Devan. He felt exposed to her, naked in more ways than one.

Lupita kept her gaze fixed on him as he transformed. Her wide eyes and attentive expression showed that she was just as enthralled by Devan's shift to human form as he was by hers. They stood opposite each other for a moment, still as the water cascaded by. Lupita stepped forward and then she was in his arms. Their bodies met. Devan was the first to meet her lips. He simply couldn't hold himself back. Lupita responded in kind, placing her arms around his neck for support as the running stream buffeted their bodies. Even though Lupita was in human form, she kissed him back with primal ferocity.

Taking his cue from her fervor, Devan wrapped his arms around her midsection and gently lifted her. She instinctively wrapped her long, slender legs around his waist. They began to move together, slowly at first but building in speed. Devan's muscled body easily bore her weight as she moved against him. The sense of urgency reached a crescendo before they both let out urgent breaths and collapsed into each other. Devan cradled her gently in his arms as she buried her head into his neck. She was still wrapped around his body and was in no hurry to let go.

CHAPTER 12

Walking back to the shore, Lupita's body still one with his own, Devan gently placed her back onto the ground. Her bare feet squished the wet earth. She leaned in and hugged him, placing her head against his hard chest.

"Now I'm *really* glad you're back," said Devan, still catching his breath.

"So you can use me for a little stress relief?" Lupita murmured back. Devan knew she was smiling even though he couldn't see her face. Her tone gave it away.

"No at all," said Devan, sounding offended. "I also need someone to bury the pack's dung, so we don't give away our position."

She snapped her head away from him then slapped him across the chest.

"Charming! And there's me spending my time away thinking about you."

Devan felt a renewed stirring down below.

"Me too," he said, as he pulled her against him. "...and mostly R-rated thoughts at that."

She gently pushed him away.

"Not like that," Lupita said.

"Then how?"

Devan began to lay gentle kisses against her neck and under her chin.

She lifted her head to savor the caress of his lips before she continued speaking.

"You said you didn't change until you were older?"

"Umm…yeah," Devan replied.

He stopped trailing his kisses and looked at her. His desire was suddenly damped by the unexpected topic of conversation. The night he first changed wasn't something he wanted to think about, much less talk about.

"Well, I asked my dad about it," Lupita said, taking his hands in hers and looking up at him earnestly.

"You told your dad about me?"

Devan felt indignation rising within him. Lupita had no right to talk to her father about him. What he'd told her was private. Now Lupertico would want to know the details. It could jeopardize the dynamics of the pack, his ability to lead.

"Lupita, I'm different, right," he said, frustration lacing his voice. "I didn't change when I was meant to. This all came to me way later than it should have. If the pack finds out just how much of a rookie I am, I'll lose my authority. They won't want to take orders from someone who's…"

"Woah, slow down, Devan," Lupita interrupted, squeezing his hands. "I didn't tell my dad about you, specifically."

Devan let out the breath he hadn't realized he'd been holding.

"I asked him about why one of our kind might possibly not change until they're much older," she continued. "Okay? I didn't tell him about you."

Lupita placed a hand against Devan's chest, where he was sure she could feel his heart hammering away.

"Sorry," Devan managed. "It's just…"

He looked away from her. He didn't want her to see him so vulnerable, so unsure of himself.

"It's okay," she soothed. "I should have explained it better."

"What did your dad say?" asked Devan.

"He'd heard rumors of it happening before," Lupita began. "A young girl. She was alone and didn't belong to a pack. Either that or she did, but her pack was wiped out and she was left alone. It's not entirely clear. Anyhow, the point being is that

CHAPTER 12

she had nobody to tell her what she was, or show her anything. There was no expectation for her to turn, so she just didn't. Not until she was in her late twenties, my dad said, though his information was second-hand. The story goes that she was attacked on the street. Some lowlife fucker tried to take advantage. Fearing for her life triggered something in her that brought forth the change."

Devan flinched a little. The story was hitting home.

"That scumbag never had the chance to attack anyone else," Lupita added.

Devan assessed her words carefully, noting the similarities with his own story. He'd been afraid when he turned, but not for himself. For his mother. There was also nobody to tell him what he was when he was young.

Lupita could see the pensive expression as his memories were dredged to the surface.

"Devan, what happened to you?"

Lupita's eyes were dark, on the verge of tears. The two of them shared a special bond beyond the already intimate connections found within pack life. She was picking up on his suffering, even though he was trying to contain his feelings. She already knew that something traumatic had happened. According to her father, it was the only way he would have turned without being part of a pack.

Devan just shook his head. He couldn't. Not yet.

"Something bad," is all he said, looking away.

"I'm sorry Devan," she replied, without pressing the issue. "I'm sorry that whatever happened, happened. And I'm sorry that you were alone when you experienced the change for the first time. I can't even imagine what that must have been like."

Devan nodded. He muttered a weak thank you, still not

making eye contact.

Lupita wrapped her arms around his waist and rested her forehead against his broad chest.

"You're not alone anymore," Lupita spoke against his skin.

Devan remained quiet.

Lupita reached up and cradled his chin.

"You're not alone anymore," she repeated.

Devan nodded, weakly.

Lupita slowly yet firmly tilted his head down, so he was forced to look at her.

"You're not alone anymore," she said.

Devan saw the iron resolve in her eyes, then nodded again, with more conviction this time.

"Whether you like it or not," added Lupita.

That shook Devan out of his funk. He wrapped his arms around her back, squeezed her to his chest and kissed her forehead.

"I like…very much," he assured.

They fell asleep in each other's arms by the stream that evening as the sun dropped delicately behind the tree-lined hills in the distance. For the first time in a long while, slumber came easily to Devan.

***

He awoke to a loud chorus of wild birds chirping in the nearby trees. Devan had to do a double-take when he looked down. He was still in human form. He had only ever slept in wolf form when out in the wild, so his own body was a slightly jolting sight. Lupita was tucked into his side, her long limbs wrapped around his body. Her breathing was deep and even.

CHAPTER 12

Devan took in her light brown skin and the taught curves of her body.

His moment of serenity was broken when Flint came darting into the clearing. His dark eyes settled on the pair of naked humans before him, entwined on the thick grass.

"We have a problem," he said, not bothering to avert his gaze.

Devan sat up. Though Flint's words were alarming, he found a moment to count his blessings that Lupita's father or brother hadn't been the ones to come and find them. He wasn't sure if it was a scene Lupertico or Lupo particularly wanted to stumble on.

Lupita was up now, roused by Devan's movement. Both of them swiftly transformed.

"What is it?" Devan asked, padding towards Flint.

"I caught the scent of something not too far away," projected the youngster, urgently. "I went out just before first light because I was hungry and found the scent of…it smells like…like…death."

Devan's knee-jerk reaction was exasperation.

"Flint, how many times?" he admonished.

The younger wolf dipped his head.

"You *don't* go bounding off alone without telling the pack," Devan shouted. "It's either going to get you killed or put the pack in jeopardy by giving away our presence."

"I didn't want to wake the others," Flint implored. "I couldn't sleep because my belly kept…"

"It's okay, Flint," Lupita interjected. She stepped forward and stood next to Devan. "It's done now, but please learn from this."

Lupita nudged Devan with her muzzle, telling him that he needed to calm down. That perhaps now wasn't the time.

"You said the smell of death, Flint," said Devan, getting back to the matter at hand, his tone more measured. "What did you mean?"

"Vampires. I think more than one," replied the teenager.

Devan and Lupita both flinched.

"But also humans. Dead humans."

Flint's stoic voice cracked for the first time.

"Nell?" Devan asked, quickly, his heart suddenly racing.

"No, not her," said Flint. "There wasn't that scent we detected back at the cabin, but others."

All three wolves were silent for a moment.

"You've done well, Flint," said Lupita. "Good work. But remember, next time it has to be a team effort. No running off. We have no idea what's out there, especially now."

Flint moved his muzzle up and down.

"Okay," said Devan. "We have to get going. Right now."

The pack ran north, crashing past trees, down slopes and across a ravine. Devan led the way with Lupita fixed at his side. They caught the faint stench that Flint had detected. Soon it became overpowering. A mix of vampires and humans. Devan could see why Flint had been so unnerved. A collective quiver ran through the pack as the wolves braced themselves for what was to come.

They passed the first body as they hit an area of marshland. A woman. Her neck and stomach ripped open and her face frozen in a perpetual scream. Traversing across the wet ground, the pack passed nine more bodies. Seven women and, horrifyingly, two children, all with ugly gouges on their throats and mid-sections.

Devan shuddered, cursing the Red Claws for inflicting such cruelty and for the fact that his pack had to witness the

CHAPTER 12

gruesome aftermath. Flint and Lupita's brother Lupo were the youngest. They shouldn't have had to witness such savagery. Such barbarism.

The pack didn't linger as they came across the bodies. Devan and Lupertico took the lead, approaching the corpses and inspecting them to confirm the cause of death.

The pack soon came across the first vampire.

She had been drained of her blood. 'Exsanguinated' as Amara would have pointed out, Devan thought darkly. The Red Claw was white as a sheet. One of her arms was missing. Clumps of blackened blood clung to her soiled clothes. Her limbs jutted out at odd angles, making her look like a broken, twisted doll. It was only a matter of time before the final drops of blood would seep into the soil and she would turn to ash.

The pack discovered more human women close by. Dead at the hands of the Red Claws. Dumped in the wild. There didn't seem to be any settlements nearby, so the vampires must have stolen them from somewhere else. Taking them away from their families and lives as they knew them to die what must have been painful and terrifying deaths.

They found another Red Claw. An older male with graying hair, from what Devan could make out from the disfigured corpse. This one was almost split in two. The gaping hole in his midsection spilled vital organs onto the ground. Thick black blood oozed out of the gap.

In all, the pack discovered five Red Claws left for dead and fifteen humans very much dead. All had been drained of their blood. Devan had no idea what to make of it. The humans, perhaps. But the Red Claws? What had happened here? A revolt? Punishment? Power struggle?

"Let's sit a while, gather our thoughts," Lupita spoke into

the minds of the pack.

Normally she would advise Devan and he would give out the order. But right now he was glad of the input.

The wolves moved to a clearing out of sight of the macabre scene. They formed a tight circle and spread their limbs on the ground, heads resting on front feet. It was Devan who spoke first.

"We have to inform headquarters about this, urgently," he began. "But first things first. The vampires must be destroyed. Heads off and turned to ash."

He was quiet for a moment. No one seemed to disagree.

"The humans," he continued, more solemnly. "We can bury their bodies to cover up the slaughter site."

"But where does that get us, son?" asked Lupertico. "The other humans must know they are gone. They'll be searching. This can't be kept hidden."

"And it's wrong," added Lupita, firmly. "Who are we to bury the bodies? These people have families. They need to go back to their loved ones so they can have proper funerals."

"Okay," said Devan, feeling out of his depth. "We wipe out the Red Claws but leave the humans untouched."

It felt obscene to just leave the bodies as they were.

"There's no good choices here," said Lupertico, with a heavy sigh, after sensing Devan's thoughts. "But I think this is the least worst option."

"Are we all agreed, then?" projected Devan, raising his head.

He didn't usually put decisions to a vote but in this instance he felt the magnitude of the situation called for collective agreement.

"Aye," came the first reply from young Lupo, followed by a chorus of 'Ayes' from the other wolves.

CHAPTER 12

With that decided, Devan's thoughts turned to headquarters. He didn't want to leave the pack at this time. The wolves were on edge and felt vulnerable after making the grisly discovery. He asked Flint to backtrack to the last town they'd passed to make the phone call, after carefully explaining to the young wolf what to do and what precautions to take. Despite the bleak situation, the adventurous youngster couldn't hide his excitement at being entrusted with the task. He literally bounded off into the forest as he set off on his solo mission.

Devan approached Lupertico. Right now he could use the wisdom that came with age.

"What do we think this means?" asked Devan. "Why kill your own?"

"The master could be losing power over his troops," suggested the old wolf. "A reaction to Klaus's treatment, perhaps. They might be rebelling against Zachariah and he's dealing with it the only way he knows…by killing."

There didn't appear to be any other logical explanation for what had happened.

"What about the woman and children?" asked Devan.

The humans had to have come from somewhere. There was no way all those people were just out in the middle of nowhere. And why scatter the bodies around the forest like that? Something didn't feel right.

"I have no idea.." said Lupertico. "…and to tell you the truth, son, I'm not sure I want to know."

Chapter 13

Life was mercifully undramatic for the wolves over the next few days as they covered more ground. The pack was subdued and the normal banter back and forth had all but ceased. One day turned into the next with the usual respite for eating and sleeping. Devan didn't have much sense of time passing anymore. His mind dwelled on the bodies they'd found. Mutilated and drained. It was hard to push the graphic images out of his mind. He knew it would be the same for the other wolves.

It was rare for werwulfs to become involved in a large-scale conflict. They preferred to live peaceful and inconspicuous lives in the wild, away from the drama of other supernatural creatures. Lupertico said vampires were the worst when it came to creating turmoil. Devan had no trouble believing him. If it wasn't for those damn blood-suckers, he wouldn't be here now. But he also would never have met Lupita, which almost made this whole thing worthwhile. Almost.

Nell flashed into his thoughts. His romantic feelings towards her had begun to ebb. The more time he spent with Lupita, the less he thought about Nell in that way. But he still felt the burning drive to save her. Not only as a friend, but as an innocent who had been thrown into something way out of

CHAPTER 13

her league simply for falling in love with the wrong person. Devan almost chuckled, knowing that the exact same thing had happened to him. That's why he found himself bounding through the Canadian wilderness right now.

The pack had been in Canada for a few days. It was easy to slip over the border without being noticed if you were a wolf. No passports or paperwork necessary, just a bit of digging in the earth. There were now over twenty in the pack. Lupita's father had been responsible for most of the new recruits. Lupertico had an easy and sincere way of communicating with other wolves, which made them quickly grasp what was at stake. Devan felt the skill came with age and experience, but also from being a father. What all creatures, supernatural of not, shared was a desire to see their offspring thrive in the world. Not threatened by murderous undead hordes. Of course, the rapidly spreading stories among the wild wolves of humans being slaughtered in the forest also helped. It served as tangible proof that the threat was real. Lupertico just had to fill in the blanks in his convincing, fatherly manner. If the Red Claws continued to grow in power and, eventually, numbers, they would do far more damage than the world had already seen. No one was safe.

The pack kept their noses to the ground as they tracked the vampires. After Klaus had revealed the Red Claws were taking Nell to Alaska, Kavisha had suggested chartering a private plane for the werwulfs. The Council had connections built up over decades and could pull a number of strings. Devan had refused. He wasn't prepared to take Klaus's word. He felt it could be a ruse to send them in the wrong direction. Following the scent on the ground was the only method he trusted.

However, it looked like Klaus was telling the truth as the pack tracked the Red Claws all the way to Yukon, the mountainous territory bordering Alaska. They reached the small town of Beaver Creek to bed down for the night. So close. So very close now. The pack hunted and slept well that night, feeling a buzz as the journey's end approached. Amara had said Zachariah's census records came from Whittier in Alaska. The city was most likely their ultimate destination, but Devan was taking nothing for granted. He was only prepared to trust what his senses could detect when Nell's life hung in the balance.

Nell's scent continued to guide the way. Meaning that she was alive. Probably not in the best of health knowing the Red Claws, but she was alive. Devan was sure he would be able to tell if she'd been killed. Her scent would be tinged with the smell of decay. He didn't want to think about that. The Red Claws had kept her alive until now, which boded well for her in the very short-term at least.

Once his pack had bedded down in an undisturbed patch of undergrowth, Devan left to contact headquarters. He made his way to a sparsely populated area and stole jeans and a pullover from his staple source of clothing — an unattended washing line. He thought about the many households across the country who were missing garments on account of him. All for the greater good, he reminded himself. Shoes were always more difficult. But he was surprised at the number of muddy pairs of sneakers that could be found outside front doors, especially if the home had a porch and steps leading up to the house. Those houses appeared to be magnets for dirty shoes left out.

Devan found a payphone at a nearby motel. He called

headquarters after reversing the charges. He wanted to find out how they were doing more than give an update on his own progress. As his pack closed in on the Red Claws, he needed to know how the army was shaping up. As much as Devan wanted to decimate the Red Claws with only his pack for support, he knew that it was wishful thinking. It would take an army to eradicate them from the world.

Two birds with one stone, as his mother used to say. Save Nell and wipe out the Red Claws, which would mean that Christopher wouldn't need to kill Nell. This was the only ending that Devan was interested in.

Christopher picked up the phone after the first ring. Devan heard him calling out to Amara.

"Hang on a minute, Devan, let me put you on speaker," said Christopher. "That way Amara won't have to breathe over my shoulder."

Devan chuckled. He knew how engrossed the librarian could get when it came to learning new information.

"Okay, we're ready," said Christopher. "Just so you know, Kavisha, Loris and Klaus are on their way, too."

That was a shock to Devan. If Klaus was being allowed to listen in on the call, then the vampires were trusting him. Devan wasn't sure how he felt about that. But he knew Kavisha and Loris had a lot of wisdom when it came to making judgment calls. Amara was no fool, either. Klaus must have proven himself useful to the cause.

"We're almost there," began Devan. "We're in Beaver Creek, which is about six hundred kilometers from Whittier, assuming that's where they're headed. The trail is still strong. As long as there aren't any nasty surprises, we'll be there in the next six or seven days. Will you guys be ready to fight by then?"

After a long pause, during which Devan imagined them looking from one to the other, Loris spoke up.

"Seven days sounds good," he said. "Vhik'h-Tal-Eskemon is almost full, but more are coming as word spreads. We need every recruit possible. Strength in numbers, as they say."

Devan let out a small sigh of relief.

"That's good to know, Loris," he said. "We have no idea what they have planned for Nell, but time is of the essence. How will you get here?"

"Some of us will fly," said Amara. "Others have a more direct approach, given their abilities. We can be with you in less than twenty-four hours once we're ready to go."

"Excellent tracking, by the way, Devan." It was Kavisha who spoke this time. "You and your pack have done incredibly well. Better than we could have imagined. How many of you are there now?"

"Just over twenty, give or take," said Devan. "We pick up new recruits along the way but sometimes others choose to go home. I honestly can't blame them. We've seen some pretty scary stuff out here."

Devan remembered the young werwulf Ashtina and her twin Talan who had decided to go back to their family after seeing the trail of corpses left by the Red Claws. He recalled the look of abject horror in their eyes. Yet Flint, who was their junior in years, stayed on. His resolve seemed to harden after witnessing the savagery of the Red Claws. Everyone reacted to tragedy in their own way. Yet Devan felt a stab of pride at the pack he'd managed to pull together.

"We're still following Nell's trail closely and rest assured she's still alive," said Devan. "But I'm not going to lie, I'm concerned that she won't be kept alive for much longer once they reach their destination. It almost feels like a trap. Like they're luring us to them."

This was the first time Devan had voiced out loud his concern about an ambush. He was disconcerted by his own words.

"Have you shared your thoughts with the rest of the pack?" Kavisha asked.

"They're aware," replied Devan. "They can sense it. They've also seen up close what the Red Claws can do."

"Yet they're prepared to follow you into the dragon's den?" asked Loris.

"Pack is pack," said Devan, as if no more explanation were needed.

God, this is a fucked up, he thought. Emotion began to engulf him as he thought of Lupita, Lupo, Flint and the rest. He took a sharp breath.

"Any more updates on your end?" Devan asked, changing the topic out of fear he might start tearing up.

"We're coming along with the strategy," said Amara. "We'll share the finer details with you when we meet up. But it's pretty simple. We'll play to our strengths. Werwulfs are strong, so you'll be our first line. This will allow the other supernaturals to come in and mop up what's left." Amara's words flowed quickly. Devan could tell she was in her element. "Christopher will swoop in to rescue Nell," she continued. "The Vampire Hunters will concentrate on Zachariah and his entourage. Without him the Red Claws are greatly diminished. I have more details to give you, but that's the gist of it."

"Let's not lose sight of the prophecy in all this," warned Loris, gravely. "If needs be, Christopher must…"

"It won't come to that," interrupted Devan. "We'll tear them to shreds so there's no enemy left to defeat. Fuck the prophesy."

Kavisha sighed.

"We can only hope it is that simple," she said. "History would tell us otherwise."

"Our team is locked and loaded," said a voice that Devan didn't recognize. Klaus? No. That wasn't something he was likely to say. Not after having slept for one hundred years.

"Who's that?" Devan asked, caught off guard.

"Oh, that's Haiden, one of the Vampire Hunters," Amara answered.

"Yeah, he's been a great *help* to Amara," Christopher said, a little slyly.

"Nice to meet you, Haiden," Devan said, picking up on the hint.

"Likewise, bud," the voice replied.

"You're a brave man," added Devan. "In more ways than one."

That brought a few low chuckles.

"Thanks, furball," said Amara. "I do hope you don't fall into a bush of stinging nettles on your way back. That would be just dreadful."

"Speaking of that, I'd better be making tracks," Devan said, realizing he needed to rest for tomorrow's leg of the journey.

"See you soon, dude. Keep us updated," said Christopher before hanging up.

Devan put down the receiver and leaned heavily against the phone, trying to straighten out his thoughts. He didn't think he was any great shakes as a pack leader and his wolves were trusting him with their lives. It was a heavy burden to bear. He sometimes caught himself imagining a future with Lupita, but always shook himself out of the fantasies. Why go there when he couldn't even guarantee that she or he would be around very much longer? It was just so unfair.

That's when the tears came, and it seemed like they would never end.

Chapter 14

Over the next week the pack crossed more than seven hundred kilometers of harsh yet beautiful terrain. The wolves traversed snow-capped mountains, ice valleys and fields of the purest virgin snow as they headed west from Beaver Creek. On the fourth day they made their camp on a mountain cap at the Wrangell St. Elias National Park. As the wolves stared out from the frosted peak it seemed the entire world lay beneath them. 'Breathtaking' was an understatement for the stunning view they briefly enjoyed. The weather was bitterly cold, with freezing winds and icy ground. Not much fun for humans but ideal for wolves, who could lap up the ground with their padded paws and strong legs. Food was abundant in the wild and the pack feasted on beavers, arctic foxes and elk.

They reached their destination as dawn broke on the eighth day. A feeling of elation came over the pack after the long trek. Even Devan allowed himself a moment of quiet celebration. Nell's scent was still strong. Stronger even, given the lack of care she had been shown. At least she was alive. Devan kept telling himself that nothing else mattered, as long as she survived. She'd hopefully have a lifetime ahead of her to make up for the suffering she had endured at the hands of the Red Claws.

CHAPTER 14

The wolves made base at Blackstone Bay, which lived up to its name with its rocky coves the color of coal. It was just south of Whittier and Devan hoped that the vast, caterwauling ocean that smashed up against the rocks and sent sea spray high into the windy air would prevent the Red Claws from detecting how close they were. All that was left to do was sit and wait for back-up to arrive. Two wolves kept watch at all times over the main thoroughfare of Whittier from the high vantage point of the rocks.

On the second day of observation, Lupita and Devan had taken the high ground, scanning their surroundings. Whittier was a tiny city with a small population, making the two vampires stick out like sore thumbs. A man and a woman, both maybe thirty judging by outward appearances. But of course that meant nothing. They could be hundreds of years old. They were dressed in black cargo pants with dark green windbreakers, no doubt liberated from a clothing store or warehouse. Their pale, bloodless faces turned this way and that, as they took in the scattered shops and fishing boats unloading their catches.

This was the first sighting of the Red Claws since the long pursuit began. A shudder of both excitement and trepidation ran down Devan's back, making some of the thick fur stand up on his neck. Lupita noticed.

"Yeah, me too," she projected.

Devan raised his muzzle and sampled the air.

"It's blustery today and the salt's thick in the air," he said. "I think it could hide us. This might be our chance to track them back to their base."

Lupita kept her eyes locked on the two Red Claws as she contemplated.

"Okay," she said, finally. "I'm not overjoyed at the prospect, but it makes sense."

"Project what you're seeing back to the others, so they're in the loop," said Devan. "You're better at it than me, but tell them *not* to follow. We don't want to give ourselves away."

Lupita nodded then went still as she sent out the message.

"Done, let's move," she said after a few moments.

The two wolves raced down the rocks, using their claws and pads to expertly traverse the hard, uneven surfaces. They quickly made it to the main road and trailed the two vampires at a considerable distance, not taking any chances. The Red Claws stopped at a boating supplies store. After a few minutes they came out. The man was holding a length of thick rope, no doubt bought using cash stolen from one of their victims. Devan's heart sank as he saw the rope. This did not bode well at all.

Slowly but surely, the vampires led the wolves back to Zachariah's home. It was hidden deep in the mountains surrounding Whittier, as the grassy verges began to frost over with a carpet of ice. It was far from civilization. No human would accidentally stumble upon the building. The terrain was too unwelcoming, as were the occupants.

It was a huge wooden fortress. A ten-foot-high fence surrounded the enclave, helping it to remain relatively obscured. Devan and Lupita scurried up a nearby peak to see over the fence. What they saw shouldn't have surprised them, but it did. The compound looked like a military base. With various smaller buildings surrounding the main one.

"Sheesh," projected Lupita. "That is quite something. It has to be well over a hundred years old, if the Red Claws just woke up."

CHAPTER 14

"Yeah," said Devan. "By the looks of it they were always planning to wreak havoc on the world. Why else would you need a fortress like that?"

Lupita didn't reply. Devan turned to her, noticing her frame was hunched. He nudged up next to her so she could feel his body.

"What's wrong?" he asked, gently.

She just kept staring out at the compound.

"It's really happening, isn't it?" she said, at last, dipping her head and placing her muzzle on her front legs. "We're actually here. This isn't some exhilarating chase through scenic landscape anymore. We're going to fight them, and we're going to lose some of our kin."

Devan took a long moment before replying.

"It's a very real possibility, yes," he said. There was no point denying it. "But nothing is written in stone here."

In all likelihood, they would lose friends and family in the battle. Those Devan knew well, perhaps even loved, would die. He nudged up closer to Lupita, gently placing a paw on her back. How would he cope if he lost her? Was she even his to lose?

"Nell's down there somewhere," said Lupita.

The statement surprised Devan. The fact that Lupita was thinking about Nell. She had joined the cause to wipe out the Red Claws, so that her kin and their way of life could remain safe in the world.

"We'll save her and do some serious damage in the process," Devan said, trying to sound upbeat.

He wasn't actually sure what to say, but the way Lupita turned away from him told him he'd missed the mark.

"Did you ever think that she might not be the priority here?"

Lupita snapped back.

Devan recoiled as though he'd been slapped. He took his paw off her back.

"She is a priority. In a very real sense," said Devan. "I want to kill each and every Red Claw. But we need Nell to remain alive so the Red Claws don't break the prophecy, as much I hate to admit it. It might be the only way to defeat them. Plus, she's a person, Lupita. A good person. No, a really fucking great person. She doesn't deserve to die at their hands. She doesn't deserve to die at all. But if she has to, Christopher will be the one to do it, for that goddam prophecy to work. But at least it will be the one she loves doing it, as completely batshit mental as that sounds. Not some filthy, hate-filled vampires. I am not willing to let her die at their hands."

Devan was taken aback that the wolf he was falling for, had fallen for, could seemingly be so callous.

"I don't know her, your extra-special Nell," said Lupita. "All I know is that my family is risking their lives for somebody they've never met. The way I see it, we have two options. Go in hard and kill all of the Red Claws, therefore breaking the prophecy anyway. There's a possibility that Nell might die in the process if we can't remove her from the battle. Or, we split up, and some of us try to save Nell. But trying to save her would make us less effective as a fighting force against the Red Claws. And if we save her, then what? Then she'll probably have to die anyway. She's dead either way, Devan. Can't you see that? That's what the damn prophecy says."

"We don't know that for sure," said Devan. "Amara and some of the others are trying to find a way to break the prophecy, or at least find a loophole, to keep her alive."

"Devan." Lupita turned to face him, her eyes hard, her tone

stern. "Why do you want to save her? You're placing so many at risk. I can't imagine she'd want you to do that if she's anything like you say."

"Because she's my friend," Devan shot back. "Because she's a good person. Because she doesn't deserve this. Any of this."

"Just a friend?" Lupita asked.

Devan's eyes widened and he lifted his head.

"Is that what you were worried about?" he asked.

Lupita puffed out a long breath, which formed a misty cloud in front of her.

"Partially," she admitted. "I want to know that you aren't risking my life, my family's lives, just because you're infatuated with her. I know you said she's with Christopher, but sometimes we can't help what we feel."

Lupita's candor startled Devan. He turned to her. Her eyes looked so sad.

"What are the right reasons to save somebody's life?" Devan asked. He sat back on his hind legs, straightening his back and lifting his head. "Because she deserves to live? To save the world? Well, Nell means the world to me, but I'm not besotted by her, Lupita." He slammed a paw onto the ground. "But that doesn't mean I'm not going to do everything in my power to save her. It's a matter of doing what's right, Lupita. Things aren't always so black and white."

Lupita sat up and stretched her back before burying her muzzle into the thick fur of Devan's neck.

"You're a good man, Devan," she said. "I'm glad I met you. I'm sorry if I upset you. I just needed to know how you really feel. You have my support, all the way."

She nuzzled the soft flesh under his chin.

"I can't wait to see Christopher's face when he finally has

Nell in his arms," she said.

She cast an image into Devan's mind of Christopher holding a generic heroine from a paranormal romance novel who didn't look the vaguest bit like Nell. The girl in the image was also pristine, with no signs of trauma, which Devan knew wouldn't be the case if (no, when) they finally rescued Nell.

It occurred to Devan that the wolves had been tracking Nell by scent, but he hadn't shared an image of her. Great pack leader he was turning out to be.

"No, like this," he said, then projected an image of the real Nell and Christopher holding each other.

"Oh wow," replied Lupita, sitting up straighter. "Cute couple. Nell is lovely, right?"

She looked hard at Devan, who had a sneaking suspicion she was looking to see whether the mental image they were sharing was causing him any unease. One final way to check that Devan wasn't risking lives to save Nell for his own selfish reasons. He wasn't. He had to admit that at the start of the journey he was driven partly by the hope that Nell would be with him one day. Maybe she'd eventually feel the same way about him. But that no longer mattered. He wanted her to survive to live a long, happy life. The object of Devan's desire had shifted.

"One more thing before we go." Devan's words were soft. He slowly and gently rested his head against Lupita's. "I love you. I wanted you to know that, now that everything is so uncertain. You don't have to say anything back."

He was scared for Lupita to remain silent. Equally scared for her to speak.

"I love you too, dufus," she replied, pushing her head more firmly against his.

CHAPTER 14

A scream echoed from below. A woman. Nell.

Devan flinched as though struck by electricity.

Another piercing scream rang out.

Devan was already barreling towards Zachariah's house. Towards the scream. Towards Nell.

He heard somewhere in his subconscious Lupita summoning the pack. Devan flew over the rocks and hard earth.

"Devan, STOP!" screamed Lupita in his mind.

He didn't slow his pace.

"The pack is on its way," she added, breathlessly. "You will only get yourself killed like this. Devan, STOP. You don't stand a chance. Nor will Nell."

That made him slow down. Then he stopped altogether, turning around to see Lupita running towards him.

"We can't do this with just the two of us," she said, hastily. "We probably can't do it with just the pack. But at least we'll stand some kind of chance."

Thank God he had Lupita, he thought, in a sudden moment of clarity. His blind rage was surely about to be the death of him, of them both.

"Okay," he said, panting hard from the exertion. "Okay. We wait."

They approached the perimeter of the high wooden fence and peered into the narrow gaps between the vertical planks. Devan couldn't see any movement in the grounds, but could easily detect Nell's characteristic scent.

Minutes seemed to last hours as they waited for the pack to arrive. Finally, they saw movement in the distance as the wolves came into view. Sleek feral shapes glided over the rocks and quickly converged on where Devan and Lupita were crouching.

"We dig our way in," Devan ordered, dispensing with the pleasantries. "I go first. Alone. I'll project what I can see. Lupita is in charge out here. Follow her orders." This was no time for lengthy explanations.

Then he spoke to Lupita directly. "I trust you. Do what you think is right. Keep them safe."

"Devan, the screams have stopped," she replied. "Maybe we should wait for…"

"You know I can't do that," he interjected. "I would never forgive myself if…if…"

Lupita nodded her understanding.

He began digging in front of the fence and was quickly joined by the other wolves. The frosted earth was hard on top but soon gave way to softer soil underneath. They made quick work of forming a rudimentary tunnel.

Devan squeezed himself inside the hole and dug the final few feet on his own, doing his best to remain as quiet as possible. He scooped mounds of soft earth with his front paws and smoothly deposited it behind him. After a few moments he saw a crack of sunlight above him as he broke through on the other side. Soft soil covered his head as he slowly emerged from the gap inside the compound. He crouched low and shook his muzzle. The dirt flew off.

He projected to the rest of the pack what he could see. A large building in the center with five smaller structures of various sizes spread around it. Dipping his nose low to the ground, Devan moved forward as stealthily as possible, his footsteps making hardly any sound on the earth. He silently gave thanks for the humid sea air, which softened the ground, making him unheard. For now at least.

Nell's scent was incredibly strong and it led him to what

looked like the oldest structure on the development. It was the largest of the five outbuildings. A cabin. The wooden exterior was badly pockmarked and stained, no doubt battered by decades of harsh Whittier weather. Devan put his ear up to the cold wood and strained to hear inside. He could make out muffled voices, but couldn't discern how many Red Claws there were. Although he could smell Nell strongly, he couldn't hear her. Not a good sign, especially after her screams. Panic rose within him. Perhaps he was already too late. There was only one way to find out. He transformed into his werwulf form and took a deep breath, bracing himself.

"WAIT!" Lupita's voice had never been so clear or so loud in his head.

Devan turned to see her, Lupertico and Flint quietly padding towards him, heads held low to the ground, doing their best to go unnoticed.

"Your blood's up, son," projected Lupertico when he reached Devan. "Don't be a hero. Let's do this together. Pack is pack."

"Pack is pack," agreed Devan, quietly glad of the support.

"The high walls are blocking the wind," said Lupertico. "We have to be quick before they detect our scent."

"The rest of the pack are patrolling the border," added Lupita. "They'll be here if we need them. How many inside?" She pointed her muzzle towards the cabin.

"Sounded like more than two from what I could make out," projected Devan. "But there could be more. I just don't know."

"We can't just go charging in, not when Nell's in there," said Lupertico. "We need to thin their numbers first. We need a distraction."

"Leave it to me," said Flint, eager to get involved.

Before anyone could utter a word, the excitable young wolf

ran to the other side of the fortress.

"Flint, don't even think ab…" Devan began.

"It's okay," interrupted Flint. "I'm the fastest…they won't be able to catch me."

"Flint, you haven't seen…"

Before Devan could finish, Flint threw his head back and gave a loud and long howl. The high-pitched shriek echoed through the compound and off the surrounding rocks of the mountains.

The response was almost instantaneous.

Red Claws sprang into action from all over the compound. They poured out of the various buildings, running towards the source of the sudden noise. Four vampires bolted from the cabin Devan stood against.

"Save her, I've got this covered." Flint's voice sounded so sure, so confident, excited even.

There was nothing for it now. Devan saw Lupita and Lupertico shifting into werwulfs. The die had been cast. They could only hope that Flint was able to keep himself safe.

The three werwulfs hastily came around to the cabin entrance and barreled inside, claws raised, teeth bared, loud growls emanating from deep in their chests.

"What the fuck?" shouted a vampire as he saw them careening into the room. A look of dismay was etched on his face.

Devan could see there were three Red Claws in total and in the far corner was…Nell. His heart lurched. She was sitting against the wall, her body slumped and her head lolling against her chest. He ran towards her, ignoring the ensuing battle around him as Lupita and her father began wrestling with the vampires.

CHAPTER 14

Devan lifted Nell's head with the flat of his padded fingers, making sure his sharp claws didn't touch her skin. Her eyes were closed and she moaned, as if she was caught in a bad dream. Her body was covered in bite marks. There was barely a patch of skin left untouched. Devan pushed down his rage. Revenge could come later. He placed his hands under Nell's arms and began to lift.

Fingernails ripped into his back, searing his flesh and forcing him to let go of Nell. She fell back hard against the wood. The pain in his back was excruciating. He turned around to see a vampire snarling at him. Blood dripped from her fingers. His blood. That's when he finally gave vent to the rage.

He slashed at her face then pushed her to the ground, using his superior strength. She tried to squirm away but he pinned her down, slashing and tearing at her neck. Devan could hear footsteps around him but he ignored them. His white-hot anger wouldn't allow him to cease the attack. He ripped and tore over and over again, taking out all his built-up fury at the Red Claws on this one vampire. He leaned down and ripped at her neck with his sharp teeth, clamping his jaw against bone. After feeling her spine crack beneath his teeth, he jerked his head backwards violently, dismembering the head from her body. She crumbled beneath him. He was left sitting on a pile of ash-covered clothes, breathing hard.

He looked up. Nell was gone. There were only bare wooden walls in front of him.

Oh God...Fuck, what have I done?

Devan quickly turned and surveyed the two fallen vampires. Lupita and Lupertico stood panting over the badly bloodied bodies. Their necks were covered in deep gashes. Lupita gave him a brief nod before reaching down and wrenching the head off the vampire. Lupertico did the same. Within seconds dark ash filled the floor of the cabin.

"Where is she?" Devan broadcast the frantic words to the entire pack.

He had one job and he'd failed. He had Nell in his grasp but had taken his eyes off her. Now she was gone. Once again he'd let his emotions get the better of him. This time it might have cost Nell her life.

"I think I have what you're looking for."

There was something strange about the words. Then it hit Devan. The voice wasn't inside his head. It was spoken aloud.

Devan, Lupita and Lupertico exchanged wary glances before slowly exiting the cabin.

Standing atop the main house was a Red Claw, holding Nell. Her body flopped limply across his outstretched arms. He was holding her like she was trash. As far away from his body as possible. As if she was contaminated. By his side was the rogue Magister, Fabian Bamford, wearing his familiar dark robe. Devan recognized him immediately from their previous encounters. Tall, skinny with a completely hairless dome of a head. The other Red Claws were assembled on the ground beside the house. They didn't attack. It seemed their leader had something to say.

"The pack?" projected Lupita.

"No," replied her father. "There's too many of them. It would be suicide."

Devan stared at the horde of assembled vampires. There must have been close to a hundred, if not more.

"Agreed," he said, reluctantly. "We don't have the numbers. Tell them to stay back, no matter what."

CHAPTER 14

"Ah, Devan. I'd like to say it's a pleasure to finally meet you," said the Red Claw holding Nell, who Devan could only assume was Zachariah.

"Fucking traitor," Devan shouted up to Bamford in his gravelly lycan voice.

The Magister had no doubt told the vampires who he was, along with a host of other information. Bamford remained impassive.

"I see you've met some of my Family," continued Zachariah. "And I understand it didn't go so well for them. That is most unfortunate for you, and for dear Nell here." He looked down at her slack body with undisguised contempt.

Devan balled his fists.

"You see, when people hurt my Family, I get angry, very angry," added the Red Claw.

"Don't hurt her," Devan shouted upwards.

It was a ridiculous thing to say, given her present state, but it just came out.

"Silly dog, of course I'm going to hurt her," Zachariah replied coolly. "But you can rest assured that I won't kill her. Not yet, anyway. Although, I can't promise the same fate for your little friend."

Zachariah made a beckoning motion with his head. Below him, a Red Claw emerged from among the sea of vampires. His long, pale arms held the still body of a wolf. Bright red blood matted its fur.

Flint.

Devan couldn't tell if he was alive or dead. Just then Flint moaned and wriggled weakly in the vampire's arms.

Lupita heaved an audible sigh of relief.

"Okay," said Devan, holding up a placating hand. "This

doesn't have to get…"

"Do it," commanded Zachariah.

The Red Claw holding Flint lifted a knee then violently slammed the young wolf's body down onto it. The loud crack echoed around the compound. The vampire dumped Flint onto the ground before reaching down and forcefully twisting his head.

Lupita screamed. Anguished howls rang out from outside the compound as the pack registered the death. A wave of shock and despair swept through their collective mind.

"You bastard!" Devan screamed at Zachariah. "He was a child. He was innocent."

"This is war. There are no innocents," Zachariah said, mockingly. He looked down at the Red Claws. "Finish them," he ordered.

Zachariah turned on his heel, walking away with Nell in his arms. The Magister raised a cynical eyebrow and gave a half-smirk before turning and following Zachariah.

"Change back," projected Lupertico.

Devan hardly registered the words. His attention was fixed on the slumped body of Flint. The young wolf had been so fearless. So enthusiastic and full of life. To see his broken body discarded on the ground broke Devan's heart.

"CHANGE BACK," shouted Lupertico.

Devan snapped out of his stupor. He turned to see his two companions already shifting to wolf form.

The mass of vampires surged forwards.

"Fall back," projected Lupita. "Now!"

Sorrow and defeat laced her voice.

Devan turned and made for the tunnel entrance near the fence, shifting form as he moved. The two other wolves raced ahead of him. In seconds they made it to the hole and quickly ducked inside. They scrambled out of the earth on the other side, where the anxious pack stood waiting.

The Red Claws wouldn't be able to fit in the tunnel. Instead, they began jeering loudly on their side of the fence.

"DOGS, DOGS, DOGS…" they shouted in a victory chant, adding insult to injury.

The pack fled back to Blackstone Bay before the vampires could give chase. Not a word was said on the way. The mood when they arrived was somber. The wolves sat silent on the cold ground, lost in their own thoughts.

Lupita approached Devan, who was sitting away from the main pack, staring at the waves crashing into the rocks below.

"You did what you could," she said, sitting beside him.

"He died because of me," Devan replied, turning to her, his eyes red. "Flint didn't have a bad bone in his body. He hadn't even seen life yet and now…and now…" He had to gather himself before he could go on. "They all hate me," he continued, turning his muzzle to the rest of the pack. "Flint died because I was reckless."

"You *were* reckless," said Lupita.

Devan looked stung, as if he had been slapped.

"Do you want me to lie?" Lupita replied, her voice stern.

"No," he said, dipping his head. He felt utterly defeated.

"Nell is part of your pack, your human one," Lupita added, more sympathetically. "I would have done the same if someone in my family was in mortal danger."

Devan took a long moment before speaking.

"That doesn't bring Flint back," he said, despondently.

"No, it doesn't," was the only reply.

Chapter 15

It had been all hands on deck at headquarters since Devan's phone call saying the wolves had arrived at Blackstone Bay. He had sounded impatient, as if he was spoiling for a fight. Amara hoped he wouldn't do anything reckless. Devan was loyal to a fault, but could also be highly temperamental.

The infrequent communication between headquarters and the wolves was something Amara struggled with. If it was up to her, she would have a live camera feed of their progress on the ground. But that was just wishful thinking. She trusted Devan to do the right thing. She also knew that in Lupita he had a trustworthy and level-headed lieutenant.

Headquarters was buzzing with activity. Supernaturals regularly roamed the corridors and on multiple occasions in a day Amara would find herself being introduced to new faces. Her favorites had to be the spell-casters, witches and warlocks, who had descended from all over the country on the grand gothic building. The Red Claws had apparently made a hell of a lot of enemies over the decades.

Amara had spent most of the morning dispatching various portions of the army to Alaska. Some via air, others by their own means. At one point she was even contemplating asking the witches and warlocks whether they in fact used brooms to travel. Loris mercifully set her straight on that point, without even having a chuckle at her expense. The small-town librarian had been submerged into a world she hadn't even thought was plausible only weeks ago. Being a voracious reader, she always had an open worldview, but this was a different league entirely.

The assembled army was large and varied. Loris said this kind of coming together of disparate factions had never happened before. Creatures of the night tended to stick to their own kind and distrusted others, as a general rule. And never ever had vampires and Vampire Hunters, their mortal enemies, had anything to do with each other. Amara felt heartened by the unity forged among those who were so different in such a grim situation. It seemed there would be at least one silver lining to come out of this battle. Though there would also, no doubt, be much loss and sorrow.

Loris had smiled when he mentioned the Vampire Hunters. Amara suspected he never thought he'd live to see the day when he would welcome them, despite being an immortal. When Loris noticed Amara smiling in response to his own wide grin, he winked at her and then hurriedly made off to carry on with his preparations. Although she was warming to Loris, Amara couldn't quite work him out. He kept his cards very close to his chest.

Chapter 16

Loris paced the floor. With war imminent, he found himself in a contemplative mood. He pondered Nell and Christopher's love for each other. It was tragic that the one vampire who could feel love, could actually experience it, was the subject of an accursed prophecy that prevented a happily ever after.

On many long evenings Loris had reflected on the nature of love. The concept felt abstract to him. Not that he'd never been in love before. He had experienced the kind of love that could shatter your heart and also make you feel like you could soar above the clouds when he was human. Would he give up being a vampire to experience that again? For love? It was a futile question. Also an impossibility. But Loris often found himself toying with the imaginary conundrum, nevertheless.

As much as he tried to bury the feeling deep within himself, Loris was jealous of Christopher's capacity to love. Very jealous. Love was the most raw and real of all emotions and it was the only one he could no longer feel. What kind of a sick joke was it that vampires could feel anger, betrayal, jealousy, envy, lust even, but not love. Love was always just out of reach. Just a stretch too far. Sometimes Loris thought that he might have felt the stirrings of love within him. It happened when he'd seen Klaus broken and bruised. But it was imagined. He was confusing his feelings of sorrow and empathy for the brainwashed vampire. Nothing more.

Loris had been ruminating about love, loss and the mixed blessings of being an immortal when he found himself outside Klaus's door. He wasn't quite sure how he had ended up there. When he was lost in his own mind at night he often wandered aimlessly around the maze-like building. Vhik'h-Tal-Eskemon was quiet in the small hours and he had the long corridors and various shared spaces mostly to himself.

Klaus had been moved from his 'cell' once Loris and Kavisha were convinced he had severed his allegiance to his old Family. Christopher was the most vocal proponent of Klaus's relocation to a more comfortable and less lockable room. That was a surprise. Loris wasn't sure what had spurred Christopher's newfound sympathy for the former Red Claw, but it was nice to see the gentler side of Christopher again. It hadn't been in evidence much since Nell had been taken.

Loris stopped his pacing and silently berated himself. What the hell was he doing here? These stirrings weren't real. He couldn't fall in love. At best, he could lust for Klaus. That was it. He turned around, ready to march back sullenly to his room. Just then the door opened.

"I thought I heard someone out there," said Klaus, smirking at Loris.

Loris wished Klaus wouldn't smile at him like that, as if his life wasn't complicated enough.

"I thought it was an assassin ready to finish me off," added Klaus. "I guess I'm of no further use now."

"That's not how we operate," replied Loris, levelly. "We aren't Red Claws."

"That you aren't," mused Klaus, looking Loris up and down.

Silence ensued as the two vampires just stared at each other.

"Well? Are you coming in or are you just going to stand there like a bookcase?" Klaus said, opening the door wider and raising an eyebrow.

"Um…sure." Loris fumbled to find the right words. He felt like a child who had been caught ringing a doorbell and trying to run away.

Loris headed towards a lone chair in the corner of the room. He sat down carefully, suddenly very aware of each of his movements.

"So, what brings you here in the dead of night?" Klaus enquired.

"I was just…um…checking everything was in order around headquarters."

Klaus gave a wry smile.

"And is everything ship-shape and to your satisfaction?"

"Yes," Loris said, fidgeting with his hands. "It appears that way."

In the name of the Omni-Father, you're a Council Elder, he thought. *Perhaps try acting like one.*

"What I said before is not entirely true," said Loris, looking up. "I came here because I wanted to talk to you."

"The truth always comes out, doesn't it?" Klaus said, not unkindly.

"Yes, it has a rather annoying habit of doing that," said Loris, quietly.

The air was thick with anticipation. Loris had no idea how to begin. He was very much out of his depth when it came to delicate matters. He decided honesty was the best policy. It seemed that Klaus could see right through him, anyway. So why tie himself in more knots?

CHAPTER 16

"Have you ever stopped to think why love is the only emotion vampires aren't capable of?" he began.

Klaus looked taken aback. It seemed this was the last response he was expecting.

"Not happiness. Not sadness. Only love," continued Loris when there was no reply. "If we were created to be predators, the apex species, surely emotions such as guilt and remorse would be the first ones to go. Now fate decrees that Christopher is allowed to feel love, and he's punished for it. It doesn't make sense to me."

Klaus's forehead creased.

"I didn't realize that Elders were quite so... soppy," he said.

"Not soppy, merely confused," countered Loris. "Every other emotion is accessible to a degree, except that one."

"And...erm...you came all the way here to tell me this because?" Klaus enquired.

"I'm not sure," said Loris, looking down at his overactive hands. "Maybe because you were part of the prophecy until recently. Or maybe..." He swallowed then looked up at Klaus. "...maybe because I think you're as lonely as I am."

The words just hung in the air, until they were enveloped by a long silence.

"I have people around me all day but I still feel lonely," added Loris. Then he shook his head. "A lonely vampire! Listen to me. In the name of the Omni-Father, how pathetic. I'll leave. I seem to be cracking under the stress. Pretend this never happened."

Loris got up and quickly strode across the room towards the door.

"I'm lonely too."

Klaus's voice was soft. Loris paused on his way out. He

stood by the door, his back to Klaus.

"My Family, the only Family I can remember, left me. I still don't know how to process that," confided Klaus.

Loris remained rooted to the spot, waiting for Klaus to continue talking. He dared not turn around, in case the spell of the moment was broken.

"I don't remember ever feeling love or being loved," continued Klaus. "The Red Claws were the closest I have ever come…and look what kind of twisted affection that turned out to be." Klaus's voice trailed off into barely a whisper.

"I remember…" said Loris, willing himself to turn around. Instead, he remained facing the door.

"Being loved or loving someone?" Klaus asked.

"Both."

Loris turned quickly to look at Klaus. Their eyes met briefly. Loris could hardly believe that only a few days ago the vampire standing before him and speaking so sincerely had been a sworn enemy. Right now he looked so fragile. Vulnerable. Loris wanted to reach out to him. But instead he did the one thing that he despised. He acted like a coward.

Loris spun on his heels and shot out of the room. The conversation, the one he had initiated, had suddenly become very real. Too real. It felt overwhelming. A feeling stirred deep in the pit of his stomach. Lust. No, not that exactly. But not love. Surely not. This was uncharted territory. It felt dangerous.

Loris walked heavily back to his room, his head down, cursing himself for crossing the boundary with Klaus. They were no longer simply two vampires united in a cause. They were confidants. Or perhaps something else. As he reached his door, Loris felt a rush of fear, and also a trickle of exhilaration.

CHAPTER 16

"Hey."

The voice snapped Loris out of his introspection.

Christopher was jogging along the corridor, concern etched on his face.

"What's wrong?" he asked as he reached Loris, taking in his troubled demeanor. "Has there been a development?"

"No, Christopher, it's not that," replied Loris, his voice tinged with emotion. He couldn't look at the younger vampire for fear that his face would betray him.

Loris's unsteady voice and odd manner signaled to Christopher that he was hiding something. The question was what.

"You *have* heard something," exclaimed Christopher, his voice raised. "Why were you out at this hour? What's happened? Stop freezing me out, Loris. I have a right to know."

Loris looked up at the indignant Christopher. In that moment he looked twice his age. Not that Christopher could ever physically appear twice his age. He was frozen as a young man for all eternity. But the way his face contorted with concern gave the impression of an older man. He was weary, Loris realized. Preoccupied with heavy thoughts. Much like himself. That was probably why he was also roaming the corridors in the dead of night.

"It's nothing about Nell," reassured Loris. "Don't worry yourself. It's...personal, Christopher."

"You're hiding something," Christopher shot back. "I know it." His accusation felt like a jab to the chest.

In the name of the Omni-Father, cursed Loris.

"Yes, Christopher. Yes, I am," he admitted.

Christopher's eyes widened. Loris quickly raised his hands in a placating gesture.

"But I swear, it's not about anything that concerns you…or Nell," he tried to reassure. "Trust me, if there was anything tha…"

Without warning, Christopher reached forwards and grabbed Loris's hands.

Chapter 17

Fury filled Christopher. Loris was hiding something. He knew it. It was written all over his face and evident in his defensive manner. Christopher wasn't going to be fobbed off this time. He was sick of being shunned. Then an idea occurred to him. Loris's emotional defenses were down right now. His usual impeccable self-control had been dented and he appeared exposed. Christopher reached forward and grabbed Loris's hands with his own. Nothing happened. Loris simply appeared bewildered by the unexpected physical contact. Then the memories came flooding into Christopher's mind.

***

Their arms were wrapped around each other in a tight embrace. Elliot felt like he was melting inside. The pair had been inseparable throughout their childhoods and now, as adults, the bond was stronger than ever. As he lay there in a state of bliss, Elliot recalled memories of them playing in the streets together when they were younger, throwing a ball back and forth in the narrow alleyway between their homes. Their bedroom windows were a mere meter apart, across the alley.

The dilapidated tenement blocks leant precariously together in London. Slum landlords cut corners and building controls were unheard of. A thick smog filled the air. The boys didn't cough or splutter, though. Luckily, they had made it to the cusp of adulthood without succumbing to the diseases that claimed so many so young.

It was because of Acton that Elliot had realized he wasn't attracted to women in the same way the other boys were. While his friends were enjoying the availability of ladies (for a price, modest though it was) in the slums of London, Elliot stayed on the sidelines. He never felt the urge to sample the women of the night and "drop his skittle", as was the parlance.

Elliot fondly recalled the evenings when Acton bathed in his family's rickety tin tub. His mother and sisters would boil the water on the stove before pouring it into the rusty tub for the whole family to use. The view was as clear as day from the bedroom Elliot shared with his five brothers. Elliot's siblings would fight for a view of Acton's sisters bathing. By the time Acton took his turn, they had grown bored and left to kick a ball in the alleyway or whack a metal wheel with a stick and chase it down the street. That's when Elliot crept quietly to the window.

The first time that Acton had turned around and caught his eye, Elliot thought he would die of embarrassment. He quickly busied himself beating the dust out of a rug that was hanging out of the window to air. When the two next met to play, neither mentioned Elliot's indiscretion. It didn't seem Acton was particularly bothered by the intrusion.

The next time their eyes locked while Acton was scrubbing down his body with a hard block of soap, he didn't look away. Neither did Elliot. He felt a wave of exhilaration at the new world of possibilities this one moment might have opened.

When they met again to play catch in the alleyway, they furtively shared their first kiss. Elliot hadn't thought such happiness was possible. His drab world suddenly took on a new color. Their relationship developed from there. In secret. The way it had to be. While a man with another man wasn't unheard of, it was roundly condemned. It was ungodly. Blasphemous. Shameful. But Elliot couldn't stay away. Neither could Acton. They explored each other's bodies, learning the intricate ways in which to make one another feel good.

Love. That's what it was. Elliot loved Acton more than life itself. They spent every moment they could together. When others were around, the tension between them was almost unbearable. Elliot longed to be in his arms.

The years passed and the two boys grew up. Elliot lived a life of quiet solitude, having become an administrative clerk in the local town hall. Acton married and had three beautiful children. It was expected of him, as the only son, to carry on the family name. It pained Elliot to see him so content with somebody else. A wife, no less. But the two men's desire for one another still burned bright. Stolen moments inside his tiny flat with Acton kept Elliot going. The hours wrapped in his lover's warm embrace made Elliot's unremarkable life worth living.

Then life fell apart.

After an evening at a pub, spending the little money they had left at the end of the month, Elliot and Acton stumbled home. In their intoxicated state, they were overcome by a fit of both passion and recklessness. They found a dark, recessed doorway to express their feelings. As they pressed their lips and bodies together, Elliot felt more love for this man than he ever thought possible.

Their embrace was interrupted, and so was the course of their lives.

"Well, what do we happen to have here?" came the voice. "Two young fellows? Well, I never."

Elliot and Acton turned in the direction of the voice then slowly stepped out of the shadows with their hands raised. They fully expected to see a policeman with his truncheon aloft and metal whistle hanging around his neck.

But this was no policeman. He was dressed in a fine blue velvet suit and had eyes that seemed to bristle with pure menace. For a moment Elliot thought he could be a puritan, one of the church vigilantes who patrolled the slums of the East End looking to cleanse the streets of vice. But this man, if you could call him that, carried no cross with him. There was also nothing remotely godly or righteous about his presence. In fact, he exuded the exact opposite qualities.

"Run," Elliot said to Acton, sensing the danger.

With one sharp look at the stranger and then a sorrowful glance at Elliot, Acton fled into the foggy night.

"Alone at last," said the stranger, wryly, as he stepped forward, blocking Elliot from escaping. "You're the one I had my eye on, but I would think it remiss if I didn't introduce myself properly to your 'friend'. All in good time, though."

"Leave him alone," said Elliot, with as much force as he could muster.

"Feisty, I like that!" said the stranger as he closed in, trailing his eyes hungrily from Elliot's face down to his neck.

Elliot stumbled backwards into the doorway.

"Wh…what do you want," whispered Elliot as he spread his

palms flat against the door behind him and twisted his head away from his assailant.

"I've been looking for someone of your particular persuasion to spend a little time with, that's all," said the stranger, playfully. "Perhaps an evening, perhaps a few days…perhaps an eternity."

The stranger launched himself at Elliot, whose world went dark.

***

Christopher snapped his hands away from Loris, his heart thundering in his chest. He slowly came back to the present moment. He took in the dimly-lit corridor and Loris standing in front of him looking dismayed.

"What happened next?" Christopher breathed. "Elliot."

Loris stumbled back from Christopher, looking shocked. It was almost a replay of the scene he had just witnessed, Christopher thought darkly. Loris even had a similar expression.

"What did you call me?" Loris's voice was raw.

"Elliot," repeated Christopher. "That's your name, right? Or was. What happened to you after the attack in the doorway? And Acton?"

Loris looked wounded at the mention of the name. He closed his eyes and took a sharp intake of breath. Old habits. When he opened his eyes again he looked directly at Christopher.

"This," Loris answered, sharply, gesturing to himself. "This happened."

"Acton?" Christopher asked.

"Dead," said Loris, bitterly. "Hunted down and gutted like

an animal."

"What's going on?" said a new voice.

They both turned. Amara languidly dragged her feet towards them in her canary yellow robe and pink fluffy slippers. Her appearance served to break the ominous mood.

"I could hear the voices from my room," she added, before yawning.

"It seems that young Christopher here has been hiding something from us," said Loris, turning to the librarian.

"What do you mean?" said Amara, who looked to Loris, who in turn looked to Christopher.

"I'm not sure how it works," Christopher began, resigned. "It's all a bit random."

"How what works?" asked Amara. She didn't like to be kept in the dark. About anything. Knowledge was her only power in a world of supernaturals.

"Sometimes when I touch a person, I can see their past," explained Christopher. "Not all of it. Just glimpses. They need to have thought of those particular events recently, I think."

Amara stared wide-eyed, fully awake now.

"It works on some people and not on others," continued Christopher. "And on some people only some of the time, when they're in a heightened state, for example. When I touched Loris I..." Christopher looked to the other vampire for confirmation that he could go on. Loris nodded, albeit reluctantly. "...I saw his life as a mortal," said Christopher. "With Acton."

"Acton?" Amara looked puzzled. "Who's Acton?"

She looked between the two vampires for an answer.

Christopher remained silent. He didn't feel it was his place to reply. It wasn't his life. Loris finally relented.

"My lover," he said matter-of-factly. "He died at the hands of the one who turned me."

"Oh…I'm sorry, Loris," said Amara, a little taken aback.

"Who was he?" asked Christopher. "The attacker. He didn't look like a Red Claw."

"That he wasn't," said Loris.

Anger crossed his features.

"Then wh…" began Christopher.

"Am I allowed to keep *anything* to myself, Christopher?" Loris said, sharply. "Or is my entire life an open book to be perused, poked and prodded at your leisure?"

The hallway went silent.

"He was not a Red Claw and his identity has no bearing on our present predicament," said Loris, more calmly. "His path and mine have not crossed for a long time…but they will," he added, cryptically.

Amara turned to Christopher.

"How long have you been able to see into people's pasts?" she asked.

"It happened the first time when I fought Klaus. As we were leaving Angel Falls, when Nell's Aunt Laura was killed."

"Klaus!" said Loris, as if he was hit by a sudden realization. "Is that why you pushed so hard for us to release him from captivity? You knew he was telling the truth. You actually saw it, didn't you? Through his own eyes."

Christopher nodded. It was a relief to finally bring his uncanny ability out into the open. It didn't feel like a grubby little secret anymore.

"I saw Nell. Klaus seems particularly suscep…" began Christopher.

He was interrupted by the shrill shriek of a phone ringing nearby.

"Fuck," exclaimed Christopher.

His cell phone. He always carried it with him but tonight he had left it in his room. He spun around and darted towards his room. Loris and Amara followed close behind.

Christopher dived across his bed and grabbed the handset before swiftly swiping on the green icon.

"Hello," Christopher shouted down the line, then he remained silent for a few moments as he listened intently.

Loris and Amara stared at his face, looking for clues as to what was being said.

"What the hell?" Christopher exploded.

"Speakerphone. NOW!" Amara instructed.

When Christopher didn't answer she went to grab the phone from his hand. He turned sharply and hissed at her from deep in his throat. Amara stumbled backwards, looking stunned.

"Christopher!" Loris said, as he jumped in between the younger vampire and Amara.

Christopher turned and launched the phone into the wall. A scream erupted from his mouth as he sank to the floor.

Loris stood over Christopher while Amara retrieved the handset.

"Hello…Devan," she said into the device, then looked relieved as she registered a voice on the other end. The phone was still working. "Hang on, I'm putting you on speaker. What's happened?"

"We failed. Shit, Amara, we failed," began Devan. "We heard her scream. Nell. I went to save her. We killed three of them but they still have Nell. Zachariah has her. She's in bad shape, Amara. She wasn't conscious. The Magister was there. We lost Flint. He's dead. We have to be quick. Zachariah said they'll keep her alive, but they're torturing her. The whole Family is there. We can't take them with just the pack. You need to get everyone here now, before it's too late."

"Okay Devan, slow down," said Amara. "You did what you could, we know that. Now, walk me through what happened."

Devan relayed everything that occurred during the short, ill-fated rescue attempt.

Christopher remained a lump on the floor. When Devan said: "...then Zachariah turned and walked away with Nell..." Christopher stood abruptly and threw himself at the wall. He actually punched right through it. Brick, stone and plaster rained down around him.

"Calm down," said Loris, placing a hand on Christopher's shoulder and gently nudging him backwards. "This isn't helping. We need you to be present, okay. Calm down."

"Get off me!" Christopher yelled.

"Not until you calm down," replied Loris. "How is this helping Nell? Seriously. Let's focus on where we go from here."

Ten minutes later Amara, Loris, Christopher and Kavisha were assembled in the drawing room.

"So, what do we do?" said Christopher, who had simmered down a little.

"We send all our forces right away," said Amara. "They know we are onto them, so what's the point in remaining covert?"

"Agreed," said Kavisha. "But we shouldn't rush in all guns blazing. We still need to plan carefully. We can't underestimate Zachariah's power and cunning. He's very old and very strong."

"I'll dispatch the rest of the army," said Amara.

"That works for me," said Devan, through the speaker of the now battered phone Christopher was holding. "We'll keep a close eye on them."

"OK, let's get to work," Amara said. Her lips formed a taut line.

For the first time, Christopher noticed how tired she looked. The deep bags under her eyes and the fine lines peppered across her forehead. She looked like she hadn't slept for days. Christopher kept forgetting that she was only human.

Chapter 18

The prisoner struggled against the binds. Lupita had managed to keep the Red Claw passive with regular bites. The werwulf saliva was doing its work. The vampire moved slowly. Healed slowly. It grimaced with pain and then spat at Devan, before trying to tug once again at the rope.

Devan watched Lupita pad forwards and take another bite on Red Claw's leg. Only a small one. But it made the vampire writhe in pain. Administering the saliva involved a careful balance. The Red Claw had to be subdued but still lucid enough to communicate.

"I bet she's regretting taking the early scout shift," Devan projected to Lupita.

The female vampire had been captured as she made her way back to the compound. It had been a spur of the moment decision to grab her. Devan and Lupita, in werwulf form, had accosted her as she left the town behind and traversed the deserted hard scrabble on her way up to the fortress. She had tried to fight back but was no match for two werwulfs. Now she sat upright against a large rock in a secluded clearing. Devan had tied her with rope he'd pilfered from the docks.

Lupita's bites ensured she remained restrained physically. However, they didn't dim her fury. Devan remained as a werwulf so he could speak to the captive, while Lupita was in wolf form to dispense the bites as necessary.

"What's your name?" Devan tried again.

He began the interrogation as pleasantly as he could, given the fact that he ideally would have loved to send her blowing in the wind as ash. But it was hard to sound friendly using his gruff, sonorous lycan voice.

The vampire, wearing stolen clothes that didn't fit her well and with dirty blonde hair matted across her face, just snarled in response. Devan thought her reply was fair enough, considering she'd been kidnapped. But she was a Red Claw, one who was clearly still loyal to Zachariah, so his sympathy extended only so far.

"Come on, I'm trying to be nice here," Devan said. "We just want information, that's all. Then you can run back home to your master, as though nothing happened. He'll never know."

"He'll know." The words emerged from the vampire's mouth through gritted teeth.

"Well, even if he does, he doesn't have to know you told us anything," said Devan. "You can say you escaped."

"He'll know everything," snarled the vampire. "Life won't be worth living if I go back having spoken to you dogs."

She hung her head down.

"Your name, please."

Devan's patience was wearing thin. All he wanted, for now, was her name. If she was willing to divulge that small piece of information, then hopefully she would open up about other things.

"What does it matter?" she replied, sounding defeated. "I'm a Red Claw. Surely that's enough for you."

She tried to blow the hair away from her face, without much

success.

"It seems rude to just call you Red Claw," said Devan with as much civility as he could muster. "And I have other questions that need answering."

The vampire remained perfectly still and perfectly silent. Lupita approached and bared her teeth while emitting a low growl. The Red claw looked sharply up at her. Fear and loathing were etched on her face.

"Zakaina," she said, reluctantly. "If you must know, my name is Zakaina."

Devan seized his chance while the vampire was talking.

"Is Nell still alive?" he asked, wasting no time on small talk.

Zakaina didn't answer. Lupita stepped forward to offer encouragement.

"Zachariah's blood bank?" said the vampire, disdainfully. "Yes, she's alive."

"What did you call her?"

Devan tried his hardest to remain even-tempered. But the phrase 'blood-bank' made his skin crawl.

"You heard me," said Zakaina, with a callous grin as she shifted her position slightly. "Zachariah has taken a liking to her... bouquet."

Devan took a deep breath to center himself. He would not let his emotions overcome him. Again.

"Is that why he's keeping her alive? Because she tastes nice?" he asked. "Zachariah can have his choice of 'blood-banks', why her?"

"That's a secret," said Zakaina. She smiled maliciously as she shifted a little more, then looked directly up at Devan. "One you'll never know, *dog*."

In a flash, the vampire shook her hands free from the

bindings and reached into her boot. She extracted an object then ran it across her neck. Devan and Lupita were rooted to the spot in shock. Thick black blood spilled from Zakaina's neck before she reached up and grabbed her own head with both hands. Lupita sprang forwards but it was too late. With a violent twist and heave upwards, the vampire took off her own head. She held it up like a prize, with that same crooked grin contorting her lips. Moments later the body disintegrated and crumbled, leaving only a pile of ash, her oversized clothes and a mean-looking hunting knife on the ground.

Devan and Lupita simply watched her drift away in the ocean breeze.

"Shit," said Devan. "I should have bound her tighter."

"I actually think she dislocated her own wrists to wriggle free," said Lupita. "You weren't to know she'd do that. Plus, it was partly my fault. She was fooling us when it came to how out-of-it she really was. It was an act. I should have gone heavier with the saliva."

"I don't think she was going to give us much more," said Devan. "She said she couldn't go back to the Red Claws, so what was left for her? She was doomed one way or the other."

He shifted back to wolf form.

"But she did give something away," noted Lupita. "When she described Nell as Zachariah's personal blood-bank, she did it out of spite, to hurt us," said Lupita. "But in her malice she revealed a connection between Zachariah and Nell."

"Yes," said Devan. "It has to be the reason why she's still breathing. But what could it be?"

"On that score," replied Lupita. "I can't even begin to guess."

Chapter 19

The evening began the same way it always did for Amara, surrounded by her books in the library. But this evening felt very different. It was her last night at Vhik'h-Tal-Eskemon before she headed up to Alaska for the battle.

She wasn't alone. Haiden was slouched in a corner, reading through material that Amara had selected for him. He frowned at the tiny text on the large page. This wasn't the usual classic literature he liked to casually while away the hours with.

They were joined by Klaus and Loris, who had agreed to read through old histories that Amara had flagged as potentially useful for their impending war. Amara herself was trying to gain further insights into the concept of 'familial amplification'. From what she'd been able to learn so far, it meant that a vampire matriarch or patriarch would gain strength if the number of family members increased. The opposite also held true. But she wasn't able to discover the mechanics of how it worked.

She looked up from her reading to give her strained eyes a break. Vhik'h-Tal-Eskemon felt eerily quiet, as most of the army had been dispatched north. Amara had booked a number of charter flights from Asheville Regional Airport in North Carolina to the small, private strip in Whittier.

Kavisha explained that the Council had plenty of funds at their disposal thanks to good investments over the years. And by years, the High Chancellor had meant centuries, as Amara had discovered. The stock portfolio values ran into the many millions. The army flew in small groups with very handsome bribes for the pilots to look the other way if their passengers appeared slightly 'kooky'.

Amara, Haiden, Loris and Klaus had less than twenty-four hours until they had to board their flight. Kavisha would remain behind at Vhik'h-Tal-Eskemon. Her disability precluded fighting battles. Amara, as a mere human, would also be of little use during actual combat. All of her input would have to come before. That's why she was so intent on making the most of her final hours at vampire headquarters. She thought more about familial amplification. If it did exist then the more Red Claws they took out the weaker Zachariah would become. So, the best plan of action might be to wipe out as many foot soldiers as possible before turning their attention to Zachariah.

Devan had described Zachariah's fortress. The plan was to attack from all angles. Surround the Red Claws. It should work. Should. But there would be casualties. Amara was in charge of planning and strategy. She couldn't help feeling that it would be her fault if any of the recruits died, especially when she herself would be safely tucked out of harm's way.

Loris and Klaus were flicking through the pages of books Amara had already scanned through at an adjacent desk. A fresh pair of eyes wouldn't hurt, especially if those eyes belonged to vampires. As a human, Amara's eyesight and visual field were limited. Vampires could take in so much more information.

CHAPTER 19

"I've found something."

Klaus's words reverberated around the room.

Amara walked over as he was tilting the book towards Loris so he could see the page.

"Is that who I think it is?" asked Loris.

"Yes," confirmed Klaus, pointing at the picture. "It's Zachariah."

Amara leaned over to look at the grainy black and white photo that was reproduced in the book. It showed what looked like two men standing next to each other, both dressed in their finery. They wore dark suits with crisp white shirts. One looked much older than the other. Klaus had his finger on the younger one.

"So who's the other one?" asked Amara.

"That's Damien," said Klaus.

"Damien? As in Zachariah's older brother Damien?" asked Amara, eyebrows raised.

"The very one," replied Klaus. "I only met him a few times over the years. He was a bit of a loner."

The paragraph below the image stated that the picture was taken in 1891 in New Orleans. It described a bloody battle between two vampire factions. The names of the two individuals in the photo were not included, but the text referred to: *'Two brothers belonging to the Griffenrougue clan who were thought to have died in hostilities'*. That was all the information provided about the picture.

Loris suddenly grabbed the book and took a closer look.

"In the name of the Omni-Father!" he exclaimed. "It can't be."

"Can't be what?" said Amara.

"Take a closer look at big brother," said Loris as he handed the book to Amara.

The librarian brought the page close up to her face and narrowed her eyes to focus better. When the realization hit her, she actually let out a small yelp, then hung her mouth open.

"Oh my God," exclaimed Amara, when she regained the power of speech. She looked questioningly at Loris. "It's the Magister, right? It's Fabian Bamford."

"Indeed," replied Loris. "Zachariah and the Magister. Brothers. I didn't expect that one. Though it explains why the snake Bamford switched sides so readily."

Klaus took the book off Amara and studied the photograph.

"I never knew Damien was a Magister," he said. "Zachariah always said that he was a hermit who didn't desire to be part of the Family. On the rare occasions that I saw him, he wasn't dressed in his Magister garb. I couldn't put two and two together. I'm sorry, I should have realized that Damien had something to do with it."

"Rest easy, Klaus," said Loris, placing a hand on his shoulder. "There's no way you could have known."

Loris turned to Amara.

"It appears blood runs deep," he said. "But does this change anything?"

Amara considered for a moment.

"It might mean that Zachariah has a weakness," she said. "One that could be exploited. Family should make Zachariah stronger. The more Red Claws he creates the stronger he gets, from what I've read. But an actual family member, one that shares the same blood as him, well that could make him vulnerable. It gives him something worth protecting, maybe something worth dying for."

CHAPTER 19

"I wouldn't hold your breath," said Klaus. "I can assure you that Zachariah considers no-one more important than himself."

"Still," said Amara, a gleam in her eye. "It's something. It's definitely something."

Chapter 20

Klaus left the library while Amara was writing furiously away on a notepad. He gestured for Loris to follow him.

"Do you think we've done enough to win?" Klaus asked when they were finally alone in his room.

"We've done all we can," Loris answered, honestly.

"Right…good," Klaus said, unconvinced.

He began pacing the floor with his hands behind his back.

"What is it?" Loris's words were soft, something Klaus couldn't quite get used to.

After decades of being berated at every opportunity by the one person he revered, it was unnerving for someone close to him to treat him with care. It felt like a trick.

"If we don't kill him, Zachariah, he'll come for me," said Klaus. He stopped pacing and fixed his eyes on Loris. "What he'll do to me will be worse than death. I know. I've been there."

"You can't know that for sure," Loris replied in his gentle tone.

"I do know," said Klaus, with venom, though not aimed at Loris. "I was by his side the longest. I thought he saw me as a brother. Perhaps something more. Now I've betrayed him. I've defected. I've told you his secrets. That's the worst thing

CHAPTER 20

I could have possibly done."

"You've done the right thing, Klaus," reassured Loris. "The noble thing."

The words gave Klaus little comfort.

"I'm scared," he admitted, looking down at the floor.

"And you have every right to be," said Loris. "But remember we're trying to keep everybody safe. Vampires included. This is bigger than any of us."

Klaus felt ashamed. Old programming was difficult to undo. He found it hard to look at the larger picture. To consider the greater good. He was thinking of himself, as Red Claws always did.

"There has to be a balance," said Loris. "Killing without any concern will only get us all killed. If the Red Claws are allowed to grow and spread then, eventually, the human race will be in peril. There might be nothing left to feed on. We die anyway. Dealing with matters now is the only option."

Klaus was even more embarrassed. Being berated by Loris was not how he'd seen this conversation going. Having been under the control of Zachariah for so long, he found it difficult to think for himself. He also didn't understand why everybody around him was being so kind after what he'd done. Forgiveness and compassion seemed like alien concepts to him. After all, if Zachariah hadn't kicked him out of the Family, he'd still be a Red Claw. He'd still be fighting for the wrong side. He'd still be intent on destruction and chaos.

He looked up at Loris as a gentle wave of emotion rippled through him. Loris who was so kind. Understanding. Patient. Klaus didn't deserve that. He didn't deserve somebody to treat him this way after all he'd done, all he would have done if he hadn't been cast out against his will.

"Has it ever occurred to you that if Zachariah hadn't kicked me out, I'd still be a Red Claw?"

Klaus's words were meant to hurt Loris. To push him away. Klaus felt he was unworthy of compassion. Why couldn't Loris see that, too? Why did he persist with this folly?

"But you're not a Red Claw anymore," said Loris, stepping closer and placing a hand on his shoulder. "You are your own person. You are Klaus. Just Klaus. There is good in you. I believe there was always good in you, but you were led astray."

The sensation he felt when Loris was near made Klaus uncomfortable. The way his stomach churned. The way he became flustered. It wasn't right. It wasn't natural. He'd felt these sparks of excitement before. But that was another time, another place, another life. Those sparks had never been reciprocated.

Loris saw the hurt in his eyes. He reached out and grabbed Klaus's hand before lifting it and pressing his lips to the cold, smooth flesh where the delicate veins decorated the surface.

"I'm not a good person," said Klaus, feeling so close to Loris that it frightened him. "I'm a murderer. A killer. If you only knew the things I'd done. You'd hate me."

Klaus began to pull his hand away from Loris, only to meet resistance.

"We all have our pasts," said Loris. "And none of us can change them. What we can decide, however, is who we are today and who we will strive to be tomorrow. You're not alone in how you feel."

Klaus thought those words had more than just a surface meaning. While he was pondering their significance Loris slowly (and unexpectedly) leaned forwards, pressing his lips onto Klaus's.

CHAPTER 20

It took a moment for Klaus to decide how to react. His heart was alight with passion, but his head was clouded by apprehension. In the end, his heart won out.

Chapter 21

The compact private jet swooped down from the air to land at Whittier's tiny airport. The plane came to a smooth halt before the passengers disembarked on a small set of steps that unfolded from the belly of the aircraft. The arrivals were met by a chorus of howls as the wolves surrounded the tarmac. Amara spotted Devan instantly, his coat a distinctive shade of deep brown. She ran over to greet him.

"Been a while, furball, good to see you," she said as she knelt down and enthusiastically ruffled his coat.

Devan pushed his head into her shoulder as his own personal greeting for pack.

The wolves led them back to camp at Blackstone Bay. It looked pretty rudimentary to Amara. But they were only staying briefly, so it didn't have to be the Ritz. The attack was planned for the early hours of the next morning. The early arrivals had bought a number of tents from a large camping supplies store in town. They were now dotted among the flat rocks as the ocean churned and crashed below. Amara would be assigned to a local motel. The freezing overnight temperatures and fierce ocean wind would be too much for her. Another pang of guilt accosted the librarian as she thought about the warm bed she'd be able to enjoy tonight.

CHAPTER 21

But first she had to discuss the plan of action with the team.

The element of surprise was key. They didn't want the Red Claws to know they had arrived en masse or how many were on their side. So they had to go at first light tomorrow, before any Red Claw scouts had the chance to spot them. Between the vampires, Hunters, wolves and other creatures of the night, they had close to one hundred. Almost a perfect match for the Red Claws. Amara thought about Nell, the friend that meant so much to her. As much as she loathed to admit it, Nell had to survive the raid in case her sacrifice was needed to save humankind.

Amara was thankful that they had werwulfs on their side. She looked around her at the docile-looking wolves in the rocky clearing. They sat in a group with their heads close to the ground, looking so placid. However, Amara knew that in a heartbeat they could shift from fluffy, elegant animals to ferocious and absolutely lethal beasts.

Amara outlined her strategy to the assembled team by the side of a campfire created by Sanya and Yansa, the spell-caster twins. The fire took on an eerie green glow that cast the entire camp in an emerald hue. Amara noticed that there was no wood or other material burning to create the flames. The fire was just there, alive and green.

There were a few snickers as Amara began talking. They seemed to come mostly from the fae, who had a tendency to see humans as weak and inferior. They had already let it be known that the Council of Elders should be leading the battle, not some mortal. The fae were here supporting the cause, Amara had to remind herself. She just had to suck it up. The librarian spoke with authority and deep knowledge as she outlined the strategy. The lips that had chuckled only moments ago soon remained tightly sealed.

Once everybody knew the game plan, Amara was escorted back to her motel for the evening. It was a cheap, out-of-the-way place called The Roadway Inn. Amara had selected the down-at-heel establishment because of its relatively remote location and also because she felt guilty. She couldn't stand the thought of enjoying a fancy room while everyone else was out in the cold.

Devan, Christopher, Haiden and Lupita had joined her, both as security escort and for moral support. Lupita and Devan wore clothes bought from the camping supplies store. The rest of the group had a chuckle on seeing them dressed for the hiking trail.

The group entered the large but shabby room and Amara threw her backpack onto one of the flimsy metal-framed single beds. She sat heavily and looked around at the stained gray paint on the walls and various faded pictures of tropical birds that adorned them. It was a strange choice of image for the harsh climate of Whittier. Haiden sat down next to her and placed a hand on her shoulder. Lupita and Devan perched themselves on the other rickety single bed that sat opposite them. It creaked and protested as it took their weight. All were silent.

The gap left by Nell felt particularly wide. Amara saw it in Christopher's eyes as he looked around at the two couples. While nobody had admitted that they were part of a couple, it was abundantly clear that both Haiden and Amara, and Devan and Lupita, were more than friends. There seemed to be an unspoken agreement not to bring this fact up to Christopher, who sat alone on a threadbare fabric armchair.

"This is it," Amara said, to nobody in particular. "Tomorrow is what we've been waiting for. Working for. The day when everything changes."

Haiden reached to grasp Amara's hand. She was about to pull it away, not wanting to upset Christopher. But she noticed Devan walking over and placing a hand on the vampire's shoulder.

"We'll get her back, man," Devan assured.

Christopher looked up and nodded silently.

From the corner of her eye, Amara caught the way Lupita looked at Devan. A mix of approval and admiration, Amara thought. It was nice to see. After everything that Devan had been through, he deserved to find somebody who looked at him the way Lupita did. Amara squeezed Haiden's hand back, wanting him to know how she felt, without having to say the words.

She didn't want him to go into battle tomorrow. She wanted him to stay by her side. But that was just selfish. She had to let him go and fight against the tyranny of the Red Claws. He said he was good at what he did. Amara would just have to depend on that. A wave of apprehension came over her. The prospect of being left alone with her thoughts this evening suddenly seemed unbearable.

"I'm staying with you," Haiden whispered to her, detecting her unease. "I'll go back early in the morning."

"Us too," the rest of the room chorused, almost as if they'd rehearsed it.

Amara was reminded of just how powerful the hearing of non-humans could be.

"You don't have to do that for me," said Amara.

She once again felt like she was letting the side down. That she was receiving special treatment and putting others out for her sake.

"I think we should be here," Lupita said, looking at the others. "Not least because you are vulnerable on your own, Amara."

"Agreed," said Devan. "I already squared it with others at basecamp. We'll set an alarm and head back in time in the early hours."

Amara felt a surge of love for her friends who, despite the enormity of what they faced in just a matter of hours, still managed to think of her.

Lupita and Devan fell asleep on their bed. Devan's arm was casually thrown around Lupita's shoulder, his face pressed into her long, dark hair. Christopher had entered his trance state on the chair, his face looking serene.

Amara and Haiden cuddled close together on their bed. Amara slowly succumbed to sleep to the beat of Haiden's heart against her ear. His warm arms enveloping her. She hoped that tomorrow evening they could fall asleep in the same way.

***

The blaring alarm of Christopher's cell phone woke the whole room while the sky was still dark. The sound signaled the end of life as they knew it. Today was make or break. Amara looked at Haiden as he blinked the sleep from his eyes. She studied his face intently, trying to etch this moment into her memory. Devan moaned against Lupita as he stirred awake.

The feeling of apprehension was felt by all as they prepared to leave. It settled heavily on the room. Amara's face as they left the motel brought a glaze to Haiden's eyes. She looked broken, bereft. She embraced them all in turn, lingering on Haiden, not wanting to let him go. He gently broke her embrace and took a step back. Devan and Lupita had already changed into wolf form and melded into the shadows of early morning as they raced off.

"Come back to me," Amara said. "I don't know what I…"

"I will," said Haiden. "I promise."

He leaned in and kissed her deep on the lips, then turned and left with Christopher, leaving Amara alone with just her thoughts once again.

Chapter 22

The wolves snaked down the rocky mountain first as a gentle warmth began to slowly infuse the inky night sky. They quickly surrounded the fortress around its high perimeter fence. Christopher could see them shifting one by one into werwulf form. They began standing on two legs rather than four. Limbs stretched out. Muscles enlarged. Razor-sharp claws formed at the end of long arms that almost reached the ground. It was a sight to behold, even for a vampire.

Their job was to rip the fencing apart and maim and kill as many Red Claws as they could in the first wave. Christopher could see Devan and Lupita leading the pack. He made a silent plea to the Omni-Father that they would come back alive.

Christopher stayed back as the other vampires and creatures of the night traversed down the rocky terrain next. They remained a good distance away from the compound. Their job was to take out the Red Claws that the werwulfs hadn't finished off. Aim for the head. Always aim for the head. Detach it from the body and, when you see a cloud of dust, then you know you've done the job right.

Then would come the Vampire Hunters. Their job was a little different. They needed to track down Zachariah and the Magister, with the aim of killing both. Or, at the very

CHAPTER 22

least, doing enough damage to incapacitate them. While Vampire Hunters were rightly feared, Zachariah and Bamford (or Damien to give him his correct name) were both very old and very strong. They would be slippery to catch and difficult to kill. This was the part of the plan that made Christopher the most nervous. Having never seen Vampire Hunters in action, he privately questioned whether they'd be able to take out the master of the Red Claws and a Magister. But if Amara thought it was possible, it wasn't his place to raise an objection.

Finally, there was Christopher himself. He had one job and one job only. Nell. That was it. In the heat of the battle he'd have to put his blinkers on and focus only on her. He couldn't allow himself to be distracted by anything going on around him. This sounded simple. But when your friends were engaged in a deadly fight, focusing on one job would prove difficult. Even if that job was to save the love of your life and, perhaps subsequently, the entire world. He would wait until the Red Claws had their hands full before sneaking in, hopefully undetected.

Christopher looked on from his high vantage point as his side moved closer to the fortress. The supernaturals swept forward in a wave-like motion, smooth and serene. It didn't look like they were readying for battle. The flowing swell of the wave gave the impression of a choreographed dance. It was eerie to watch from the side-lines, rather than being in the thick of the bodies.

His thoughts were distracted when the werwulfs began ripping at the fencing, a silent command having spread through their minds. The werwulfs attacked from all sides simultaneously. They wedged sharp claws in between the tall vertical planks before using their powerful muscles to rip at them. Some planks came clean away while others were left torn and splintered. Soon there were multiple entry points along the long perimeter wall. The werwulfs charged in, a collective deep growl filling the air.

Red Claws ran from the various buildings to meet the attack, kicking up swathes of dust in their wake. They met the werwulfs in a swarm of chaos. The werwulfs were feral, all teeth and claws. They were vicious and unrelenting. Christopher watched transfixed as they tore into the vampires, sending limbs and some heads flying. Christopher picked out Devan and Lupita in the melee and observed them closely. He wanted everybody on his side to survive the battle, that was a given, but Devan and Lupita had become close to him.

His hopes of everyone surviving the fight were quickly dashed when he saw a werwulf crash to the ground and then pounced upon by three vampires, who tore at his flesh. One of the Red Claws wrapped his arms around the werwulf's thick neck before twisting and heaving backwards with all his strength. Christopher had to look away. When he looked back the werwulf lay still on the ground. His attackers had moved on to other targets. Christopher saw two other werwulfs lying bloodied and unmoving on the ground.

He focused back on his friends. Lupita was ravaging a Red Claw who was writhing on the ground. She bit into his neck savagely. Christopher's crystal-clear eyesight was aided by the growing light flooding into the sky as the day dawned. He could make out the grimace of agony on the vampire's face as Lupita sank her teeth deep into his flesh. Christopher recalled that werwulf saliva was excruciatingly painful to vampires.

He scanned the battlefield for Devan. Panic rose in his chest when he couldn't see him. He narrowed his eyelids and looked more closely. The swirling clash of bodies made it difficult to pick out individuals. Finally, he caught sight of his friend emerging from a pack of Red Claws. Devan held the stump of a leg in his mouth. Christopher could swear he could see his friend smiling, despite the bloodied limb wedged in his teeth. Christopher breathed a sigh of relief. A leftover reflex from his mortal life.

The werwulfs ripped and tore at the vampires. Many Red Claws lay bloodied and battered on the ground, while a good many others were now no more than dust carried in the wind over the unforgiving ocean. The werwulfs' strength was their advantage and they were making the most of it. However, they were outnumbered by the vampires, who were swarming them. Werwulfs were being taken down by three or four vampires at a time, who would launch coordinated attacks. Devan raised his muzzle to the sky and let out a high-pitched howl that reverberated around the rocky mountainside.

The other supernaturals and vampires now took their turn. They charged in with the aim of taking out the weakened Red Claws. Christopher looked up to see the spell-casters soaring above the compound. Their bodies undulated through the air, dipping and diving, like eagles honing in on prey. When they came close to a Red Claw, they would make a rhythmic circular motion with their hands and then point their palms out at the vampire. Christopher could see they were chanting something repeatedly all the while. He watched in amazement as the Red Claw would simply stop in their tracks, as if frozen in time. This allowed the werwulfs and others to attack them with impunity.

The fae, some accompanied by imps, waded into the battle as though moving to a hidden beat of music. Each movement was purposeful, poised, elegant even. The vampires, although known for being nimble and graceful in battle, looked clumsy and awkward by comparison. Christopher found the fae were the most difficult to watch. Where they had been elven and beautiful before, when they attacked their faces twisted into macabre snarls with pointed teeth protruding from grossly enlarged mouths. They went from ethereal to hideous in the blink of an eye. The near instant shift was part of what made them so deadly. You were drawn in by their alluring appearance and, before you knew it, they were greedily feeding on your soul, leaving you an empty husk.

The fae fought in much the same way as the werwulfs, ripping and tearing at their victims. The only difference was that the werwulfs were much stronger. The fae (very wisely) were concentrating on finishing off the badly wounded Red Claws that lay helpless on the ground. Seeing them in action felt disturbing to Christopher. Wrong. Though they were helping the cause, Christopher found it difficult to change his impression of the fae.

The reinforcements enveloped the Red Claws and werwulfs, streaming into the mass of carnage and confusion. Christopher was mesmerized by the battle. The spell-casters' aerial maneuvers were particularly enthralling to watch.

He had to peel himself away when he saw the Vampire Hunters running into the compound in their black combat gear. They avoided the main fray and instead spread out around the fortress, seeking out Zachariah and his brother. Their entry on the scene was Christopher's cue to start moving.

He ran towards the compound, deftly traversing the rocky terrain. When he reached the perimeter he made sure to enter

CHAPTER 22

away from the fiercest fighting, though smaller battles had broken out all over the sprawling complex. He saw Haiden running towards the main house with two other Hunters. They were intercepted by a Red Claw who came charging out of the building. Christopher stopped in his tracks. The vampire lunged at Haiden.

Without missing a beat, the Hunter ducked out of the way before spinning on his heels and extracting what looked like a scythe from his weapons belt. As the Red Claw turned to face him, eyes wild with fury, Haiden swung the weapon in a smooth arc with his outstretched hand. Time seemed to stand still momentarily. Then the Red Claw's head rolled off his body and bounced on the ground before coming to an abrupt stop. The rest of his body landed in an unceremonious heap next to it. Christopher looked on as the flesh disintegrated and then turned to ash.

Haiden looked back at Christopher.

"You joining the party?" he asked, with a smile.

Christopher followed behind him.

This part of the plan assumed that Nell would be located close to Zachariah. Christopher had to work with the Hunters to scope out the compound and retrieve her. His only focus was Nell. The Hunters would look after all other matters. From what he had just witnessed, Christopher felt more secure in their ability to hold up their part of the bargain.

Screams echoed around him as the vampires, Red Claws, werwulfs and other creatures went on the attack and also sustained injuries. It was hard to make out the battle cries from the screams of pain. It all merged into one furious cacophony.

Christopher knew his orders. Keep away from the heart of the battle. Circumvent the bloodshed. Focus solely on

Nell. Yet he struggled to tear his eyes away from the carnage unfolding around him. It was a literal bloodbath. But he noticed that most of the blood was blackened and irregular. Thick and sludge-like. It was the blood of vampires. It went against his natural instincts to revel in the death of his own kind, but he hoped that the blood spilled on the ground had previously run through the veins of the Red Claws. He also couldn't ignore the thinner, brighter blood splattered in patches on the ground. It meant that some of his side was injured. Dead.

Christopher pushed his grim thoughts aside and followed Haiden into the main house. More Hunters had joined him and the black-clad group began searching the rooms systematically. Christopher followed in their wake, his senses on high alert. He inhaled deeply and closed his eyes. Concentrating. Yes, there it was. He could detect Nell's essence, her unique scent. She had been in this building. But was she here now? That was the crucial question. He heard fighting up ahead of him as the Hunters dispatched two Red Claws who were hiding in the shadows. Soon the ground floor had been searched and cleared of enemy vampires.

The group proceeded up the rickety wooden stairs to the upper floor, Haiden leading the way. Christopher could still detect Nell's scent in the air. The Hunters moved as one through the large property. Like gymnasts, they deftly navigated any obstacles in their way. The Vampire Hunters moved cohesively. As one. Men and women, old and young, it didn't matter. Years of training allowed them to focus with tunnel vision on the task at hand. The top floor of the house was deserted.

Shit, thought Christopher. *Where are they?*

CHAPTER 22

The group quickly exited the house and were met by a werwulf. His fur was mottled gray and white. He was less muscular and slightly more stooped in posture than the others. Christopher deduced that he was getting on in years.

"I'm Lupertico," said the werwulf, catching his breath. Christopher noticed the thick black blood on his claws. "Nell...her scent," he went on. "It seems to be everywhere. We can't pinpoint her."

"Makes sense," said Haiden, looking from Lupertico to Christopher. "They've probably used her blood to lay a false trail so we can't hone in on her. They probably deposited drops of it all round the complex. It buys them time."

"That's assuming they're here at all," said Ezra, the older Vampire Hunter who was built like a brick outhouse.

"Then there's nothing for it," said Christopher, with renewed urgency. "We search every inch of the compound. No stone left unturned."

Haiden and Ezra both nodded and the troop set off for the next building. The battle continued to rage around them.

After Nell's scent had taken the Vampire Hunters and Christopher on a full circuit of the compound, the group realized that something was amiss. Neither Nell nor Zachariah were here. The scent simply went round in circles. A never-ending infinity. An infinity without Nell. It struck Christopher as darkly poetic. A metaphor for his life.

"We could have missed something," said Haiden, looking at Christopher's pained expression. "A hidden room or compartment, something. Let's try the main house again. It's the most likely hiding place."

As the Hunters headed back towards the main building, Christopher decided to try a different approach. He was sure he would have been able to find Nell if she was in the grounds. That could only mean one thing. He ran out of the compound, leaping over the remnants of the wooden perimeter fence in a single bound. He scrambled up the nearby rocks and lifted his head, inhaling deeply. Nothing.

He looked back to see the destroyed fence of the compound and the fierce battle raging within. He saw the spell-casters hovering in the air, now firing what seemed to be multi-colored streamers out of their upturned palms. When the magical streamer, energy field, or whatever it was, hit a Red Claw, they would collapse to the ground writhing in agony.

Christopher turned back to the task at hand. Time was of the essence. He ran higher up the rocks, almost losing his footing at one point. He noticed the wind changing direction and once again lifted his head and inhaled deeply. It was there. Nell's scent. It was faint, but it was there. He locked on to it and began running faster. He tracked the scent higher and higher, further and further, until he had traversed several hundred feet and came to the ridge of a rocky peak.

The scent was very strong now. Like she was here. He looked around frantically. There on the ground about twenty feet away was a bright white object that jarred with the natural colors of the surroundings. He raced towards it. Then stopped dead in his tracks. His eyes grew wide. Nell's T-shirt was on the uneven earth. Crumpled and discarded. Dirty and bloodied. So much blood. He fell to his knees and grabbed the garment. He pressed it to his face. Despite the blood and mud, it still smelled like Nell. He let out a scream of anguish.

"Now now dear," came a sickly-sweet voice. One Christopher recognized immediately. It made the hairs on the back of his neck prickle. "There's no reason for hysterics," the voice went on. "It doesn't befit a brave, young vampire such as yourself. It sounds so pathetically...human."

He looked up to see Miss Odette.

Her topaz eyes shone in the morning sun. Her blonde hair was tied in a halo around her head, soft curls falling at the sides. She wore a skin-tight green velvet dress. It was low-cut to show off her ample bosom. The skirt puffed out dramatically. Not so much as a single hair was out of place. She looked immaculate. Yet here she was. In the middle of nowhere. Clothed in a ballgown, no less. Dripping with jewelry and wearing black lace opera gloves. Her pet, Master August, stood by her side, reaching only to her hips. He wore his usual white trousers and white shirt with the top button fastened, his jet-black hair was slicked down. His face was contorted into a rictus grin of happiness. It was wrong. A man-child portraying an emotion he knew nothing about.

Dragging himself to his feet, Christopher stared at the pair.

"This isn't real," he said under his breath.

"Oh, but my dearest, of course it's real," Miss Odette insisted.

Her eyes were too bright. Her smile too wide. Her teeth too white. Everything on the surface was meant to entice you. But Christopher knew the truth. Beneath the flawless skin and perfectly symmetrical features was another face. One that was twisted. Gruesome. Unearthly. Under the captivating exterior was a beast ready to gouge, rip, bite and drain you dry of your very life force.

"You look a little confused, child," she went on when Christopher failed to respond. Then she laughed. Her high-pitched cackle sent shivers up Christopher's spine.

"Don't call me child," he said, coldly.

Christopher straightened and squared his shoulders.

"Touchy today, aren't we, child?" she replied, in her same affable tone. "I want to help you out. We can be friends, Christopher. Let's put our previous little…misunderstanding… behind us. What do you say, my dear?"

Her words rang like a siren song in his ears. It was like she was reciting poetry. Even though he knew he couldn't believe a word that left her perfectly plump, pink lips, they were delivered so alluringly that it was difficult not to get drawn in.

"Where is Nell?" Christopher demanded, crossing his arms in front of his chest, as if that would protect him from her charms.

"She's not here, *obviously*," said Master August in his reedy child's voice. "Unless she's invisible…or perhaps buried under my feet." He did a sinister little jig on the ground.

Christopher lost it. He launched himself forward, grabbing the imp then spinning his skinny body around. Christopher wrapped an arm around the imp's scrawny neck and pulled him backward.

"I wouldn't joke if I were you," he snarled, tightening his grip.

Master August let out a choked gasp.

"Let go of him at once!" Miss Odette's voice was terse.

She looked enraged. Her sickly-sweet demeanor had cracked and she was showing a glimpse of what really lay underneath.

With one final squeeze for good measure, Christopher slackened his grip on the little fiend, who gulped down lungfuls of air.

"Nell," Christopher prompted.

"The manners of the youth these days," Miss Odette bemoaned, overdramatically. "And we call ourselves superior beings."

"Nell," Christopher repeated. "Or your little friend here becomes a snack for my furry friends down there." Christopher looked down at the compound.

The fae looked from Master August to Christopher.

"Keeping company with vermin," Miss Odette mused. "It's no wonder your standards are in the gutter. Anyhow, that's your business. As for little Nelly, Zachariah decided to keep his prize with him. That's what you do with pets, right? Keep them on a short lead. You don't want them to go wandering off, now."

"You'd know all about that," said Christopher, looking down at the imp and then shoving him hard towards his mistress.

"Oh, but Master August is so much more than that," she protested, as she enveloped him in her arms. "He's my big little lovely. I don't know what I'd do without him."

The imp grinned manically at her as she patted his head. It made Christopher's stomach turn. He waited for Miss Odette to continue. It didn't take long. He knew she liked the sound of her own voice.

"Zachariah Redclaw, a close personal friend of mine, has entrusted me to perform a most important and delicate task. Namely making contact with you. He'll be very happy to know that I was successful." She beamed with self-satisfaction. "All it took was little Nelly's shirt. It was so simple, yet so clever. You see, Christopher, sometimes what you need is a bit of grace and subtlety to get what you want. Brute force is not the only answer, as I told my dearest Zachariah."

"So, you're on their side now?" Christopher spat.

Miss Odette pouted her bottom lip in an over-elaborate

display of indignation.

"I joined the winning team," she insisted. "A girl has to take care of herself in such a harsh and unforgiving world. When it became apparent that your side was weak and misguided, I thought it was better to cut my losses and run."

"That's not quite how I remember it," said Christopher, an eyebrow raised.

"Irrelevant details," Miss Odette said, waving a hand dismissively. "The fact is that Zachariah has been very accommodating to me. He knows talent when he sees it."

She took a step closer to the vampire.

"It's time you took a leaf out of my book, young Christopher," she continued, her voice slow and husky. "There's still time to put yourself first."

She reached out and gently touched his face with her gloved hand.

Christopher snarled. He lost his composure. She didn't have the right to touch him like that. Her blatant denial of being kicked out of Vhik'h-Tal-Eskemon along with the fact that she had joined the Red Claws made him see red. Her sheer audacity in stroking his face was the final straw. He wasn't another one of her little pets.

As quick as a flash he jerked his head and then took her index finger in his teeth. He bit down hard, severing the finger clean at the knuckle through the lace glove. Miss Odette screamed then retracted her hand, whipping off the glove with her other hand. She held the injured finger in front of her face and stared wide-eyed at the bloody stump. Christopher spat the severed end onto the ground. He nearly gagged at the taste of her fae blood.

"You bastard!" she screamed, her hand shaking.

CHAPTER 22

Fae didn't have the ability to re-grow body parts. Her butchered finger would serve as a permanent reminder of their encounter.

"I was here to help you," she whispered, incredulously. "I was offering you a way out and…"

"Don't ever touch me," Christopher interrupted.

Miss Odette stepped away from him, still holding up her injured hand, mouth agape.

"You'll regret that, you foul blood-sucker." Her voice was cold and devoid of all emotion.

Then her face shifted. The masquerade of beauty fell away. She turned from goddess to grotesque in a heartbeat. Stained yellow teeth jutted out from a wide, misshapen mouth. Her soft pink skin became gray and cracked. Wide bloodshot eyes stared angrily at Christopher. Her eyelashes and eyebrows disappeared, making her look almost alien.

"You'll never see the human again."

It wasn't Miss Odette who spoke these words. It was Master August, having stepped in front of his mistress. It was a rather comical sight seeing the man-child squaring up to Christopher.

"Congratulations, you've just signed her death warrant," he added in his creepy shrill voice.

Before Christopher could react, the imp turned and grabbed Miss Odette's uninjured hand before quickly leading her away from the vampire. The fae appeared to be in a state of shock. She continued staring at her damaged finger as she was whisked away. Christopher thought about giving chase but instead turned back to look at the compound. It was suddenly very quiet. Too quiet. The lack of noise and movement below rattled him. He had a decision to make. He raced back down.

When he had left the compound there was a fierce, bloody battle raging. When he returned there was stillness. The fight was over. Christopher surveyed his surroundings. Bodies lay strewn haphazardly on the ground. Christopher frantically searched the grisly arena for Devan, Haiden, Lupita, Loris, Klaus. When his eyes fell on each of them, his heart skipped a beat. All alive. All accounted for. All also surveying the scene of devastation.

Klaus was looking up, seemingly mesmerized, as waves of ash cascaded away in the wind. The final remnants of some of his old Family members. His shoulders were hunched. Loris had an arm around his back, stopping him from falling. Whether that was because he was injured physically or mentally, Christopher could not discern.

Christopher approached Haiden.

"Nell?"

Haiden shook his head. Christopher grimaced in frustration.

"We put up a good fight though," added Haiden, by way of conciliation. "So far we've estimated thirty-seven dead Red Claws. The rest have fled. We're not sure how many were here to start with. Zachariah could have created more while he was on the road. We just don't know. But we have to assume we've taken out a chunk of his army."

"What about us?" asked Christopher. "How many?"

"Too many," answered Devan. "Six from the pack." He looked to Lupita, who hung her head down. "Three vampires," Devan continued. "Two spell-casters and one Hunter."

Christopher felt ashamed for not fighting beside them. He'd been led on a wild goose chase and therefore had been entirely

CHAPTER 22

useless during the battle.

"Fuck," Christopher said, scanning the unmoving bodies on the ground.

Devan knelt over one of his fallen. Lupita beside him. Other werwulfs knelt beside dead members of their pack. Heads were bowed. Some howled a sorrowful lament towards the sky.

"I'm sorry, man," Christopher said to Devan, knowing that he wouldn't receive an answer. Devan just shook his head and returned his gaze to his fallen comrade.

Christopher ran his fingers through his hair as Haiden approached.

"Her name was Emmeline." Haiden spoke softly.

It took a moment for Christopher to realize that Haiden was talking about the Hunter who had died during the battle.

"She was only nineteen," continued Haiden. "A nice person. Too nice to be a Hunter, you could almost say. But she loved this stuff," he gestured around the battlefield.

Christopher shot a questioning glance at the Hunter. How could anybody love this stuff?

"Well, not this exactly," explained Haiden. "But being a Vampire Hunter. Being in the mix. Risking her life to save humans. She loved it, Christopher. Really loved it. It was her calling, she would say. She was the youngest of us, and now she's gone. Doesn't seem fair."

"It's not fair," Christopher answered, sincerely. "None of this is fair, Haiden."

Christopher took a long moment to glance around the compound again. Before he'd only been concerned with taking stock of the dead. Only now did he notice the number of injured. The walking wounded. Some grasping at huge gashes across their bodies, or bite marks littering their necks. Others had more serious injuries, missing limbs or broken bones, limbs twisted at angles that made Christopher feel queasy.

It was also only now that Christopher noticed the long, angry gash down Haiden's face. It ran all the way from his temple down to his top lip. A piece of loose skin flapped open revealing the pink flesh underneath.

"It's nothing," said Haiden, after noticing Christopher assessing him. "One more to add to the collection."

"Sure," was all Christopher could muster.

"We need to help the wounded and take the dead back to camp," Loris said, approaching from behind. "They deserve an honorable send off."

Christopher and Haiden both nodded.

"We'll get her next time," said Haiden, patting Christopher on the shoulder as he walked off to attend to the wounded.

The thought of a next time made Christopher's skin prickle.

Chapter 23

The atmosphere in the camp was heavy. The dead had been buried in the soft earth by the ocean with only small crosses made from sticks to mark their final resting places. Sanya had created a fire, red this time. Her twin sister, Yansa, had died in the fighting. Sanya hadn't spoken a word since the battle. She looked completely desolate, despite many of the group trying to comfort her.

Surprisingly, Haiden was the only one to get Sanya to look up from the fire. He hadn't said a word. He simply took the spell-caster's hands in his own and studied the shape of the flames alongside her. Their faces were lit in a dark red glow. Amara looked on with deep affection. She had chosen well, she thought. Not that she'd had much choice. Her feelings for Haiden had come out of nowhere. He'd annoyed her into submission.

When Christopher recounted what had happened with Miss Odette, Amara observed the faces of those listening. Many of the makeshift army were huddled around the campfire, toasting lost comrades. She wasn't sure where the bottles had come from. She wasn't sure what was in them. But she wasn't going to dissuade them from drowning their sorrows. Maybe it was just what the doctor ordered. Did supernatural creatures even have doctors?

Amara's attention was distracted by Klaus. It was a small mercy that drinking didn't affect vampires in the same way it did humans, because he'd drunk a truckload. Tipping another bottle against his lips and realizing it was empty, Klaus placed it on the ground and walked away from the campfire. Loris trailed in his wake. Amara had a sneaking suspicion that something was going on between the two of them. They'd spent a lot of time together since it was decided that the former Red Claw was no longer a threat. Amara often saw them whispering together, a secret conversation meant only for their ears.

The sight of Klaus and Loris together gave Amara a bittersweet feeling. It was vexing that vampires couldn't love. Maybe the world would be a better place if they could. Less violent, at the very least. Love was the most important thing in the world, Amara thought. Everything else came second. What was a life without love? Wasted. Hollow. Devoid of color. She smiled at Haiden, the angry gash down his face illuminated by the red flames. Despite his assurances that it didn't hurt (much), Amara still worried about him.

She thought back to their reunion after the battle. When she'd opened the door to her motel room and seen him standing there, she had fallen into his arms like a damsel in those classic movies. Amara hadn't thought you could actually go weak at the knees. She thought it was just a figure of speech. But she'd proven herself wrong. The librarian didn't notice his wound as she buried her head in his shoulder. When she pulled away to take him in she gasped with shock.

"You should see the other guy," Haiden had said, trying to reassure her. "I got off lightly." He dipped his head. "Especially compared to some of the others." A tear escaped his eye.

Haiden filled her in on the battle. The dead. Their failure to save Nell or find Zachariah and the Magister. Amara had been trying for a long while to hold it together, to be strong for the team. But with only Haiden in the room, it was easy to let go. She let out her emotions with heaving sobs. This moment of release had been weeks in the making. She held on tightly to Haiden, fearing that she might lose him if she ever let go.

Eventually, Amara wiped her tears away. Then she did the same for Haiden. Together, they traveled the short distance back to the campsite. Amara wasn't sure if she was needed, or even welcome, there. Her plan had failed. But she had to face the others. To be with them at this time of sorrow. Though she would completely understand if they wanted nothing more to do with her. Perhaps the fae were right and a mere human should never have been left in charge.

Amara breached the circle of the campfire as Sanya was staring despondently at the dancing flames. The uninjured were burying the dead. The remaining spell-casters and a few of the witches were treating the wounded with various elixirs and ointments. One spell-caster hovered her hands over a nasty looking fracture on the leg of a werwulf. She chanted an incantation over and over again as her eyes seemed to roll back in her head. Amara looked on as the werwulf let out a long exhalation and then leaned back to rest on the ground, his taut muscles relaxing. The spell-caster was helping to ease the pain, and hopefully healing the broken bone.

The best Amara could do was gather sticks to form the crosses. She didn't think they were religious signs, more a universal symbol of respect for the dead. As she went about her work she received nods and faint smiles. Her fears of being shunned or cast out were unfounded. Yet she still found it difficult to look the others in the eye. Loris approached her when he spotted the librarian.

"Nobody questions the work you put in and your strategy, Amara," he said, no doubt noticing her wariness. "Without you, we would have lost a great many more lives."

"Thank you, Loris," said Amara, quietly, looking around her. "And I'm sorry."

"There's no need," replied Loris. "If Nell was there, we could have retrieved her. It is no fault of yours that she was not. The strategy was sound."

Amara straightened her spine and took a breath.

"Thank you," she said again, though she felt she was undeserving of any praise.

Chapter 24

The next two days dragged by. More respects were paid and the injured were given time to rest and recuperate. The mood in camp remained somber. Despite some discussion on the way forward from here, no one really knew what to do. Observers were sent out to watch the Red Claw compound from a safe distance.

There were signs of life around the fortress. Some Red Claws who had fled during the battle returned. The perimeter fence was being rebuilt. But there was no sign of Nell. No sign of Zachariah. No sign of the Magister. Each watcher said the same thing when they returned to Blackstone Bay. Nothing significant to report other than a few vampires entering and exiting buildings and making repairs. Some damaged furniture was being burned in open fires. Not much more.

Christopher suggested raiding the compound again and taking out any Red Claws that they found on the grounds. Amara wasn't convinced that the potential gain was worth the risk. It would bring them no closer to Nell. Christopher was still feeling guilty about not taking part in the previous battle. He was spoiling for a fight, especially since the Red Claws still had Nell. His bloodlust wasn't shared by the librarian, who took a more considered approach.

Devan suggested taking a prisoner and questioning them as to Zachariah's whereabouts. Christopher didn't have long to dwell on the suggestion as a ripple of gasps rang out into the cold air. He looked up to see the source of the commotion. Then his mouth dropped open. He had to blink hard and shake his head to believe what his eyes were registering.

Sauntering brazenly into the camp was Miss Odette, accompanied, as ever, by her pet imp. She was quickly surrounded. The crowd appeared ready to tear her and her acolyte limb from limb. Loris held up a hand in a gesture of caution.

"What are you doing here?"

His tone made it crystal clear that she was not welcome.

"Now, now, Loris dear. Don't be like that," Miss Odette replied.

Her own kind, the fae that hadn't switched sides, hissed at her. Christopher could see their faces contorting as rage overcame them. Sharp teeth were bared and bloody eyes stared daggers at her.

"I come bearing news," Miss Odette said quickly, obviously unsettled by the hostility of her former brethren.

She made eye contact with Christopher as she spoke. He looked down at the missing tip of her index finger and felt a tinge of dark satisfaction. Devan, in human form and dressed in his camping gear, placed a hand on Christopher's shoulder, grounding him.

"You heard Loris. You are not welcome here," said Christopher. "You've made your bed, now lie in it, and take that little creep with you."

Christopher registered the characteristic defiance and arrogance in her features. But just under the surface there was something else. Fear. Deep fear. Not because she was presently surrounded, Christopher felt, but because she was forced to come here. Forced to enter the lion's den against her wishes. Christopher looked down at her pet imp. For once Master August looked concerned rather than smug.

Miss Odette looked around nervously.

"Not even if I bring news that your beloved Nell is dead?" she announced, then flashed an unconvincing smile at Christopher.

Christopher shook off Devan's hand and stormed forward. A few of the fae pounced too, grabbing Miss Odette and Master August and pinning them in place. Christopher drew his hand back and made a fist. Miss Odette turned her head away and winced. Christopher could see she was in an emotionally charged state.

He looked back at Loris, who nodded in assent at the silent question. *Yes, Christopher, you know what to do,* he could imagine Loris saying.

Christopher brought his fist down quickly. Then slowed his motion. He opened his fingers and gently grabbed Miss Odette's bare hand. The thoughts came rushing in.

***

Humiliation flooded her along with red-hot anger as she and Master August were ejected from the Council headquarters. It was bad enough that she had wasted her time there in the first place. But to be kicked out for professing what everyone knew was true, that humans were a lesser species, well that was beyond the pale.

The days spent wandering around the country aimlessly were difficult. There was a war coming and now she had no allies to protect her. She was out on her own with just her beloved Master August. They were vulnerable.

She thought she would be safe and highly respected at Council headquarters. It was nothing less than she deserved, after all. She had answered their call for help and selflessly taken time out of her busy life to support the cause. A cause that would involve saving lesser creatures that meant nothing to her. The ingratitude was astounding. They would regret it in the end. But what was she to do now? She was an outsider with no friends.

It was actually Master August who suggested a way forward. He was a bright little button and she loved him oh so very dearly. Both vicious and loyal, her perfect comrade. Also her only one at present. They had been together for longer than Miss Odette cared to admit. It was rude to discuss a lady's age. But it was before the founding of the country they now called home. Before William Shakespeare took quill to paper. Before the fall of Constantinople. They had traveled the Earth together. Now it felt like they were alone on the planet. The very ones who needed them the most had pushed them away. Idiots. It was their loss. Ungrateful vermin.

The answer was a simple one. If you can't beat them, join them.

"There's only one thing left for us to do," suggested Master August. "Let's give the Red Claws a visit."

He had the voice of a child but the mind of a wise old man, she felt.

The various filth and lesser species assembled at Vhik'h-Tal-Eskemon would be sorry. Couldn't they see that her allegiance would be the deciding factor in this battle? Were they too ignorant and blind to accept that fact? They would, in time.

CHAPTER 24

"You're absolutely right, August darling," she said, patting his head. "No point moping around, eh? The Red Claws will do anything to have m…us…on their side. We can ask for any terms we choose." She smiled broadly. "We'll win the war for them and then reap the benefits. Can you imagine the look on the Council of Elders' faces when we crush them into the ground? They'll be sorry. That alone will make the entire effort worth it. Plus, I'd quite like to see that human woman dead. That will show them just how much she's really worth."

It took almost a week for Miss Odette and Master August to catch up with the Red Claws close to the Canadian border. They followed the trail of the dead and missing. Once in their vicinity Miss Odette found it straightforward to track the vampires' movements. They left behind a trace that the oldest of the fae were able to feel. Energy waves in the ether. When a creature of the night moved in the human world, they left a trail, an emanation, behind. It was a wispy, almost mist-like substance. That was how it appeared to Miss Odette, anyway. Other fae elders described the phenomena as 'shedding'. Either way, the result was the same. It meant that it was fairly easy to track a supernatural creature if you happened to be one of the sensitive fae.

The Red Claws had taken over a remote hunting lodge. Unluckily for the owners, two retired doctors from Mankota in Saskatchewan, they had chosen that particular weekend to load the pick-up and drive down for a weekend of shooting in the unspoilt wilderness. The hunters had become the hunted.

Approaching the lodge with Master August, Miss Odette made herself known. She projected confidence. Powerful men responded to confidence, she had found throughout her long life.

"Which one of you is Zachariah?" Miss Odette's voice echoed off the upright wooden logs that formed the walls of the lodge.

The vampires were coiled like springs, ready to attack. They surrounded her. She raised her head, showing that she wasn't scared.

"Come on now, darlings, there's no need for that," she said, stretching her lips into a practiced smile. A smile that usually sent men wild. "I'm here to guarantee your victory."

"We have no interest in joining forces with fairies," said a tall male at the back.

Miss Odette had to stretch her neck to see him past the Red Claws that stood in front of her. He had black hair, dark eyes and a young angular face, but the demeanor of a much older man.

"I have a feeling that I might be able to change your mind on this occasion," she replied, ensuring that her voice took on her trademark sultry cadence.

The vampire simply laughed.

"Do you really think your crass tricks will work with me, Pixie?" he said. "Do I look like some besotted baseborn human?"

Miss Odette was flustered. This wasn't going at all like she had envisioned. She had to change tack.

"You perhaps might be interested to know that I have been at Vhik'h-Tal-Eskemon for the last few weeks and have gained a startling amount of knowledge that could be of significant benefit to you," she said, dispensing with her breathy voice and adopting a matter-of-fact tone. "But, if you're not interested, that's fine. As you were vamps." She waved a dismissive hand. "We shall take our leave."

CHAPTER 24

Miss Odette turned on her heel to walk away, her imp in tow.

"Wait," the vampire called behind her.

Miss Odette turned and arched a perfectly shaped eyebrow.

"I am the one you seek," continued the vampire, his tone moderating. "I am Zachariah."

"Call off your pets," Miss Odette instructed, hoping to win the unspoken power struggle taking place around her. She glared at the assembled Red Claws. It was only then that she noticed the human woman slumped in the far corner of the room, guarded by two vampires.

"The pets you refer to are my Family," said Zachariah, coldly. "And you would do well to moderate your tongue, Pixie," he warned, looking at her hand. "Or we'll be happy to deprive you of more than just a finger."

Miss Odette swallowed hard. Her butchered finger twitched involuntarily as she recalled the searing pain when Christopher bit deep into her flesh.

"My dear Zachariah," she said, adopting a sickly-sweet tone and clapping her hands in front of her ample chest. "Can we not be friends? I assure you there is more to be gained in solidarity than enmity."

"We can talk," replied Zachariah, coolly. "That much I shall grant you."

Miss Odette strutted forwards, parting the vampires in front of her like the Red Sea. She felt powerful in that moment. All those pesky blood-suckers dutifully moving out of her way. She could get used to it.

"Be quick," said the Red Claw leader. "We have no desire to linger here."

She told Zachariah what she knew, leaving out one or two

details she wanted to keep in reserve.

"You've wasted my time as well as your own," Zachariah said when she had finished speaking. "All you've told us is that the Council have managed to recruit some werwulfs, witches and fae on their side. We knew that. Your knowledge is as shallow and vacuous as you are."

"How dare…" Miss Odette began.

She was cut off by Master August, who stepped forward. It was most unlike him to interrupt her.

"We do have something else," he said, in his shrill voice. "Something that I'd wager you weren't expecting. But I'm going to have to ask you not to speak to my mistress in that wretched way. She's been nothing but polite to you."

Zachariah looked at the imp with disdain.

"I know not what manner of Devil creature you are, boy," he began, bending slightly. "But I assure you…"

"Vampire Hunters," Master August interrupted. He spoke slowly and clearly.

Zachariah's reaction was instant.

"What did you say?"

"Vampire Hunters," repeated Master August. "They have joined the Council's side."

"How many?" Zachariah's face seemed to turn an even paler shade of white.

"When we were there, maybe ten or twelve," answered the imp. "But who knows how many there are now?" He was using his high-pitched voice to ramp up the drama.

Miss Odette felt so proud of her little munchkin. He was so clever and resourceful.

"What else do you know about them?" asked Zachariah. "Did you see their faces? Would you recognize them again?

How were they armed?" He fired off the questions without pausing for breath.

"Now now, my dear Zachariah," Miss Odette said. "We're not going to give away all our little secrets. Not until you offer us something in return."

The Red Claw leader huffed. He didn't enjoy being in a position of weakness, especially in front of his brethren.

"What is it you want?" he asked, eyeing her coldly.

He was talking terms. At last. It was so satisfying.

"Protection," Miss Odette said, simply. "We join your side and you keep us out of harm's way while you fight your tedious war." She looked at the human slumped in the corner, her head lolling in all directions as her chest heaved for breath. "And that human," added Miss Odette, pointing at Nell. "I'd very much like to suck out her soul. Call it a personal favor to me."

"Out of the question," snapped Zachariah, looking disgusted. "She is not yours to feed on."

Miss Odette didn't expect him to agree, of course. She was just upping her asking price in the hope that Zachariah would compromise on giving her protection, which was all she really wanted.

Zachariah considered the fae and the imp with his coal-black eyes.

"No, you can't join us," he said. "You are no Red Claws." He spread his arms around him. "These are my children. My brothers and sisters. A fairy and an…abomination…have no place among us."

"Fae," corrected Miss Odette, failing to hide her annoyance. "We are called fae, not fairies. And Master August here is an imp."

"I couldn't care less," countered Zachariah. "You are not Red

Claws and that is the only salient point here."

Miss Odette was flustered. Once again her expectations were not matching up with reality. Not even close.

Master August spoke up again.

"I can tell you how the Council plans to attack," he said. "I know their strategy."

Zachariah turned to him. So did Miss Odette, trying her best to conceal her confusion.

"How?" asked the Red Claw leader.

"It's very easy to blend into the background when you're my size," said the imp, with a sinister grin.

Miss Odette knew Master August was bluffing. He hadn't been privy to the Council's strategy meetings. She knew that. But Zachariah didn't. Perhaps there was a way this gamble could work. There were precious few other options.

"And what is it they have planned?" asked Zachariah, eyebrows raised.

"All in good time, my dearest Zachariah," said Miss Odette, brightly. "All in good time."

And with that, an uneasy alliance was cemented.

The next few days were tense. An undercurrent of resentment pervaded the atmosphere. None of the Red Claws were happy that Miss Odette and Master August were tagging along.

Disgust was soon added to the litany of negative feelings the vampires harbored towards their strange new associates. Miss Odette and Master August were accustomed to a diet of raw flesh. Human entrails were a particular favorite of the imp.

Vampires drank blood. Their kills were clean. The victims were drained of life but their bodies were left undesecrated.

CHAPTER 24

The Red Claws were sickened by the sight of Miss Odette and Master August feasting on the insides of the humans. To them, it was vulgar and indecent.

Also, as the Red Claws would feed, Miss Odette had a habit of hovering over the victim. She would lean down and inhale deeply through her wide-open mouth. Whatever she was sucking in from the dying body was invisible to the Red Claws. Yet the fae shook with an almost sexual ecstasy as she imbibed the stream of whatever it was. It annoyed the Red Claws to no end. Vampires didn't play with their food.

The first hunting trip was to a remote fishing town, during which the Red Claws were very careful about choosing victims. They ensured the humans were isolated and lived alone. The vampires looked on with revulsion as the fae and imp feasted upon an elderly man. But what really incensed them was that he was left in the middle of the road after they were done.

"You can't do that," Zachariah admonished. "Are you trying to get us caught? Haven't we got enough to deal with right now?"

Miss Odette was nonplussed.

"I didn't think you Red Claws felt so tenderly towards your meals."

She laughed at her own attempt at humor.

"We do when we are trying to transport a hostage undetected," said Zachariah, urgently. "The last thing we need is Hunters on our trail. You will dispose of your food properly."

After the second and third feeding trips, when the Red Claws realized their guests were still not following the rules, Zachariah came up with a compromise. He offered to bring a batch of bodies deep into the woods, somewhere secluded. That way Miss Odette and Master August didn't have to join the hunt. Essentially, table service. The corpses would be hidden from human view while the fae and imp could gut them to their hearts' content, ensuring an ample supply of 'packed lunches' for the road.

The new arrangement delighted Miss Odette and Master August. They dined messily amongst the dense trees and left their prey scattered over the forest floor. They ripped and tore, taking what they needed for the trip to Alaska.

A few days later, Miss Odette noticed that the number of Red Claws seemed to be dwindling. Faces that had become familiar were now missing from the group. She decided to confront Zachariah about the falling numbers.

"Do not concern yourself with it," Zachariah said, shrugging off the matter and attempting to walk away.

But you didn't walk away from Miss Odette before she was finished talking to you. It was basic manners.

"Where are they, Zachariah?" Her voice was stern, without a hint of the sultry siren.

Zachariah turned and marched right up to her, invading her personal space.

"Dead," he said. A smile crept across his face.

"Elaborate, dearest," said Miss Odette, trying to match his smile but failing.

"They disappointed me. I killed them," said Zachariah. "That's what I do with those who disappoint me." His cold dark eyes bored into her.

***

Christopher tore his hand away from Miss Odette's warm, smooth skin. He took a step away from her. A stream of profanities were spilling from her mouth. She was furious about being manhandled, demanding they let go of her.

Christopher was still reeling from seeing Nell held captive. She looked so weak and miserable. He wasn't sure how much more she could take judging by how she appeared in the vision. Christopher glanced back at Loris, ready to share everything he saw.

"Not now, Christopher," said Loris, holding up a hand. The words seemed harsh to Christopher. "We'll talk about this later," added the older vampire. "Just tell me one thing. Is she telling the truth? Is Nell dead?"

"I don't know," Christopher said. "I saw her, but it was some time back. She didn't look in good shape."

Christopher cursed the fact that he couldn't control how his 'gift' worked. All he'd wanted was to see Nell now. Alive. Instead, he'd witnessed Miss Odette making a pact with the Devil.

"She's on their side," he said to Loris. "That much I know. She's working with the Red Claws."

Loris considered for a moment.

"Then we have to do what we must," he said, somberly.

"No, no, I lied! I lied!" Miss Odette screeched.

The other fae tightened their hold on her as she writhed in their grasp.

"Then why did you tell us she was dead?" asked Loris.

"You know me," she replied, feigning levity. "I bore easily and like to keep myself amused. I was just having a little…"

"Miss Odette," said Loris, giving her a deathly glare. "Do we seem amused to you?"

Miss Odette looked at the ground. She appeared lost. Her inflated self-confidence had evaporated. Master August looked to her with concern.

"Tell us the truth," demanded Loris. "Or we have no further use for you. Believe me, I would be very happy to…bring this situation to an end."

"Fine," she huffed, looking up sullenly. "I told you Nell was dead because Zachariah told me to do it."

"The gamble didn't pay off, did it?" said Christopher.

Miss Odette looked at him wide-eyed. Loris looked confused. A hush descended on the camp. Only the crackle of the red flames could be heard.

"Your pact with Zachariah," explained Christopher. He pointed a finger at Master August, who looked subdued, defeated. "This little one here claimed that he knew our plans, that he had important information for the Red Claws. But it soon became apparent that it was a lie. You had nothing useful to offer Zachariah. So, he put you to work, didn't he? You became his servants."

Master August looked away. He couldn't meet Christopher's eyes.

"He sent you to lure me to him with Nell's shirt after we stormed the compound," continued Christopher. "But that mission didn't go according to plan, did it? He must have been furious."

Now it was Miss Odette who couldn't meet his eyes.

"So here you are, sent on another errand for your master. Right into the heart of the lion's den, like the dutiful serfs he's turned you into."

Miss Odette pouted like a child.

"If you hadn't attacked me like the animal you are, things could have been different, for all of us," she protested.

"Yes, very different," Christopher mused. "Both me and Nell

would be dead right now."

"No," she countered. "That's not what he said."

Christopher chuckled.

"And he would confide in you?" he replied. "Someone who tricked him. Someone he had come to loathe. Someone he considered a lesser being?"

That sparked the fire and fury back into Miss Odette.

"A lesser being? ME??" she screamed. "How dare you! Zachariah has the utmost respect for me. He knows my worth. He knows that I'm the key to this infernal battle. I'm worth more than all of you scum put together!"

Klaus, who had watched the proceedings in silence up until now, stepped forwards. He approached Miss Odette slowly. Christopher was glad. He felt he wasn't getting anywhere fast and was only antagonizing her.

"Let me tell you something," Klaus said, addressing Miss Odette. "You think you're one of them. You think you're a Red Claw. One of the Family. But you're nothing to Zachariah. Less than nothing, in fact."

She glowered at him with a mix of anger and humiliation.

"Do you know why he asked you to come to us?" Klaus continued. "Because he wants you out of the picture. He sent you here with no back-up to tell us Nell was dead. Think about that. Do you think it was part of some clever ploy? Some brilliant strategy? He knew all it would do was enrage us. He wants you dead, along with your precious imp."

Miss Odette turned to look forlornly at Master August.

"I was his Family for decades and he threw me away like I was nothing," Klaus went on, his anger rising. Haiden stepped up beside him, in case he lost control. "He made me," Klaus spat. "Then he discarded me. I was Family. You? You're nothing more than a leach. A succubus."

Klaus turned around to face the assembled crowd while Miss Odette and Master August remained stunned into silence. She was no longer hurling insults or thrashing around. Klaus had evidently got under her skin.

"I say we kill her now," announced Klaus. "She doesn't know anything and we can't have her going back to the Red Claws after tracking us here."

"I know where she is!" shouted Miss Odette. "I found out!"

Klaus whipped back around to face her.

"They're in the tunnels," she went on, looking around desperately. "Under the compound. The Magister, Zachariah and the human woman. August overheard them. They're in the tunnels, the ones carved into the very rock. My August is so very resourceful."

The imp gave a wan smile to his mistress.

"See," Miss Odette pleaded, wide-eyed, looking around frantically. "See. You need me! You need us! I can be your savior. I can hand you victory."

"Just like you promised to hand Zachariah victory?" said Klaus. "And look at you now?"

Fury enveloped Miss Odette. Her face contorted. Her mouth widened into a gaping hole filled with sharp stained teeth. Her eyes grew bigger and reddened, making her look demonic.

"You," she seethed at Klaus. "You vermin! You absolute scum! Zachariah told me about you. How you betrayed him. I would never do that. I'm more Family to him than you ever were."

Klaus gritted his teeth and balled his firsts. Haiden placed a placating hand on his shoulder.

CHAPTER 24

"He said you were never a true Red Claw," continued Miss Odette, globs of spittle flying from her mouth. "You were stupid, useless, pathetic. He was ashamed someone like you were ever…"

In a flash Klaus reached down and grabbed the scythe from Haiden's belt. He swung it in an arc in front of him.

Miss Odette was silenced. She stared at him wide-eyed. Then her head rolled off her body.

Master August screamed. The piercing shriek nearly shattered Christopher's eardrums. He had never heard anything like it. He had to clamp his hands to his ears to stop his brain from melting. Christopher saw the others doing the same, pain etched on their faces.

He saw a flash of movement in front of him. Then the scream died. It was a blessed relief as he tentatively removed his hands from his head, ears still ringing,

In front of him another head thumped to the cold, rocky ground.

Master August had joined his mistress for all eternity.

Chapter 25

The bodies of Miss Odette and Master August were buried together, far away from those fallen in battle. Devan had suggested just burning them, but the fae wanted to give one of their own a decent burial. It was an honorable send off for someone who had not shown much of that quality in life.

The mood around the camp was anxious. The group felt exposed and vulnerable. If Miss Odette had managed to find them, then there was every possibility that the Red Claws could arrive en masse, looking for revenge. They needed to act, and soon.

The sense of imminent danger and lingering aftermath of the previous battle had served to bring down barriers in the camp. Before, each kind would stick to their own, sitting in groups. Slowly, the groups had merged together. Vampires and Hunters mingled. Spell-casters and fae spoke animatedly about how they could combine their skills in the next attack. They talked about what the war meant for their communities, but also the supernatural world at large.

Sanya, still recovering from the death of her beloved sister Yansa, had become a much-loved member of the mismatched army. The fae had taken a particular shine to her motherly wisdom. It was almost as if she had become what Miss Odette should have been to them.

Devan and Lupita came bounding into the camp. Even as wolves, Amara could tell they looked excited. Devan shifted into werwulf form. Despite the camp witnessing the transformation of the wolves on numerous occasions, it never failed to mesmerize. The way a creature could so elegantly and naturally shift from one form to another was almost magical.

"Nailed it," said Devan in his deeply resonant lycan voice. "I know where the entrance is."

He and Lupita had been keeping watch over the Red Claw fortress all morning.

"The smallest building on the compound, the wooden shed," continued Devan. "I was keeping an eye on it. Vamps were coming out over the course of the morning but I didn't see any going in. It has to be the way in and out of the tunnel complex."

Lupita was wagging her tail next to him.

"Great work, Devan," said Amara. She turned to the assembled army. "We go again today, after dark. I know it's asking a lot, but time is of the essence now. If any of you are not ready, or have had second thoughts, I perfectly understand. There's no shame in it. We have already asked more from you than we had any right to."

The camp was quiet. Many faces were staring at the ground, lost in contemplation.

Sanya stepped forward. A few sharp intakes of breath could be heard.

"I have lost something more precious than my life already," she said, looking around her. "Nothing could hurt me further. I know many of you feel the same way after losing friends and kin." She paused, looking out at the sea of somber faces. "But

I say let's make their sacrifice mean something. Let's finish what they so willingly helped start. Let's rid the world of this disease called the Red Claws, so we can be free and safe. The alternative is a life of darkness and constant fear. A life not worth living, if you ask me. Together we can make a difference. We can make tolerance and understanding our guiding lights going forward. We can make a future worth fighting for. So let's fight for it!"

Cheers erupted around the compound. Sanya received a flood of hugs. Amara's face was wet with tears. Haiden embraced her tightly.

"We need to get you back," he said, over the continued loud cheers.

Once again guilt flooded Amara. She would be safely tucked out of harm's way while everyone else was risking their life. She looked anguished.

"Ssshhhh," said Haiden, rubbing her back. "I know. I know. But we need you. Alive. There's more to do, more to figure out, and that's where you shine bright. We're depending on you. I'm depending on you." He leant down and kissed her softly on the lips.

"Promise me..." she began.

"I promise," Haiden finished for her. "I promise I'll come back to you." Though he wasn't sure it was a commitment he could guarantee to keep.

Chapter 26

The compound was eerily quiet when the army approached. Not a single Red Claw in sight. A bright almost-full moon illuminated the landscape and a canopy of stars was spread across the dark sky. The wild ocean wind whipped hard against Christopher's ears, making a whooshing sound. It was as if nature itself was on edge. He looked up and caught one of the stars twinkling. He didn't know what kind of omen that portended.

The army was split into two groups. The first would tackle the Red Claws in the compound and try to concentrate the fighting above ground. A smaller core group would venture into the tunnels to find Nell and hopefully take out Zachariah and his brother. Well, that was the plan, anyway. Devan, Lupita and Haiden would orchestrate the battle in the compound while Christopher, Klaus and Loris would lead the contingent underground.

Whereas before they attacked at first light, now they were storming the fortress at dusk. It was hardly a revolutionary element of surprise, but they were hoping that the Red Claws weren't anticipating their arrival. Much of their plan seemed to revolve around hope, Christopher thought. But there was no way around it. Their information was limited. They'd just have to 'hope' for the best.

The army snaked down the mountainside, trying its best to remain covert. The dark shadows slowly converged on the compound. Fractured pieces of wood lay on the hard ground, remnants of the tall fence that had once surrounded the buildings.

Christopher led the way stealthily to the smallest building. His team followed behind in single file. The structure was hardly bigger than a garden shed. Not much good for storage or for living in. Its sole purpose appeared to be concealing the entrance to the underground tunnels.

Christopher gingerly opened the door and stepped into the dismal, musty shack. Rusting barrels of what looked like fuel stood stacked up at the back haphazardly. On top of them was thrown some old netting, which was covered in gray cobwebs. To the side sat a stone casket running the length of the shack. Christopher recognized it right away. It was a sleep pod. The kind that once filled the old house in Angel Falls when Christopher was caretaker of the slumbering Red Claws. His former peaceful and solitary existence seemed like a lifetime away now.

Christopher quickly peered inside to ensure there wasn't an occupant. The casket was empty, barring the small black spiders running across the intricate matrix of webbing. Christopher quickly turned his attention to the ground. He spotted it right away now that he knew what he was looking for. A faint square outline where the earth was pushed either side of the four lines. They missed it the first time they stormed the compound and searched the grounds. They were too focused on finding Nell and avoiding attack to consider looking closely at the ground. Plus, this little shack seemed so

CHAPTER 26

sad and useless that it couldn't have been of any significance. Christopher was quickly learning that looks were deceiving. The seemingly angelic fae were a case in point.

He stuck his head out of the door, where his team was assembled outside, crouching low to remain inconspicuous.

"It's here. I found it," said Christopher in a hushed but urgent tone.

Loris nodded back. Klaus stood behind him, his expression resolute. Christopher took a moment to peer around the compound. Still no sign of Red Claws. His own ragtag army was spread around the grounds. Werwulfs, fae, spell-casters, Vampire Hunters and imps stood in the lengthening shadows. Poised. On alert.

Then it happened.

The Red Claws came crawling out of the woodwork. Literally. They emerged from within the other wooden buildings, atop roofs and behind walls. They charge towards the assembled army. Christopher stood transfixed, rooted to the spot.

He felt a hard shove to his chest.

"Let's get moving," implored Loris, wide-eyed. "We have to trust the others to handle matters here. This is not our fight."

Christopher was jolted out of his stupor. He quickly turned and bounded back into the shack. He bent down and swept the earth away from the trap door with an urgent hand. He found four holes in the thick wood. He placed his fingers inside the grooves and yanked upwards. The trap door swung open easily on metal hinges. Christopher retracted his fingers from the wood and the door came crashing down with a thud, sending earth and dust into the air. It revealed a gap, with a dark chasm beyond.

There was nothing for it. Christopher lowered himself into the open space feet first and then retracted his arms from the cold earth. He didn't know how far down he would fall. But time was of the essence now. The moment for a careful and considered approach was over. Luckily, his feet soon landed on the hard granite below. He was met by complete darkness. Utter blackness. The kind that you don't realize exists until you've experienced it. For a human at least. Christopher's enhanced eyes slowly began to adjust. As the others landed in quick succession behind him, he could start to make out the hazy outlines of his surroundings in high-contrast black and white.

The tunnel was narrow, less than an arm-span wide. The ceiling was low. It reminded Christopher of an ant colony for some reason. He led the way, having to crouch down as he moved. There was no sound down here apart from the shuffling footsteps echoing off the stone walls. Christopher felt uneasy. Something was off. Why had no one been guarding the shack? Why was no one down here barring their progress? It didn't seem to make sense. But still he kept moving forward. What other choice did he have?

He finally arrived at a small wooden door. It was unadorned with a simple round wooden knob for a handle. Two metal latches held the door in place. Christopher paused. He leaned forward and inhaled deeply. Vampires. Nell. The scents were unmistakable. He grabbed the knob and pulled open the door.

Nell sat in the middle of a cavernous stone room, tied to a post that was protruding from the ground. The room was lit by two burning torches on the far side. The moving flames sent ominous shadows dancing across the large space. Nell was unconscious but breathing. Barely.

CHAPTER 26

Christopher sprang across the room towards her, failing to take in the rest of his surroundings. His focus was only on Nell. He failed to see the Red Claws emerging from the adjoining tunnels. He failed to see Zachariah standing on a stone ledge just to his left. Not until it was too late.

Fuck. It was a trap.

His mind flashed back to Miss Odette back at Blackstone Bay. She had revealed the existence of the tunnels when she thought her life was in peril. A last trump card to ensure her survival, or so Christopher had thought at the time. But was it a ploy all along? A scheme cooked up with Zachariah to ambush them. It was immaterial now. No answers would be forthcoming from her.

Zachariah stood atop the stone ledge and looked down imperiously on the ensuing chaos. The Red Claws attacked the intruders in a flurry of teeth and claws. Screams echoed off the stone walls to form a chorus of bedlam as blows were landed and flesh was ripped. Though who was gaining the upper hand, Christopher could not tell. His focus was entirely on Nell. This close to her, the smell of vampire saliva was rife. All over her body. He could hear Nell's heart working too hard. Thumping away to keep her emaciated body supplied with what precious blood she had left.

Christopher frantically looked around him, seeing his comrades fighting against a sea of Red Claws. It was chaos. Carnage. A werwulf hurled a vampire across the room. A Red Claw bit into the neck of a young fae.

A figure swooped down on top of Nell's body. Christopher jerked his head upward.

The Magister. Bamford.

In his hand was a blade. Scythe was a more accurate term.

Orange flame from one of the burning torches reflected along the length of the menacing curved metal. Christopher stared wide-eyed as Bamford retracted his arm then swung the weapon in an arc towards Christopher's neck.

Instinct took over. Christopher shot out an arm and grabbed Bamford's wrist, slowing the motion of the blade until it came to a halt just a hair's breadth away from his exposed neck. Bamford's face contorted into a snarl and he screamed out in anger. Any trace of the genteel, refined scholar was gone. He was now a feral predator. Christopher tightened his grip on the Magister's wrist.

Then the noise and chaos around him began to recede and colors began to flash into his mind's eye. The colors began to form images. Unwanted. Unrelenting.

Fuck, not now, Christopher thought as his mind began to betray him and take him out the present moment. But he had no control over his gift. There was simply no choice in the matter.

***

Damien and Zachariah as young boys. Laughing and playing together with a worn leather ball in a sparse field. The hot sun radiates its warmth high in the sky and the two boys are bathed in a bright light as they chase the ball among the weeds and hard scrabble. A deep love emanates between the pair. Damien is much older than Zachariah, yet the two feel like equals. Two sides of the same coin.

Flash forward. Another tableau. This one very recent.

Zachariah with his lips pressed against Nell's neck. Then her thighs. Then her breasts. Nell writhing in pain and calling out, then going silent and still.

"Brothers share," says the Magister, looking on hungrily.

"That they do," says Zachariah, smiling. "Blood before all."

"Blood before all," repeats Bamford before swiftly kneeling down and partaking of the feast.

When the brothers finally lift their heads, their eyes blaze red. Their skin glows almost silver. They no longer look like ordinary vampires, if there can be said to be such a thing. They are something else.

Another flash. New images.

"You must abandon him, Zachariah," the Magister says, urgently. "He is not as we are. Not truly. He will betray you. You think he is a dutiful serf but his future is unclear. I cannot discern it. Something has shifted."

"You are mistaken, brother," replies Zachariah. "Klaus would never forsake me. I am the one who gave him life. He is as…"

***

The connection was suddenly broken. Christopher was violently plunged back into the here and now. Screams echoed around him in the cavernous underground room. He saw he was still holding on to Bamford's wrist. He trailed his eyes upwards. Then his breath caught in his chest.

There was an empty space where Bamford's head should have been. A bloodied stump of neck was all that remained. He sensed movement on the ground and looked down to see the Magister's head skitter across the floor. It came to an unceremonious stop in a corner of the room, looking like part of a child's macabre doll that had come apart.

Christopher turned to see Ezra, the huge Vampire Hunter,

standing over him with the Magister's scythe now in his large hand. Ezra gave a quick nod before rejoining the fray, hacking and slashing at the Red Claws with his new weapon.

Christopher's grip on Bamford's wrist loosened and then dissolved. He was left clutching a handful of dark ash.

"Noooo," came the wild scream from above.

Christopher looked up to see Zachariah swoop down from the ledge. His face was a mask of rage and shock.

"Damien! Damien! You killed my brother!" screamed the Red Claw leader. "Now you die."

Zachariah launched himself towards Christopher, who stood quickly to parry the attack. Christopher wanted to kill Zachariah so badly, but he needed to protect Nell and get her to safety. He couldn't lose sight of his primary objective. He remembered the last time he turned his attention away from her at the compound. She had disappeared from sight.

Christopher raised his fists in front of chest and braced himself. A blur flashed before him and suddenly Zachariah was pinned back against the jagged rock wall under the ledge. His assailant turned his head and glared at Christopher.

"Get her out of here," Klaus ordered, as he held Zachariah in place using all his strength. "Go. Now!"

Christopher didn't need to be told a third time. He stooped down and ripped the bindings that held Nell in place before picking her up. She weighed hardly anything across his muscled arms. He turned and ran back through the small wooden door, ducking his head low and holding Nell close to his chest. He ran down the dark tunnel trying his best to ensure Nell didn't bump up against the hard rock. She felt so fragile in his arms.

More screams sounded from the chamber behind him. But

CHAPTER 26

he didn't look back. Not once.

Chapter 27

Klaus looked into the eyes of his master as he struggled to restrain him. That was still how he thought of Zachariah. His master. The realization made him feel disgusted with himself. Klaus slammed Zachariah back against the wall, using his self-loathing as fuel. He had only managed to pin Zachariah in the first place because he had taken the older vampire by surprise. But now rage was helping to work his muscles.

"So, you're one of them now?" Zachariah spat.

The words cut Klaus to the core. They should have had no effect. Klaus wasn't a Red Claw in thrall of his cruel master any more. Yet still the words stung viciously.

"I was warned about you, but didn't believe it," continued Zachariah. "But look at you now, how low you have fallen, consorting with scum. I'm surprised the dogs didn't butcher you."

Fury overcame Klaus. He leaned forward and ripped flesh from Zachariah's neck with his sharp teeth, exposing tendons and cartilage. It would heal, but it would hurt.

"Yes, I'm one of them," Klaus hissed. "And proud of it. Those you call dogs have more integrity and decency than you ever had."

Zachariah stared at Klaus wide-eyed, genuinely taken aback.

"Do you even hear yourself?" said Zachariah, wincing in pain from his neck wound, which was oozing thick black blood. "To think that I once thought of you as closer than a brother."

The words were like an emotional gut-punch. Klaus knew he was being manipulated, but it seemed old bonds were hard to sever.

"Tell me something, Zachariah," breathed Klaus. "Why did you choose her over me? I would never have left you. We were family." He felt pathetic, ashamed, yet he needed answers. Tears stung his eyes. He hated himself for having this reaction to Zachariah.

"I didn't choose her. She's nothing. Less than nothing. She's human trash," said Zachariah. "It's her blood that I want, that I need." His face seemed to soften, despite the pain from his wound. "Come now Klaus, did you really think that I'd chosen a human over you? Over my Family, my confidante, over my beloved Klaus."

Klaus was accosted by a barrage of conflicting emotions. Affection, hate, betrayal, shame, anger, guilt. The heady mix threw him off-balance. He tightened his grip on his former master.

"Then why?" implored Klaus, leaning in. "Why, Zachariah?"

"Damien," said Zachariah, simply. "He can see things. He said you would betray me when I needed you the most. That you would be my Judas…and look where we both stand now. See for yourself, Klaus."

The two of them were silent for a moment, just staring at each other. Then Klaus turned his head to take in the chaos that continued to rage around them. The Red Claw numbers had thinned. Ash piles littering the stone floor served as testament to their fate. But Klaus also took in the dead and wounded on his side. A werwulf lay torn to shreds on the ground and a Vampire Hunter was clutching a gaping stomach wound, trying to stop his innards from spilling out. Klaus winced as he turned back to face his nemesis.

Zachariah held something in his hand. Klaus's eyes widened as he focused on the object.

A weapon? No.

A glass vial. It contained a liquid. Red. Blood.

Before Klaus could knock it out of his hand, Zachariah quickly tipped the glass to his lips, gulping greedily. Klaus realized that Zachariah's supposed heartfelt words had simply been a ploy to distract him long enough to extract the vial and drink its contents.

Fooled again. Zachariah always had the upper hand.

Then something truly strange happened. Before Klaus's eyes, Zachariah began to heal. Quickly. Too quickly. The ripped and severed tendons in his neck knitted back together in mere seconds. The thick black blood retracted into the wound. Then fresh skin closed over the gaping flesh. It looked like Zachariah had never suffered an injury.

Klaus stared at the Red Claw leader in disbelief. He noticed Zachariah's eyes were glowing a crimson red and his skin seemed almost translucent. He also seemed to grow in stature. His shoulders broadened and his head cocked sideways as a smile spread over his face.

It's her blood that I want, that I need.

Klaus recalled Zachariah's words. It was why he had chosen her over him, why he kept her alive. Nell's blood. There was something special about it. If it had this startling effect on Zachariah's appearance, what would it do to his abilities? It didn't take long for Klaus to find out.

Zachariah whipped out a hand at lightning speed and clamped it around Klaus's neck. The grip was tight as a vice. Then Zachariah lifted Klaus off the ground, using just the one hand. Klaus could only stare back in disbelief as his feet dangled in the air.

"Blood," said Zachariah, his voice deeper and more resonant now. "Blood connects all. Blood is the liberator. Blood is the destroyer. Blood is the answer."

That was all the explanation Klaus received before the torment began. The attack was savage and unrelenting. Zachariah pulled Klaus towards him like a rag doll. He tore at his skin with his razor-sharp teeth, slashed at him with his vicious claws and landed blow after devastating blow to his body, all with a ferocity and speed that was astonishing, even for a vampire.

Klaus didn't even have a chance to defend himself, let alone retaliate. The attack was too quick, too powerful, too merciless. Zachariah ripped clumps of hair, skin and flesh from Klaus's defenseless body. Each snarling bite, punch, kick and tear seemed more devastating than the previous one.

Klaus crumpled onto the stone floor. His stomach had been ripped open by the long talon-like fingers of his creator. He turned his head and saw the stone around him matted with dark blood. It was as black and thick as tar. His blood, he realized, with both shock and amazement. There was just so much of it. Like slow lava flowing from his body.

With a hard kick to the face, Klaus's jaw snapped in two. The pain was excruciating, indescribable. He raised his hands in a vain attempt to defend himself. Zachariah was on top of him now, straddling his chest. Klaus tried to push him away, but it felt like he was pushing against a granite boulder. Zachariah didn't budge. He just kept swinging his fists against Klaus's already battered face and tearing at his neck with his teeth.

With each tear, each broken bone, Zachariah's smile grew both wider and wilder.

"A fitting end for you, Klaus," he seethed. "How dare you betray your Family? How dare you betray me? Death before dishonor. That's our way."

With every utterance, Zachariah ripped and tore at Klaus's body. The pain was blinding.

"You won't win," Klaus managed to splutter through his wet, broken mouth. The words felt muddled and slurred as they exited his bloodied lips. But it was his final small act of defiance before eternal darkness overcame him.

Klaus begged for death now. Death was the only way out of this relentless agony. With a final effort of mind he offered a silent prayer to the Omni-Father that Loris was kept safe, then closed his eyes as the darkness came rushing in.

***

"Klaus! Klaus!"

The words were dull, muffled. They seemed to come from a million miles away. But they were steadily growing louder and clearer.

"Klaus! Can you hear me? Are you there? Klaus?"

With a monumental effort, he opened an eyelid just a fraction. What he saw brought a moment of sweet relief amidst the rekindled agony of his broken body.

Loris, kneeling over him, looking stricken.

CHAPTER 27

"Klaus, stay with me," he implored. "You need to stay with me."

Loris's voice washed over him, bringing a measure of calm amid the torrent of pain.

Loris. My Loris...my love, Klaus thought.

Being on death's door helped to push aside any inhibitions. Klaus realized then, as he half opened both eyes, that he loved Loris more than anyone else in the world. Love. He loved Loris. That wasn't strictly possible, but it was true. Loris who accepted him unconditionally. Loris who showed him patience. Loris who showed him kindness and grace. When he didn't deserve any of it.

Klaus tried to lift his head but it wouldn't budge. It felt like it weighed ten tons. He was weak after losing most of his blood in the attack. The end was near, he could feel it. He was still bleeding out and there wasn't enough left inside him to sustain the lifeforce of his body. He would soon be nothing but ash littered on the unforgiving ground. He had craved that sweet oblivion as he was being attacked by Zachariah. But now, looking at Loris, his cherished Loris, he wasn't so sure.

"Stay still," said Loris as he reached down and held Klaus's hand.

That was an easy instruction to obey. Klaus couldn't move anyway. He opened his eyes slightly wider. Loris still hovered above him, worry and anguish etched on his face. It was then, looking into Loris's horrified eyes, that Klaus knew he was as good as dead. He remembered Zachariah's savage and relentless attack. How he tore and ripped at Klaus's neck as he sat on his chest, pinning him to the ground. Klaus knew that his neck must be almost completely severed. Perhaps one or two tendons were keeping his head attached. Zachariah hadn't finished the job. Was he stopped just before landing the fatal blow? Did he flee thinking he'd done enough to end Klaus? What did it matter now anyway?

Loris cradled Klaus's head. Holding him together. Quite literally. Keeping his head attached to the damaged flesh underneath.

"Shit, shit, shit!" Loris's voice was hysterical.

Klaus felt like he was in a dream. The pain seemed to subside a little. Was he going into shock? Was his body preparing for the end? With Loris by his side, he didn't feel so afraid. It was a small mercy in his final moments.

"I love you," Klaus muttered, weakly.

"I know," replied Loris, with tears streaming down his face. "I know. I just want to stop you from hurting? How do I do that?"

Klaus was silent. There was no solution to that question.

Loris began to mutter vaguely familiar words to himself. Klaus was barely able to listen. He felt strangely calm at that moment. Safe in the hand of Loris, whose voice echoed off the stone walls. The words floated in the air. Klaus tried to focus on what Loris was saying.

"Salvation lies in one soul. A death-walker turned young...He will endure a betrayal, a loss and an awakening. He will love, as no other of his kin has before. He will abandon those he serves. He must drain the one he loves, filling his essence and ending theirs. This act alone brings forth the genesis."

Klaus recognized the words. They were from the prophecy that was meant to foresee the final destruction of the Red Claws. But why was Loris reciting that now, in their final moments together?

CHAPTER 27

Loris suddenly stopped his muttering and looked down urgently at Klaus.

"It's not about Christopher."

Klaus was more dazed than ever. He had no idea how to respond.

"The prophecy," continued Loris, breathlessly. "We've all assumed it was about Christopher and Nell, but it doesn't just apply to them." He was rushing his words, as if he was racing against the arrival of death itself, which in a way he was. "Why would it involve a human? That part never made sense to me. This is old vampiric folklore. It never mentions a human. But you, Klaus…us…"

Klaus's mind was thick and foggy. For a moment he thought that Loris was suggesting that the prophecy was about the two of them. But that couldn't be true. It was about Nell and Christopher. Everyone knew that. It was why Zachariah had kidnapped Nell.

But something stirred deep within Klaus. Slowly dawning realizations that were making their way to the surface. He was turned at a young age. He had endured betrayal, lost his Family and awakened to a new way of living. He had also literally awakened from a one-hundred-year slumber. He had abandoned those he once served. He had felt strong, overwhelming emotions again…and he had found his one true love. On that point he was certain.

Is it me? Was it my destiny recorded in that ancient book?

Klaus wasn't sure whether he'd said the words aloud or not.

"It's about us," said Loris, tenderly now. "I'm sure of it, Klaus."

Klaus thought back to words of the prophecy. *'He must drain the one he loves, filling his essence and ending theirs. This act alone brings forth the genesis.'*

But if that were true it would mean…Klaus refused to contemplate the thought. No. Never.

Loris saw the torment etched on Klaus's face and gently stroked his head before speaking softly.

"My Klaus, if I am your one true love then you know what must be done."

Klaus clamped his eyes shut. He would not be party to this. He willed death to finally come and claim him. He wouldn't countenance what he was being asked to do.

"Shhhhhh Klaus," soothed Loris as he continued to gently stroke his face. "Shhhh, my love. Fate has been cruel to us. Yet we cannot turn away from it. I've only just found you, yet it appears now we must part…for the greater good…for the fate of all. We should have had eternity, but we are only left with now."

Klaus kept his eyelids squeezed shut. But while he could block his vision, he couldn't stop his thoughts from racing. If he was the one, the death-walker turned young as mentioned in the prophecy, then his dying here and now would be in vain. No. More than that. His death would condemn humankind as well as vampires and all other beings. There would be no defense against the Red Claws spreading, multiplying, conquering, killing.

"I'm old," said Loris, wistfully. "I've seen a lot of life. It grows tiresome after a while. But you brought new color to my world. You gave me an exquisite joy I have never known before. To have felt that, I can leave the world content. My time is now, Klaus, we both know it, in our hearts, we know it. Drink of me, fully, as it must be. That way I will always be a part of you. I can never leave you, and never will. My blood is ancient. It can heal you. Do what must be done, my love. Do it quickly. Do what must be done."

Klaus opened his eyes. Loris quickly bent down and kissed him tenderly on the lips. With one final look into Klaus's mournful eyes, Loris ran a sharp nail deep across his own neck. Thick blood began to pour from the wound. Loris leaned down and placed his neck to Klaus's lips.

Klaus felt repulsed. He tried to turn his head away. He couldn't do this. But as the warm blood trickled over his lips and seeped into his mouth a primal hunger overcame him. With tears streaming down his cheeks, he began to drink. Lightly at first. But as the life-giving blood energized his senses, he began to gulp it down. He slowly regained the strength to lift his arms and cradle Loris as his true love made the ultimate sacrifice. For Klaus. For all.

Klaus just held him tight and drank and drank and drank.

Chapter 28

Bodies were littered across the compound. Devan's heart sank as he took in the injured and dead. Looking at the scene it appeared that only his side had suffered losses. But he knew that a good number of Red Claws were now no more than particles of dust carried on the turbulent currents far over the North Pacific Ocean. Hearing the groans of injured and dying comrades around him, the fate of those Red Claws brought little comfort.

By his rough estimation they had killed about half the Red Claws that had been present in the compound. The rest had escaped when they realized that the battle wasn't going their way. Zachariah had fled seemingly unscathed, which was a failure. But they had Nell back, which could only be viewed as a success. Devan recalled feeling elated in the midst of the battle as he spotted Christopher whisking her away from the grounds in his arms. Whether her rescue outweighed their inability to take out the Red Claw leader, only time would tell. But in the pit of his stomach Devan had an uneasy feeling.

Devan's eyes were drawn to his pack. They were huddled around the body of a fallen werwulf. He could make out Lupita, with her rust-colored fur and distinctive markings. Her head was dipped. Devan's heart sank even further. He didn't want to see anyone on their side die, but it was worse when it was one of the wolves. One of his pack. He always felt responsible, which of course he was. He had brought them into this battle in the first place.

Though they had fought as werwulfs, the pack was now assembled in wolf form. It was how they felt most comfortable, most connected with nature and one another. Devan followed suit and shifted into his wolf form, then he tentatively padded over to the huddle. He dreaded what he'd find, but he could not avoid the grim task.

He slowed as he reached the group and came to a stop next to Lupita. It was then that he saw who had fallen. Young Lupo's body lay still and bloodied on the ground. One of his legs was bent at an obscene angle. The pack had formed a tight circle around him, heads lowered, hind legs bent as if in supplication or prayer. A wave of grief spread around the pack, engulfing their collective mind. Heads were raised one by one and long, harrowing howls rang out into the surrounding mountains. Lupita remained perfectly still, head bowed. She couldn't avert her eyes from her dead younger brother.

"I'm so sorry," Devan projected into her mind.

Lupita's lips curled into a snarl. She turned to face Devan, teeth bared, a deep growl emanating from her chest.

"Lupita..." he began.

"DON'T SPEAK TO ME," she shot back. "This is *your* fault."

Her words cut him to the core. Because they were true, and the truth hurt. Had it not been for Devan, Lupo and his family would still be quietly living off the land in the forests of North America.

"She needs some time alone, son," rang the voice in his mind.

It was Lupertico. The old wolf had just lost his son and yet was reassuring Devan, the very reason why his boy would remain still and silent for ever more. Devan felt guilty and ashamed.

"This isn't your fault and she knows that, deep down," Lupertico added, no doubt tuning into Devan's pulsing emotions. "We knew what we were signing up to. She'll come around... eventually."

"I'm so sorry, Lupertico," said Devan, knowing his words were vastly inadequate as they left his mind. But it was all he had.

He gave one final glance to the distraught Lupita before slinking off, feeling sorrow and remorse like he had never known before. He tried to distract himself by making a tour of the compound, seeing if they missed anything.

While inspecting the smallest building he padded over to the trapdoor in the center and dipped his head into the dark chasm. He heard something. Devan pricked up his ears and focused his senses. A low moaning. He could just about make it out. He had assumed that the tunnels were deserted after the Red Claws had fled and his army had extracted their dead and wounded. But someone was still down there, and it sounded like they were in pain.

Devan shifted back into a werwulf before lowering himself into the trapdoor. He retracted his long arms and then fell a few feet before landing on the granite floor. The tunnel in front of him was narrow and low. He had to crawl along its length before reaching a small wooden door. It was wide open so he squeezed inside and came out into the large stone chamber beyond. Burning torches illuminated the space.

He saw piles of ash spread across the floor. The only good Red Claws, he thought. Just to the left, underneath a wide ledge set into the wall, was someone very much alive. They were hunched over a pile of rags on the floor. The clothes were covered in the all-too-familiar dark ash. The survivor's shoulders were heaving up and down as wailing sobs echoed off the walls.

"Hey," said Devan, not knowing what was appropriate in the circumstances.

The mourner looked up, a river of tears staining his face.

"Klaus?" said Devan.

It was him, yet not him. Something had changed. Devan couldn't quite figure out what, though.

Devan remained still and silent now that he knew he wasn't facing a threat. His wariness was replaced with awkwardness as Klaus continued to clutch at the clothes and weep. Devan had no clue what to do. He knew that Klaus could be fragile and combustible.

The sobbing began to cease and Klaus took in huge, heaving breaths. The vampire looked back up at Devan, his face raw with anguish. Devan noticed he couldn't see any cuts or other injuries on Klaus. Had he survived the entire battle down here unscathed? When the fighting must have been at close quarters. It didn't seem likely.

"I had to do it…he…he…made me do it," stuttered Klaus.

"Umm, right," said Devan, clueless and completely out of his comfort zone. "And…um…what did you have to do?"

Klaus was silent. His eyes bored into Devan. For an eerie moment, Devan thought that Klaus was seeing into his soul, or reading his mind. The look was so intense.

When Klaus didn't answer, Devan tentatively walked over, as you might approach a terrified dog that had been mistreated by its previous owner. He crouched down and very slowly reached out a hand and placed it on Klaus's shoulder.

"Hey, Klaus. It's okay, dude," he said. He was trying to sound reassuring, but his gravelly lycan voice sounded anything but. But he didn't want to switch to human form and stand there naked. The scene would go from merely awkward to downright absurd.

Devan braced himself for a snarl like the one he'd received only moments ago from Lupita. Instead, Klaus simply continued to look at Devan. Frightened and confused. The vampire looked brittle, breakable, almost child-like.

"I had to," he mumbled.

Klaus's eyes pleaded for Devan to understand. Though what he was referring to was far beyond Devan's comprehension.

It wasn't until Klaus peeled himself away from the garments on the floor that Devan saw what Klaus was protecting. Loris. These were the clothes that Loris was wearing when he entered the compound. He was dead, Devan realized with shock. Turned to ash…and Klaus was admitting responsibility.

"You bastard," screamed Devan, adopting a fighting stance. "You killed Loris! You were supposed to be one of us, but you never could be, could you? How stupid we were to believe you. It was a trick. A ploy all along. You fucking Red Claw."

Devan crouched low, claws raised, teeth bared. Ready to strike.

"I loved him," Klaus murmured.

That stopped Devan in his tracks. He was caught off-guard by the frankly bizarre statement. Instead of lunging he snarled.

"That's impossible and we both know it," said Devan, through gritted teeth. "You think your lies will buy you time. Well…"

CHAPTER 28

"I mean it," implored Klaus. "He died to save me. The prophecy. It's not what you think. If you kill me now, then you doom everyone. It's the very reason why Loris sacrificed his life, his very blood."

Devan went from confused to downright bewildered. This was all way above his pay grade. But his anger still simmered.

"More of your lies," Devan said. But his words weren't convincing. He wasn't completely sure of anything right now.

"We had it wrong, wolf," replied Klaus, holding the clothes tight to his chest, as if he could embrace the body that had once been contained within the fabric. "I'm the one in the prophecy. Look at me."

"What do you think I'm doing?" said Devan, slightly bemused. "I haven't taken my eyes off you the whole time."

"No," replied Klaus. "Really look at me."

Klaus gestured to himself. Devan wasn't sure what he was supposed to be looking at.

"Zachariah nearly killed me," said Klaus, when no reply was forthcoming from the werwulf. "He tore me to shreds. Loris held me together. Literally. Look, now." He gestured to his own body again.

Devan remained quiet.

"Not a mark. Not a scratch. I am whole again," continued Klaus. "But I'm not as I was before. I'm different."

Then it hit Devan. That something about Klaus that had changed. He hadn't been able to pinpoint it before, but now it stood out.

"Your face, your hands," said Devan, sweeping his eyes across Klaus's skin. "The deathly vamp pallor is gone. You don't look like a walking corpse anymore. You look almost…almost…" Devan couldn't say the word. It seemed just too absurd to say out loud, to give it tangible form.

"Human," Klaus finished for him. "I look human."

Devan's mouth was a gaping 'O'. He couldn't process what was going on. Had Klaus just reverted to a human after drinking Loris's blood? Was he the chosen one mentioned in that crazy prophecy?

That would mean that everything had been for nothing. The war to save Nell. All that death. Of course, Devan would have willingly fought to save his friend. But the grand battle. The big cause. Had it been a mistake based on a false assumption?

"Zachariah?" Devan asked, his thoughts churning. "He still thinks the prophecy is about Nell and Christopher?"

Klaus contemplated.

"Yes, I can't see why he would think otherwise," he said. "He knew nothing of Loris and me."

Devan's mind was working overtime, ticking over with new questions, new thoughts, new fears.

"So, she's still in danger? Still a target?" he said.

"One would assume so," replied Klaus, somberly.

"When, in fact, you were the savior of the world all along?" asked Devan.

"I'm not sure I'd quite put it like that," said Klaus, his cheeks flushing.

Devan saw the color rising in his face. Proof, if ever there was, that the person before him was no blood-sucker. Not anymore.

"We need to get you out of here," said Devan, a new urgency in his voice. "This is going to take some explaining but we need to hand it over to brains that are way bigger than mine. I'm out. But I'll keep you safe. You've suddenly become quite valuable."

CHAPTER 28

Devan turned away, expecting Klaus to follow. When he didn't, Devan turned back.

"Just a moment more," Klaus said, sitting beside the sad remnants of his former lover.

Devan could not deny him that.

Chapter 29

Christopher burst into Amara's motel room holding Nell's limp body. She hadn't woken up. Hadn't muttered a word. He'd seen her eyelids flutter a few times. That was it. Her pulse was faint, but it was there. Her scent was wrong. A wasting, decaying odor. Christopher almost expected her to rattle as he carried her. She seemed nothing but a hollow bag of bones.

"What the…" began Amara, startled by the sudden intrusion. Then she quickly realized what was happening. She bolted over to the pair. "My God, Nell! Put her on the bed."

Christopher was reluctant to place her down. He'd only just got his hands on her again. The last thing he wanted to do was let her go. He just stared at her face, willing her to wake up.

"Christopher! The bed!" Amara almost screamed.

He snapped out of his trance and gently placed her on the mattress. She was on the single bed closest to the window. The moonlight cast her in a spectral glow, making her skin look waxy and ashen.

"What do we do?" said Amara, looking at Christopher, who was running his fingers through his hair.

He took a moment before he spoke. It was a last chance

to reassess his course of action. To choose a different road. But looking down on Nell's fragile, wasted body, he knew his options had dwindled down to just one.

"I can feel a pulse," explained Christopher. "She's alive. But barely. She won't make it on her own. They've taken too much out of her."

"So, what then?" asked Amara, frantic now.

"I have to change her," said Christopher, resolute. "I can't see any other way."

Amara looked horrified. She lurched forward, pushing Christopher back. She placed herself between the vampire and her friend.

"No," she seethed. "That's not your choice to make."

Christopher looked stricken.

"Amara," he said, trying to keep his voice calm, though he felt torn apart inside. "I love her just as you do. That's why I have to save her. There's no other choice. She won't make it on her own. She's too weak. I either change her or we lose her. It's as simple as that."

Amara turned and sank to her knees in front of the bed. She reached out and gently cradled Nell's emaciated hands in her own. Tears stained her face as she surveyed Nell's hollowed out eyes and the shallow rise and fall of her chest.

"I'm not sure how much time we have left," added Christopher, gravely.

Amara gently placed Nell's hands back on her chest then stood, before backing away from the bed. Her eyes never left her friend.

"Do what you have to," she said, quietly. "Save her."

Christopher didn't waste any time. He knelt down and leaned over Nell's body before sinking his teeth into the paper-thin skin of her neck. He had to pierce through scar tissue underneath. A remnant of her brutal time as a captive. Christopher's anger flared at the thought of the Red Claws feeding on her. Treating her like a piece of meat. But he forced himself to push the fury aside. He needed to concentrate. The procedure was finely balanced. He couldn't afford to make a mistake. Yet thoughts still invaded his mind.

What if Nell didn't want to be a vampire? What if changing her meant the prophecy wouldn't work. Didn't it state that he needed to end her life? Was he being selfish? Would the Red Claws now destroy humanity? What would Nell want him to do?

Christopher knew that Nell would much rather die than risk the lives of so many others. But she wasn't able to make that choice. And he didn't want to live without her. He couldn't live without her. On and on his thoughts raged.

Maybe because I have to drain her first, the prophecy will still be fulfilled. Her human life will end. Does that count? I can have Nell and still fulfill the prophecy. Can't I?

It was futile, he realized. He had no answers and he also had no time left. He would just have to act and be damned. Act and the whole world be damned, perhaps. At this point he didn't care. Let the dice fall where they may. He wasn't prepared to lose her. Not after coming this far.

He closed his eyes and drank deeply of her. The blood flooded into his body. It was like nothing he had felt before. He felt suddenly exhilarated. Energized. He had drunk of humans before. More times than he cared to admit. But it was never like this. Never so intimate, so invigorating. Was it because it was Nell? His Nell? That was part of it. But there was something more. Something about her very blood. Goosebumps decorated his skin. Small hairs at the back of his neck stood on end. He could feel her very essence entering his body.

Christopher reached up and placed a hand on Nell's face, caressing her skin as he continued to imbibe her life force. He felt so awake, so alive. It was an almost sensual experience. His senses were on fire. A raw, animalistic energy coursed within him, pulsating. He was vaguely aware of Amara standing over him, looking down on the scene. It felt intrusive, voyeuristic, like she was intruding on a deeply private moment.

He didn't have time to dwell on those thoughts. He could sense Nell's heart slowing now. Her life force ebbing away. She was nearing the end. Yet he couldn't pull away. Her blood was intoxicating and his body craved more. But the rational part of his brain sensed her pulse rapidly dwindling. It was so faint. Any moment now it would cease altogether.

With a monumental effort of will, Christopher tore his mouth away from her neck. The highly-charged connection was broken and he was thrust fully back in the room. He looked around wildly to reorient himself, taking in the cheap, austere furniture and flaking paint on the walls. He heard Amara gasp loudly. She was staring at Nell's deathly pale, seemingly lifeless body. There was no time to waste, Christopher realized with alarm. He had to act now or risk losing Nell forever.

He ripped at the skin of his own neck with a pointed nail, then leaned down to position the open wound above Nell's cracked lips. The blood began to flow. Thick and dark. It coated Nell's lips and began to slowly drip down her chin, staining the old, yellowing mattress. Yet Nell didn't move. She just lay there like a statue.

Christopher panicked. Was he too late? Had he taken too

much from her, waited too long to offer his blood?

He stared wide-eyed at Amara, alarm etched on his face.

"Mouth...her mouth," he shouted, incoherent in his hysteria.

The librarian caught his meaning, thankfully. She quickly knelt beside Christopher and gently parted Nell's lips. She then slightly repositioned the vampire's head so the flow of blood landed directly into Nell's mouth.

Nothing happened.

The blood began to slowly fill her mouth but Nell didn't react in the slightest.

"Nell...please Nell," pleaded Amara, gently stroking her forehead with the flat of her fingers. "Please..."

Then it happened. Nell's throat contracted ever-so slightly. Then again, more pronounced this time. She was swallowing, taking in the thick liquid.

"She's doing it," announced Amara, relief lacing her voice. "She's drinking."

Christopher closed his eyes and gave silent thanks to the Omni-Father.

Nell was drinking heartily now, her throat contracting rhythmically as the blood continued to flow into her open mouth. Weakly, she lifted a trembling arm and placed her hand on the top of Christopher's neck. He felt her trying to pull him closer to her, but she had so little strength it was like being caressed by a toddler.

But as the seconds slowly ticked into minutes, Nell's strength began to grow. Christopher could feel her grip tightening on his neck. He was now held firmly in place as she continued to greedily drain his life-giving blood.

Christopher felt weak and hazy. His vision began to swim. The balance of power had shifted. Nell had the strength now

CHAPTER 29

while he was rapidly weakening. He had to pull away. Quickly. If she kept taking from him he would soon pass the critical point where his body could no longer preserve its integrity. His flesh would disintegrate into a pile of ash.

He tried to pull away but her grip was vice-like. He didn't budge even a millimeter. He raised his shaky hands to her face and tried to push himself away. Nothing. He was locked in place as she continued to feed. More and more she drank from him. The room began spinning and bright stars began to flash in his vision. So, this was the end. She would kill him. It was the prophecy in reverse, he thought darkly.

With his last trickle of energy he reached a hand out to Amara, his fingers splayed and trembling.

"Ama...Am...I..." was all he could whisper.

For the second time that evening the astute librarian read the situation correctly and sprang into action. She quickly wrapped her hands around Christopher's shoulders then pulled back. But Nell held him firmly in place. He was going nowhere.

"Shit," shrieked Amara. "Nell, let go. It's Christopher. You need to let go."

Amara took a deep breath then heaved back with all her might, straining the muscles in her biceps. Christopher was suddenly released from Nell's dangerous embrace. He flew backwards, still held tight by Amara. They both landed in an unceremonious heap on the floor. The librarian took the brunt of the impact. Christopher was still in her arms, like a child wrapped in his mother's protective embrace. Then his world went black.

Chapter 30

Nell awoke gasping for breath. She instinctively shot out her hands in a vain attempt to fend off her attackers. It never did any good, but her body did it anyway.

She opened her eyes. No one had their teeth clamped to her neck. That was unusual.

She looked down. Sweat and dirt clung to her body. Layers upon layers of grime.

Something else was unusual. The relentless pain that tormented her flesh was…gone? Really? She took a moment to feel her body from the inside. The tiredness, fever, soreness, weakness, pain and haziness that were the background to her very existence. Where were they? Was she dead? Was this heaven?

Her eyes took in the drab, stained mattress beneath her and peeling paint on the wall. Heaven was really oversold in the brochures if this was it. But she wasn't complaining. Respite from the constant agonies of her body was her own version of heaven.

So, Zachariah had moved her again, it appeared. She searched her memory. The last thing she remembered was being carried over his shoulder into a large stone room. She thought it was underground, but she couldn't be sure as she

CHAPTER 30

kept slipping in and out of consciousness.

"Nell?"

The voice belonged to Christopher. She looked up. There he was. Right in front of her. His hand reaching out and grasping hers.

Ah...so there was the explanation. Simple really. Another dream. Now that she knew it was a dream it wouldn't be long before her consciousness was thrust back into the broken and battered body lying on that stone floor. But she resolved to enjoy the final few moments she had left in her fantasy world. She often dreamed of Christopher. She'd woken up calling out his name countless times, and was consequently ridiculed and humiliated by the Red Claws.

He seemed different this time. Weaker and thinner than she remembered. But his eyes still shone that radiant blue.

"Hey dream boy," she said. "We don't have long, kiss me quick, so at least I can wake up with a nice memory."

Christopher looked taken aback, confused. He just kept staring at her, as if he couldn't quite believe what he was seeing.

Strange dream this one, Nell mused.

"How do you feel?"

Another voice. Female this time.

Nell swiveled her head. There sitting on another rickety single bed was Amara, as real as life. The librarian was staring intently at Nell.

"Amara!" Nell said, brightly. "How lovely you've joined my little dreamscape. I've missed you so much, amigo!" She wagged a playful finger at Christopher. "I guess a smooch just became out of the question, lover-boy. But a hug from my two besties would go a long way."

Christopher and Amara just stared at her.

"How do you feel, Nell?" Amara asked again, tentatively.

This really was the strangest dream, Nell thought. But she rolled with it, taking a moment to fully consider the question. She felt pretty damn good, if truth be told. Better than she had for a long, long time.

"I feel really pretty great, as it happens!" replied Nell. "Shame it can't last, but I'll take it all the same. Now about those hugs." A grin crept across her face as she sat up in the bed. She had almost forgotten how to smile. She hadn't used those face muscles for so long. Nell held out her arms like a toddler asking for a 'hugsy'.

"Oh Nell." Christopher jumped onto the bed with childish enthusiasm and enveloped her in his arms. "Oh God, I've missed you. I've missed you so much. Don't you ever do that to me again."

Tears fell down her cheeks as Nell melted into his arms. It all felt so...*real*.

Amara came over and joined the hug, turning it into a three-way embrace.

"Now that's what I'm talking about," beamed Nell. "This'll keep me going for a while. Until I see you again, for real hopefully."

Amara gently pulled away and began stroking Nell's hair.

"You still don't get it, do you?" she said softly. "This *is* real, Nell. You *are* here with us now. Christopher rescued you from the Red Claws."

Could it possibly be true? She doubted it. But then again if this were a dream then surely she would have woken up by now. That's how it always went. Whenever she had the realization she was dreaming, it would signal the end of the fantasy and she'd wake up. But that hadn't happened. She was

CHAPTER 30

still here…and it felt *so* real.

She looked from Amara to Christopher, dumbfounded.

"It's true," reassured Christopher, cradling her face in his hands. "This isn't a dream. You're right here, right now, with us, and we're never going to let you go again."

Nell shot out her arms and grabbed his shoulders, checking if he was real, feeling the solidity of his body. Then she reached out a hand and placed her palm against Amara's face. The librarian looked amused. But Nell needed to feel the heat of her flesh, her very aliveness.

It was then that it hit her. She was with the two people she cared about the most. Safe. Away from the Red Claws. They had really done it. They had rescued her.

Nell pulled them both in for another tight group hug as the tears flowed freely once again. She didn't want to let them go, just in case the moment evaporated and she was thrust back into her life of squalor and captivity. But as the seconds passed her new reality became more and more solidly established.

"I just never thought I'd see you again," said Nell, still clinging to them. "I tried to hold out hope, but it seemed there was only darkness ahead for me."

"Shhhhh," reassured Amara, stroking her back. "There's no way we would ever give up on you, girl. Sorceress Sisters stick together, remember."

That elicited a little chuckle from Nell.

"But there's more, Nell," added Amara, her tone more serious now. "More you need to know."

Nell pulled away and searched Amara's face.

"Devan!" said Nell, suddenly alarmed.

"No, no," replied Amara, holding up a palm. "He's okay…well okay as can be considering what he's been through. This concerns you, Nell."

The librarian looked hesitantly at Christopher.

"There's...something...we need to talk about," said Christopher.

He was hesitant and chose his words carefully. Nell studied his face and realized that he was scared. She had never seen him like this before. It only served to make her more apprehensive.

"When I found you, you were in really bad shape," continued Christopher. "Like, really bad. What they'd done to you...you wouldn't have lasted much longer if I hadn't..." He exhaled and scanned her face closely. "If I hadn't changed you."

"Changed me?" she said. "What do you mean?"

"For you to live...to stand a chance," continued Christopher. "I had to change you...into a vampire."

The bottom dropped out of Nell's world upon hearing that last word. The room began swaying in her vision.

"It was the only way to save you," continued Christopher, hurriedly.

He reached out and grabbed her shoulders to steady her.

Christopher continued to splutter out words, but Nell couldn't register what he was saying. It sounded distant. Muffled through cotton wool. She remained perfectly silent and perfectly still, just staring at his face.

"Nell...Nell...Nell," she heard him repeat over and over again, concern knitting his eyebrows together.

She slowly came back to herself. It was like coming up from the bottom of the ocean.

"So I'm dead?" she whispered.

"Well, um...technically, yes," replied Christopher. "Your mortal life has come to an end. That's why your body is no longer plagued by the injuries you sustained. You can heal now. Quickly. There's so much more..."

"Perhaps..." interjected Amara, placing a gentle hand on Christopher's arm. "...we can leave it at that for now. It's a lot to take in and Nell has got the main point."

Nell looked into Christopher's worried eyes. He had brought her back to life. He'd fought for her. Saved her. But she was now changed. Forever. She didn't have the slightest clue what this would mean. But they would figure that out. Together.

Chapter 31

An anemic stream of lukewarm water sputtered from the rust-stained showerhead and drenched her skin. Though she was in a tiny, shabby bathroom of a budget motel, to Nell it felt like sheer paradise. She gently scrubbed the caked dirt away, revealing ivory skin underneath.

Nell had always been on the pale side, hailing from pasty European stock, but this was something else entirely. It looked like she was made from the purest alabaster. Nell marveled at her own body as the rapidly cooling water washed away the grime and revealed more of her flesh. Even more remarkable was the fact the countless bites, bruises, welts and scratches that marked her body were gone. Healed without a trace, as if they were never there in the first place. She looked as unblemished as a newborn.

There was more. It seemed she could hear every individual drop of water as it bounced off her skin and landed on the cheap, scuffed shower tray beneath her feet. Whereas before a shower sounded like a constant drone of water, now there were nuances, different tones and inflections as the various drops impacted on the cheap plastic of the tray. It was actually mesmerizing in its own way.

Though she was different now, on the inside she felt like

CHAPTER 31

the same Nell. The girl who ran away to save the world. But she couldn't escape this new reality. The fact that she was a vampire. She knew now that not all vampires were evil. But they had to drink blood. That fact was inescapable. They had to kill. They were predators. The apex of the food chain. Did that mean she would have to kill? Was it the only way to survive?

Before her thoughts could spiral down, Nell heard voices coming from the room beyond. That was another thing that astonished her. Though the pitter patter of the shower was loud and the bathroom door was closed, she could still easily make out what was being said in the main room. Also who was saying it.

"Where are you hiding her?"

Devan's distinctive voice carried across the room.

Nell quickly shut the water off before grabbing the frayed towel hanging on the shower screen and patting herself dry. She hurriedly dressed in Amara's spare jeans and a canary yellow jumper. She swam in the clothes but didn't care. Anything clean was a luxury. She exploded out of the bathroom and into Devan's arms.

"It's good to see you, furball," Nell breathed into his chest.

"You too, you walking blood-sucker buffet," Devan laughed, hugging her tightly.

Nell was vaguely aware that there was someone else in the room but it wasn't until she spotted the Red Claw that she tore herself away from Devan, backing up against the far wall.

"Red Claw!" she shouted, pointing a shaking finger at the red-haired vampire.

He was the one who had killed her beloved Aunt Laura, she realized with horror. He had also been Zachariah's most trusted follower while she was held captive. He looked a little different now. It must be the gloomy yellow light thrown by the overhead bulb that was altering the color of his skin, she reasoned. She couldn't believe he was standing in front of her right now. It made no sense.

"Hey, it's okay, it's okay. He's on our side now," Amara explained, stepping forward. She turned to the Red Claw. "Klaus, meet Nell."

The vampire stepped forward with his hand extended. Nell pushed herself further against the back wall. When she realized there was nowhere to go she quickly crouched low, ready to go on the attack. She didn't know where this urge to fight suddenly came from, but her body felt galvanized, like it would do whatever it took to ensure her survival. She felt capable and resolute. Her senses were honed on the Red Claw, blocking out all distractions. A hiss emanated unbidden from her throat.

"Woah, woah," said Christopher, stepping in between a poised Nell and flustered Klaus. "Let's just cool it for a second, so we can explain." He turned to face Nell. "A lot's happened since you've been away. We need to get you up to speed."

"On that subject," added Devan. "Klaus here has a tale to tell, and you're going to want to sit down for it, trust me!"

"I suggest we all sit down," said Amara, lowering her palms by her side in a placating gesture. "And talk this all through. Calmly."

They all looked at one another, then Klaus walked over to the threadbare armchair. Christopher led the still-rattled Nell to one of the rickety single beds. Amara and Devan took the other. The cheap bed springs protested as they sat.

The room was quiet. Christopher spoke into the silence.

CHAPTER 31

He brought Nell up to speed with events since she willingly walked out of Vhik'h-Tal-Eskemon in the Blue Ridge Mountains all those weeks ago. He covered Devan's pursuit of her trail, the assembling of the army, Klaus's unlikely conversion, the journey up to Whittier, the first unsuccessful storming of the compound and her eventual rescue from the underground chamber.

He left out much of the fine detail, otherwise they'd be there all night, but managed to convey the main points of the winding story. Nell listened in stunned silence. Tears stung her eyes at certain parts as Christopher spoke. When he finished, there was yet more quiet.

"So many died because of me," Nell said at last. "Because I made a rash, impulsive decision."

"The war was coming anyway," said Devan. "Sooner or later there was going to be a showdown with the Red Claws."

"And it's not over yet," added Amara, grimly. "Far from it. Those who died did so for a bigger cause. For the sake of us all, you could say. But there will be more bloodshed ahead. This cannot end until the Red Claws end."

Silence enveloped the small room once more as everyone mulled the heavy words.

After a few moments Nell stood and walked over to Devan, before once again throwing her arms around him.

"Thank you," she said. "For coming after me."

"It's the pack you need to thank," he replied. "I'd be nothing without them. Just a kid lost in the wilderness. They saved me."

"I can't wait to thank them all in person," said Nell. "Plus the Hunters, the fae and all the others."

Amara was suddenly animated.

"We need to call Vhik'h-Tal-Eskemon," she said. "I should have thought of it earlier. I'm sure Kavisha and the Council have a thousand questions for Nell about...."

"Hang on, hang on," Devan interrupted, holding up a palm. All eyes turned to him. "Before you do that you need to hear what Klaus here has to say. It might just change everything."

The attention shifted to Klaus, who squirmed slightly as he sat uncomfortably on the edge of the chair.

"Go ahead," said Devan, turning to him.

Klaus let out a long breath then began speaking. He was hesitant at first but slowly the words began to flow. As he recounted his story everyone in the room remained perfectly still, transfixed by the tale. Eyes widened and a few gasps were heard as he made his points. When he finished talking, nearly every mouth was wide open.

Devan looked around, a little self-satisfied.

"Lived up to the billing, right?" he said.

"That's impossible," Nell breathed, ignoring Devan's quip. "The prophecy is about you and Loris? Not me and Christopher. You've become human again and my blood, my blood... it's some kind of super-serum?"

Klaus looked anxious as he spoke.

"As for the prophecy, it appears we misread it," he said. "We jumped to conclusions based on the information we had at the time. But it wasn't the whole story. There was more to it."

Amara reached for her backpack in the corner of the room. She rifled through the front pouch and pulled out a piece of paper. It was a copy of the prophesy that had been provided by the Magisters, from their own edition of the *Adumbrate Invictus*. She held it up and began to read aloud.

CHAPTER 31

"Salvation lies in one soul. A death-walker turned young. One of tainted blood. He will endure a betrayal, a loss and an awakening. He will love, as no other of his kin has before. He will abandon those he serves. He will develop abilities unknown while reverting to the origin. These abilities can corrupt and besiege, for they stem from the transmutation of loss, the most powerful emotion. He must drain the one he loves, filling his essence and ending theirs. This act alone brings forth the genesis."

She dropped the paper on the bed and looked at Klaus.

"Reverting to the origin," she mused. "It might mean becoming human again, but we don't know for sure. The language is cryptic, and it's probably a translation from old Romanian."

"What about my blood?" asked Nell, looking from Amara to Klaus. "What's the story with that?"

Klaus's eyes scanned the room before he spoke. He looked more troubled than ever.

"When you were our...their...captive, at first all the Red Claws fed from you," he said, looking in the direction of Nell but with his head bowed. He couldn't meet her eyes. "But Zachariah must have quickly realized the effect your blood had. That's why he claimed you as his personal prize. Only he was allowed to take from you. Do you recall that?" He raised his head to look at her.

Nell simply nodded.

"When Zachariah tried to kill me in the chamber, he swallowed a large vial of your blood. It was a bigger dose than he would take when he fed on you," continued Klaus. "His wounds healed within mere seconds. He grew stronger. He began to vibrate with power. I could almost feel it in the air."

Klaus suddenly looked at Christopher, a realization dawning.

"When you drank of her, during the transmutation," he said. "I presume you felt it too, something different, something... potent?"

Now it was Christopher's turn to lower his head. He remained still, other than the slightest nod.

"I didn't realize...I thought..." he said to the ground.

"It's okay, you weren't to know," said Nell, reaching out and grabbing his hand.

"I'm sorry," he mouthed.

"What for?" Nell replied. "You did what you had to do. You saved me."

"I thought it was part of the prophecy or something," said Christopher, finally looking up. "Why it felt different. I thought perhaps it might be because we were in love."

"The vial that Zachariah had in his hand turned him into a monster," said Klaus, turning back to Nell. "He must have more of your blood stored away. It all makes sense now. I always wondered why you looked so drained constantly, when he was feeding on you only sparingly. It wasn't because he was drinking the blood, it was because he was preparing a stockpile."

"But I'm still alive...sort of," replied Nell. "I still have blood running through me, right? Can't we use that to fight him."

"You're different now," said Christopher. "That includes your blood. It's thicker, darker. Whatever was contained in your human blood might not have survived the change."

"So now Zachariah is more dangerous than ever," said Devan. "A killing machine."

CHAPTER 31

A heavy silence permeated the room yet again.
Their work wasn't finished. It had barely even started.

Epilogue

For Amara, life seemed like a dream. Only a few months ago she had been in a dingy motel room in Whittier, Alaska, helping to orchestrate a supernatural war. Now she was thrust back to 'real life' in Angel Falls, Georgia. She found herself standing behind the polished mahogany desk of Henry Freeman Memorial Library with a book scanner in her hand. It felt surreal.

She had never felt more alive than when she was hunting blood-thirsty rogue vampires, plotting a war and attempting to save humanity in the company of her preternatural friends. Now here she was in her gray slacks, white formal shirt and burgundy cardigan having just scanned *The Complete Guide to Pot Plant Care* and *101 Easy Knitting Patterns* for Dolores Schofield from the town's senior center.

She gently placed the scanner down and looked across the library. The round window on the far side showed dark clouds forming in the sky. They served as an apt metaphor, the librarian thought.

The council had lost sight of Zachariah and his remaining few Red Claws, despite their best efforts to track them. It was as if they had simply evaporated into the ether. Hopes were that Zachariah had been killed (unlikely) or decided to refrain from further bad behavior (even more unlikely). Amara stared out at the gathering clouds again. A storm was brewing. In more ways than one.

Amara often thought of Nell. She'd only seen her friend once in the past month. Christopher had been keeping her out of harm's way, teaching how to live while being undead, so to speak. He had to keep her away from humans, in case her burgeoning hunger grew overpowering and she did something decidedly reckless. She had a steep learning curve ahead of her, but was in good hands.

They had met three weeks ago at the funeral of Nell's Aunt Laura. The first thing Nell did upon returning from Alaska was give her dear aunt an honorable send-off after having to hastily bury her by the side of a road in Angel Falls. Amara stood on the leafy grounds of St Mary's Church with Haiden and Devan. Nell seemed to materialize out of thin air, with Christopher by her side. Amara had looked up and suddenly there they were. Amara had a suspicion that Christopher was teaching her how to use new abilities to move unnoticed. Their pale skin stood out against the black clothes. Christopher wore a suit while Nell wore a flowing full-length dress. She held herself with confidence, elegance even. Whereas before Nell had a tendency to fade into the background, there was no ignoring her now. She had been pretty as a human, Amara thought, but as a vampire... it took her breath away. She was radiant, ethereal, exquisite. Although none of those words truly did her justice. Her and Christopher made a stunning couple.

Amara's memories were interrupted by muffled mumbling. She turned her head to track down the culprit. Dozing in a wingback reading chair in the corner of the library was

Haiden, the open pages of a classic novel splayed over his thigh. She smiled to herself. Their relationship had been forged under intense pressure. Coal turning into a diamond, she liked to think, but had never said that to him. It sounded a bit mushy. With Zachariah having vanished into thin air and a truce declared between the Hunters and other vampires, Haiden had some time on his hands. However, Amara had a feeling in the pit of her stomach that he would soon be recalled. Dark clouds gathering. The feeling was hard to shake.

Klaus had moved to Angel Falls, where he could be protected and watched. He had taken over the old Red Claw mansion on the rural outskirts of town. The shielding talisman had been fortified for his protection. He rarely left his home. He was depressed, it was clear to see. Losing Loris and the implications of the prophecy had broken him. He was a shell of a man. Man, Amara mused. It was still hard to believe he was no longer a vampire. Amara and Haiden had tried on a few occasions to visit him, but he wouldn't even answer the door. She had wanted him to know he still had people on his side. A family of sorts, after losing his first one. But to no avail.

Amara's phone buzzed on the small counter attached to the main desk. She had it on silent but the vibration caught her attention. She never took calls while on duty but, looking at the number displayed on the screen, she quickly grabbed the handset. Luckily it was just her and Haiden around at the moment.

"Amara, turn on Channel 11."

Kavisha was straight to the point. No small talk.

Amara had been in touch with the High Chancellor regularly to keep abreast of the hunt for the Red Claws. This was the first time that she'd not wished the librarian good afternoon or asked how she was, or even said hello for that matter. Ice suddenly ran through Amara's veins. She knew that something was wrong.

Amara dropped the phone and then fumbled for the TV remote. She called out to Haiden as she pointed the controller at the TV on the far wall of the library. It normally showed a text display of new releases available at the library along with a scrolling ticker of local town news.

She switched to Channel 11 and turned up the sound.

The newsreader, a smartly dressed woman in her fifties wearing a blue blazer, was seated in the studio outlining events.

"Our international sources are reporting no less than ten locations across the globe that have been wiped out by the brutal attacks, carried out simultaneously. At first it was suspected to be a coordinated terrorist assault, but new information tells us a very different, and frankly unbelievable, story. To repeat, entire cities have been decimated with no signs of life remaining within their boundaries. The closest affected location to us here is San Luis in Arizona, where our crime correspondent, Serena Marshall, reports from the boundary line."

The scene cut away to a young woman holding a microphone standing in front of what looked like a hastily erected police cordon.

"Thank you, Jane. Yes, I am currently standing at the edge of San Luis, Arizona. A small border city known for its agriculture. However, it is now a literal ghost town. No signs of life remain. I have been reliably informed that a police helicopter has recorded footage of bodies scattered all over the streets. The authorities are not sharing those images with us at this present time. Government officials and police are trying to keep the cause hidden, so as not to cause widespread panic. However, we at Channel 11 believe you have a right to know what is going on. Cell phone footage from affected areas is already being shared widely across the globe, so Channel 11 has made the editorial decision to give you the facts now."

The reporter paused before continuing, the camera zoomed in closer on her face.

"Vampires. Yes, you heard correctly. Vampires have been swarming cities, wiping out entire populations, decimating every human life in their path. These deadly creatures were once relegated to the realms of fiction, but the devastating events of today prove that they are in fact real and a clear and present threat to humanity. They have come out of hiding and already killed hundreds of thousands, if not millions, in the space of one day."

Amara stared at the screen open-mouthed. She had to hold on to the desk to steady herself. Haiden was standing beside her now. He put an arm around her shoulder for support.

"This…this…can't be real, can it?" Amara said, her voice quivering.

The thought of so many people dead, wiped from the planet in one day, was too much.

Haiden's phone rang in his pocket. He fished it out and put it to his ear.

"Yeah, I'm watching it now," he said. "Why didn't we know? That's meant to be our job."

Amara was transfixed by the TV. The scene had cut back to the newsreader in the studio, who was saying something about exclusive footage.

EPILOGUE

Shaky cell phone video filled the screen.

The bodies were everywhere, strewn at odd angles on sidewalks, some in the middle of the road after being dragged out of their vehicles. Deep gouges and tears were visible on their necks. Some of the wounds were blurred out by the TV channel, but they hadn't done a thorough job in their rush to broadcast the footage.

The owner of the phone was running now. You could hear their labored breathing and the images moved quickly. They turned into a narrow street then came to a dead stop. At the end of the road was a scene that knocked the air out Amara's lungs.

A pile of bodies rose from the ground, like a human bonfire. It was at least five feet tall. None of the bodies were moving. There was somebody standing atop the mound, like a demonic climber who had reached the summit of a mountain in hell. The camera zoomed in on their face. Though the image became slightly distorted as the phone camera reached its maximum zoom, the face was clear enough to make out.

Amara gasped. Haiden dropped his phone.

"No, no, no..." muttered Amara as she took in who was standing over the carnage.

Looking back at her from the TV screen was Nell.

***

Dear Reader,

Thank you for reading my second book. I'd again like to make a humble plea.

As a part-time indie writer with a full-time job, I would be truly grateful if you could leave me a review on Amazon, as I have no other way of raising awareness. Even just one simple sentence would be perfect. Thank you so much in advance.

If you would like to contact me for any reason (such as to point out a mistake!) or simply to say hi, that would be great. My email address is:

anyakelner@gmail.com

The story continues

Legacy: the stunning conclusion to the Red Claw saga.

The forces of darkness spread their deadly shadow far and wide.

Nell, Christopher, Devan and Amara are torn and tested.

Can the 'One of tainted blood' turn the tide, or is all hope lost?

Lives, loves and the future of all vampires are at stake.

Anya Kelner delivers a stunning conclusion to the acclaimed Rise of the Red Claws series.

Printed in Great Britain
by Amazon